Killer Serve

A Tennis Team Mystery

JEANNE MEEKS

Chart House Press
New Lenox, IL

KILLER SERVE - A TENNIS TEAM MYSTERY

Retirement isn't all tennis, golf, and Mahjong. After Packi Walsh finds a stranger stretched out on the tennis court with a hole in his chest, the ladies' tennis team uncovers a seamy side to their tropical paradise.

ISBN-13 978-1545560808
ISBN-10: 1545560803

Published by:
Chart House Press, New Lenox, IL
Direct inquiries to: ChartHousePress@aol.com

Cover design by Les Solot, GermanCreative, at Fiverr.com
Cover vector by Leonido at Depositphotos.com
Author photo by: Donna Hinshaw

Other works by this author:
Backcountry Mystery series: *Rim to Rim - Death in the Grand Canyon*
Wolf Pack - Mystery on Isle Royale
Tennis Team Mystery series: *Gator Bait*
Short Stories: *Eternally Yours, Robert* and *Home Run*

ACKNOWLEDGMENTS

Special recognition goes to my #1 fan, Marie Woods, my mentor, model, and Mom. Thank you for encouraging your friends to read my books.

Thanks also goes out to Liza Perez, RN, emergency room nurse extraordinaire, for answering my trauma questions, sharing her ER experience, and keeping me sharp on the tennis court. Another big thanks goes to Kay Duddleston, RN, who accompanied on my research forays.

I also greatly appreciate my Beta Readers: Sherry Scarpaci, a terrific author; Cheryl Stillwell, Bev Ferris, and Jan Homolka

The Women of Mystery, my critique partners, are a great group of talented ladies. Lydia Ponczak, Sherry Scarpaci, and Helen Osterman encourage me and keep me on track. They are also good cooks—well, not Lydia. She's the one who stores sweaters in her oven. Thanks, WOM!

I love involving real people with the stories I write, so I asked readers for interesting character names. They came up with some great suggestions. Thanks to: Kathy and Mark Eversman, Janet Bontz, Marianne Hospadar, Vicki Chiapetta, Joan Fitch, Jo Rexer, Morgan Pearce, Carol Pearce, Cheryl Stillwell, Mary Beth Hafner, Marilyn Wyrick, Mary Baker, and Nancy Sorci.

Thanks also to my Florida friends for their stories about personal experiences with fire ants and to Jan Homolka for arranging speaking engagements for me and for getting her book discussion group excited about my novels.

NOTE:
If any mistakes of fact or procedure found in this novel, they are my own and not the fault of the professionals with whom I consulted. I try to get it right, but errors could arise from my own misinterpretation of their excellent information.

Forget not that the earth delights to feel your bare feet

and the winds long to play with your hair.

-- Khalil Gibran

1

The sun had not yet risen above the slash pines and cypress trees, but heat radiated from the pavement. While the rest of the country enjoyed the colors of autumn, Paradise Palms began another sweltering day in southwest Florida. The streets were quiet, though lawnmowers scurried over the rolling hills, manicuring the course before the first golfers teed off.

"Wait up!"

Packi looked over her shoulder and coasted to a stop. She leaned on the handlebars of her Schwinn and watched her tennis partner pedal like crazy toward the intersection. Kay's short skirt fluttered behind her and the tennis bag on her back swayed side to side. Behind her head, two racquet handles stuck up like turkey feathers.

As Kay neared the corner, Packi raised her hand in greeting. "Hey." She mounted her bike and accelerated. "What's got you up so early?"

Kay pedaled alongside Packi without breaking a sweat in the early morning humidity. "Gotta warm this old body up before practice. I'll pull something if the new pro drills us too hard. I hope to get a half hour on the ball machine."

"That's where I'm headed." Kay's pace tested Packi's limit. She measured her words to conserve her breath. "I reserved the machine for seven o'clock." She drew air into her aching lungs. "We'll share the court, if you can program the machine for two players."

"No problem, partner." Kay slowed her speed and coasted alongside.

She's been to the stylist again, thought Packi The sun highlighted new streaks of red in Kay's golden-brown hair. *Where does she find the time?* Packi chanced taking her hand from the handlebars to tug on her own stubby ponytail and tuck a stray hair behind her ear. Gray had started at her temples and seemed to be multiplying, but Packi hated the thought of spending time in a salon. She was comfortable with her ashen blond, even though it had lost its sheen sometime back. Twice a year she went to chop it off. That was enough.

"So, any good gossip?" asked Kay. "This husband-swapping thing should be good for some juicy stuff. What do you hear?"

"Nothing." Packi laughed at the way Kay tried to turn simple exchanges of expertise and work hours into salacious stories. The trades were merely practical and economical, or so she assumed. "They seem to be working it out. I wouldn't mind borrowing someone's husband to clean my pool filter."

"Mike will do that for you," Kay offered but then wagged her finger at Packi with mock severity. "But I get to choose what the swap is."

Unsettled by the small, territorial look in her friend's eye and the flash of her own imagination, Packi almost lost her balance on the bicycle. "I wouldn't . . ." She decided Kay was teasing, and she had to play her part. "Well, I don't have a man to swap."

"What about Mark?" Kay waggled her eyebrows. "He's a handy guy."

Talk about Mark Hebron, teasing or not, was a big step into Packi's personal space. She hid her blush under the wide brim of her cap and concentrated on her pedaling, Months ago, she'd mistaken Mark for a volunteer at the food pantry. Now questions about the homeless man disconcerted her.

"He's very busy."

Truth was, Packi seldom saw him. He worked all hours trying to rebuild his life. "Besides, I don't know him well enough to trade him off to do odd jobs. How about I barter homemade zucchini bread for an hour of your husband's time?"

Kay cocked her head as if listening for clues to Packi's life but let it go. "Sold. I love your zucchini bread." Her nostrils flared as if the aroma of toasted bread drifted past her nose. "I'll send my hubby over to look at your filter later today."

They biked the next block in silence, but Kay then again pulled abreast of Packi's bike and pointed her finger. "Speaking of Mark, Marilyn said he's collecting blankets or quilts or something. What's that about?"

"Yes." Packi ignored Kay's eagerness to bring the subject back around to Mark. He deserved his privacy. "Blankets. He didn't give me details, but he wants them for people living on the street."

Kay bobbed her head as if picturing Mark in his act of kindness, then shrugged. "I'll check my closets. I'm sure I have several. Cotton okay?"

Packi wished she had listened to Mark's explanations, but sometimes his endless energy wore her out. "I'm sure cotton is fine."

With the question of blankets and the pool filter settled, the women cruised through the landscaped streets of Paradise Palms toward the clubhouse. Kay chatted in a sassy, teasing manner which still rattled Packi. A lifetime of reserve couldn't be changed with a few months of tennis and friendship. Kay didn't seem to notice her discomfort, or maybe she felt it her civic duty to draw Packi out.

The cyclists wheeled into the empty parking lot of the main clubhouse where groundskeepers tended lush beds of pink impatiens. Others lopped off low-hanging palm fronds. An aproned employee skirted the spray from sprinklers and headed toward the kitchen entrance where a garbage truck lifted a dumpster over its back to shake the contents into the maw of the truck. The lid banged and crashed, metal upon metal, destroying the serenity of the tropical morning. Packi covered her ears until the noise abated and then hefted her bike into the rack outside the tennis courts.

"Looks like we have the place to ourselves."

"Dave's on Court Three." Kay pointed toward a stocky maintenance man who was busy grooming the courts. "Maybe we can get enough practice in before he gets to Court Nine."

The women quickened their steps along the concrete pathway. The last court in the row was reserved for players practicing with the ball machine or as an overflow court when matches filled the main courts. Packi preferred Court Nine because she could practice where people couldn't see her. Plus, in the heat of the day, the surrounding trees offered a few feet of shade.

"Shoot." Packi stopped with her hand on the gate. "Somebody already has the court. There are balls . . ." She squinted through the windscreen. "Oh, no!"

At the far baseline, a man lay on the gritty surface with his back to them. Packi threw open the gate, intent on getting to him. With Kay on her heels, she ran as if in a fog, down the sideline, around the net post. Halfway across the court, Kay grabbed Packi's arm and spun her around.

"Defibrillators on Court Four. Get them." Her bony fingers dug into Packi's skin and pushed her toward the exit. "I'll do this."

Packi pulled her focus away from the man and tried to understand what Kay had said. "Defib. Court Four," she repeated dumbly. The meaning clicked in when she remembered Kay was a nurse. Packi jumped at the idea and raced for the defibrillators. She got as far as the gate before Kay's flat voice caught her.

"Never mind," Kay said. "We don't need them.""What?" Packi hung onto the fence for support.

Kay, on her knees at the man's back, gave her a frantic wave. "Just call nine-one-one."

"Okay. Okay." Adrenaline had Packi's heart beating double-time. "Call nine-one-one," she said to herself to focus on her task. *Do I have my phone?* She unzipped her tennis bag, dumped its contents on the ground, and untangled her phone from her sweat rag. She swiped at the screen and punched in the numbers.

"What is your emergency?"

"Hello. Hello. We need an ambulance. Heart attack." It was a good assumption. Heart problems were not uncommon in the community.

"Your location?"

"Paradise Palms. South of Colonial, west of Treeline, off Osprey Boulevard. On the tennis courts. Court Nine, way at the end."

"I'm dispatching now. Can anyone there start CPR?"

"Yes, my friend is a nurse." Packi heard the relief in her own voice but then glanced back at the man. Kay still knelt beside him, her hands clasped in her lap. She closed her eyes and shook her head.

"Oh," Packi whispered, grasping to make sense of the scene. "We're too late." The phone slipped from her ear. Guilt crept in from somewhere. "Please come anyway," she begged the dispatcher. "He must be dead."

2

Packi ended the emergency call and dropped the phone into her pile of stuff. She rushed across the court to Kay's side, but no closer, and scrutinized the man sprawled on the ground. "Are you sure he's dead?"

"He's as cold as stone." Kay kneaded a headache into her forehead and gave a sad, ironic laugh. "Cold means dead, and probably for some time."

"Oh." Packi stared down at the body, wishing it was a prank, someone's idea of a bad joke. "Do you recognize him?"

"I'm afraid to look."

Packi clenched her teeth and tiptoed around the body. One arm was beneath him while the other was extended above his head, half hiding his face. His one visible eye was blank, his skin waxy. Grit had embedded in his upper cheek as if he had slid across the court surface.

Packi sucked in a long breath. "It wasn't a heart attack."

"How do you know?"

"Come around this way."

Kay brushed clay from her knees as she rose. She took her time, making a wide circle around the man's feet. She pursed her lips and scowled down at the victim. "Definitely not a heart attack."

A large, brown bloodstain had bloomed across the man's chest, soaking his white nylon shirt. A tennis racquet lay on the ground, a foot from his outstretched hand. Several tennis balls, stained with the same red-brown color, were near the body. Kay nudged one out of the way.

"Be careful." Packi pressed her arms against her stomach to fight off a rising nausea. "We have a crime scene here. The police will want to see everything as we found it."

"Sorry," Kay muttered. "This is upsetting. Not like the hospital with staff and monitors and . . . It happened right here." She put her hands under her armpits and stooped to look at the man's face, then sighed and turned away. "I don't know him."

"Me neither. Could be new or a renter."

"It's possible he's a golf member. I don't know many golfers."

"But he was here practicing tennis. Could be a guest."

"True."

Their dispassionate discussion helped to quell Packi's queasy stomach, but the incongruous scene struck her. How odd to stand over a bloodied body while morning dew dripped from the palm trees, the sprinkler system sent rainbows over the golf course, and an entire community awakened to a new day. *How could this have happened?*

Packi tilted her head to get a different perspective. He would never have been caught in this vulnerable position in life, she thought. Spread out and awkward. Limbs splayed, out of control. Something in the tone of his muscles, his athletic build, his high cheek bones suggested he had lived with confidence and command, always in authority.

Yet, he had died alone.

The sound of sirens drifted in from the main road. The thread of intimacy between her and the victim thinned. Urgency crept into Packi's thoughts.

"We should get off the court." Kay stepped backward toward the gate.

Packi nodded but sank to her knees to study him before EMTs broke into their isolation. A prayer to send him on his way seemed in order, but none came to mind. Too late. She dragged her gaze away from his face to make mental notes: Graying at the temples. A few years younger than herself, mid-fifties perhaps. High-end tennis clothes. Athletic, not real tall, but it was hard to tell with him lying in this position.

"Kay, is there some medical reason he'd bleed from his chest; something internal?" Packi looked over her shoulder to where her friend shuffled from foot to foot.

Kay's eyes darted to the wound, then to the cloudless sky as if to recall memorized text. "Skin is an excellent barrier to hold blood in the body. A puncture wound would break the barrier. A knife, glass, a stick, a bullet." Her hands fell to her sides in frustration. "Geez, Packi, I don't know. I was a pediatric nurse. Let the professionals take care of this. You shouldn't even consider getting involved."

Packi shared her friend's discomfort but ignored the scolding. She rose from her knees and backed away from the body, deep in thought. Footprints. Where were his footprints? None trampled the clay except hers and Kay's coming from the gate. It was as if the man had been dropped into his death pose from above.

Perplexed, she widened her survey. The ball machine on the opposite side of the net had launched its entire bin of balls and now stood silent. The thought of the machine continuing to feed balls to a dead man made her queasy. She bit at her dry lips and forced herself to estimate the number of tennis balls on the court, note their positions, and counted those stained with his blood.

Though Packi had practiced with the team on Court Nine for almost a year, she'd never studied its details. Along the west side, shrubbery screened the metal storage shed used by the maintenance crew. A row of royal palms grew on the opposite side between the court and the golf course. No golfers were in sight. The whooping sirens grew louder.

A metallic odor scented the air around the corpse at her feet. Blood, Packi figured. The last body she discovered had been hundreds of feet away. Pond water had masked the smell. Now her nose twitched.

"I'll go wave the ambulance crew in," said Kay.

Packi blinked to give approval and watched her teammate jog toward the parking lot. She questioned Kay's puncture theory. *Shouldn't there be more blood?* Television crime shows always talked about blood splatter and large pools of red. She ruled out a messy stabbing.

If he was shot, Packi challenged herself to consider, where would the killer have been? She turned in a circle to study the fence surrounding the court. She then scooped up her phone and other stuff and followed her own footprints back through the gate.

"Mizz Walsh?" Deputy Teig's gruff voice contained suspicion and accusation as he marched toward her. "What are you doing here?"

Packi stopped as if caught trespassing. She was peeved she couldn't complete the search of the fence perimeter. "Billy! I'm so glad you're here." His uniformed bulk, layered with police paraphernalia, reassured her. She hadn't seen him in months and tried to smile, but stress turned it into a grimace.

He met her at the corner of the court, his face flushed from his hurried walk. "Was it you called in a medical emergency?"

"Yes, I did." She got the impression he thought the call was an overreaction. "It *was* an emergency. He's over there." Her finger quivered as she pointed into the tennis court.

"We're too late," Kay said, rushing up behind him. "He's gone."

The sight of the body jolted the deputy out of his skepticism. He squinted through the windscreen and back at the women. "You touch anything?"

"Only to check for a pulse," said Kay in a firm, professional tone. "He's been dead for hours." She raised her chin, ready for a reprimand. "And I may have kicked a ball."

Teig pursed his full lips. "Stay outside this gate," he ordered and hustled onto the tennis court.

The women watched as the deputy bent to put his fingers to the dead man's neck and then straightened up to speak into his radio. The phalanx of EMTs hurrying up the sidewalk toward the court must have received his radio message. They slowed their advance, filed through the gate with their equipment, and made their own determination of death. Soon afterward, plain-clothed officials began their painstaking process of documenting the passing of a human life. Deputy Teig strung yellow crime-scene tape across the sidewalk to hold back tennis players and curious neighbors.

"Packi!" Beth Hogan rushed along the sidewalk toward the growing crowd at the side of the tennis court. "What's going on?"

Marilyn Scott trotted alongside Beth, keeping pace with the team captain's long strides. "Somebody sick?" She and her fellow nurse, Kay, exchanged professional glances.

"Oh," Marilyn said. "Who was it?"

"Don't know. We guess he's a renter or a guest," said Packi, "but could be wrong. I don't know half the members of the club."

Held back by the crime scene tape, Beth stood tall and craned her neck to see the victim. Her mouth dropped open. "I see blood."

"Shhh." Packi glanced at the cluster of people gathered behind them, but they were busy speculating among themselves about the dead man. She moved closer to Beth and Marilyn. "Someone murdered him."

"How terrible!" Marilyn covered her face and spoke from behind her hands. "Why would you think it was murder?"

"A lot of blood," began Packi, "and . . ."

"There was *not* that much blood," argued Kay. "A splotch on his shirt, that's all. Could have gouged himself with his tennis racquet; or his pacemaker poked through his skin when he fell."

"Pacemaker?" Beth snorted but then clamped her hand over her mouth to cover her lack of reverence in the presence of death. "That's far-fetched."

"I'm just saying there may be an innocent cause." Kay's voice fell to a whisper. "A tragic death, yes, but not murder. Not in a place like Paradise Palms."

"I hope you're right." Packi eyed the tennis court. "But I think there's more going on here."

Beth's eyebrows shot up. "You found clues? Something to help the cops again?"

"Oh, no." Marilyn crossed her thin arms over her chest. "We got in enough trouble last time Packi solved their case for them." Her defiance withered beneath a sharp glance from Beth. "Well, anyway, we shouldn't get involved."

"Hey, it worked out." Beth's commanding voice drew glares from the crowd, so she ducked her head and lowered the volume. "Besides, if we can put a murderer behind bars, we'd do some good. Don't ya think?"

"This isn't a murder," insisted Kay. "I can't believe such a thing."

"Of course, it was an accident," said Marilyn. "Right, Packi? An accident that . . ."

Beth sniffed. "Here he comes." Her sardonic comment turned the women toward a commotion on the walkway.

A wiry man with a graying crew cut ran toward Court Nine as fast as his little legs would take him. His corporate tie and starched white shirt set him apart.

Vincent Pearce, the club manager, reacted to issues with an abundance of energy, but his flustered attempts to control and organize never impressed the club membership. Vince was always on the hot seat and caught grief from every side in any argument or issue. He was a man afraid for his job and now came late to the scene, clutching a defibrillator system and a first aid kit. Deputy Teig stopped the frantic man at the gate of Court Nine.

While Teig dealt with the club manager, Packi motioned for her teammates to move even further from the onlookers. "Take a look around. Wouldn't a man practicing tennis bring his gear to the court?"

In unison, the three tennis players leaned to the right to see the court-side bench.

"There's nothing there," said Beth. "Where's his stuff? His extra racquet?"

"Yeah." Kay massaged her dimpled chin as she thought. "A jacket? Extra balls? Everyone carries a tennis bag for their stuff."

"Exactly." Packi made a sweeping gesture over the tennis court, now swarming with officials. "What happened to his bag?" As her teammates considered the possibilities, she stepped through the low shrubs lining the court fence. "While Billy is busy with our club manager, let's check out the area."

"Get back here, Packi," hissed Kay and put her arm out to deter the other women from following. "Deputy Teig said to stay here."

Packi stopped, knee deep in variegated Crotons. "Billy said to stay *outside the gate*," she pointed out. "He didn't mean for us to stand still. We can help their investigation by searching beyond the crime scene for things they'll overlook."

She marched through the landscaped plantings, determined to go it alone if need be but hoped her friends would join her. Within seconds, she sensed someone behind her. She didn't let her relief and pleasure show.

"What are we looking for?" asked Beth.

"I don't know." Packi gave a vague wave to a row of ten-foot high azaleas. "Something that doesn't belong." She continued to scan the base of the hedge but lifted her eyes as Kay and Marilyn joined them.

Kay gave a huge, martyred sigh. "What should we do?"

Packi sent a glance of thanks to her tennis partners. "Let's look for his bag. Maybe the killer grabbed it, took out valuables, and tossed it away."

"Something in his bag was worth killing him?" Marilyn grimaced but bent low to peer beneath the azaleas.

"Who knows." Beth shrugged and suggested they spread out to search.

Packi had concentrated on the immediate area and now appreciated her team captain's broader view. "You're right. Let's each search one side of the court and maybe a hundred feet back. I'll take the golf course side. That's a perfect spot for a killer to hide and shoot from outside the fence."

She frowned as she considered other scenarios that ended in the murder of the unknown man. "Look for anything out of order. Avoid stepping on soft dirt and look for fresh footprints near the fence." She glanced at the crowds milling around the court. "Beth, check out around the maintenance shed back there."

"Yes, Boss." Beth saluted and headed to the west side.

Packi shuddered at the thought of being the boss but pushed on. "Kay, please search the area between the fence and the road. Marilyn, can you make your way through the crowd and see what you can find on that end?"

With her troops dispatched, Packi hurried around to the golf course side of the court. Five-inch thick Bermuda grass slowed her pace. Her view of the crime scene was obscured by long panels of windscreen, attached to the fencing and printed with the club logo. At a gap in the screening, she peeked inside the court to watch the evidence technicians process the scene. She wondered if the investigators even considered the outside of the court as a possible source of clues. Apparently not, or they would have taped off a bigger area.

Billy Teig had his back to her, taking notes and questioning the club manager. She vowed to help the deputy by finding . . . She cringed at her own audacity. *Finding what? Something.*

3

Deputy Billy Teig was used to emergency calls from Paradise Palms and several dozen other retirement communities in his sector of Lee County. Every day senior citizens fell, got sick, or succumbed to old age. It was the demographic. He thought of the circle of life as in *Lion King*, his son's favorite movie. Mikey had seen the Disney film dozens of times.

Teig blinked away pleasant images of his son to focus on the club manager pacing in front of him. *Nervous little critter.* He itched to get away from the annoying man.

"One last question, Mr. Pearce." Teig closed his note pad. "Do you have security cameras covering this area?"

Vincent Pearce gawped for a moment but then sniffed. "I assure you, Deputy. We don't spy on our members."

Teig ignored the man's pompous attitude and slipped a business card from his shirt pocket. "If you hear or see anything that might help this investigation, call the sheriff's department." He pushed the card into the manager's hand and looked at him hard. "And keep this area taped off until further notice."

"This is bad," said Pearce, raking his fingers through his bristled hair. "The membership wants everything in pristine condition." He shot a look at the crowd of club members gawking at the crime scene. "This is unacceptable. You have to clean this up. Now. The club has a reputation to uphold."

Patience, Teig told himself. He interrupted the man's rant. "Calm yourself, Mr. Pearce. The investigators are processing the scene and will be gone soon." He hid his irritation beneath a bland countenance and spoke in monotone, underscoring his next words with a warning. "Do *not* disturb any part of this crime scene."

The man glared upward at Teig. "I demand you . . ."

The arrival of a television news van gave the deputy a reprieve from the club manager's agitation.

"Oh, Lord." Pearce ran to intercept the reporters.

Teig opened his notepad again and put a question mark behind Vincent Pearce's name. He filled his chest with heavy, tropical air and surveyed the crowd. He groaned when he spotted four women poking around beyond the fencing of the tennis court. They reminded him of pink and white birds—spoonbills maybe, pecking in the muck for crayfish. "She's at it again."

He trudged along fencing to the far end of the tennis court and rounded the corner. "Mizz Walsh!"

She jumped when she heard his yell. *Good,* he thought. *I'll instill some fear, assert my authority*. But she raised her skinny arms in what appeared to be joy. The sturdy little woman in her silly tennis outfit ran toward him, barely denting the thick grass. Mizz Hogan, on the other hand, followed behind, sinking into the grass up to her ankles. He assumed a command presence and braced himself.

"Wait until you hear what I have for you!" Mizz Walsh called.

Something about her freckled shoulders, sun-burnt nose, and spritely movements reminded him of quilts, pots of stew, and fierce hugs. "What'd I tell you?" he demanded, interrupting her happy dance.

She stopped short with the rest of the gaggle behind her. "You said to stay outside the gate." She blinked big, innocent eyes and enveloped herself in a pink aura. "Never mind that, Billy. You have to go after the garbage truck."

"What?" His gaze followed her point to a waste-hauler lumbering into a nearby street. "No."

"We've looked everywhere for his bag, but it's not here." She steepled her fingers as if schooling a six-year-old. "The killer must have thrown it in the garbage bin behind the club house. I saw them empty the bin into the truck ten minutes ago. That's where his bag is."

"Whoa! That's enough." He hated any loss of control, and she did it to him every time. "Now get back to the rest of the crowd and stay out of this."

"Think about it, Billy." Mizz Walsh stepped in the right direction but persisted. "Tennis players always have a gear bag. His is missing. I figure the killer took the bag for its contents—or to hide the victim's identity.

He bit. "What was in the bag?"

"Well, I don't know *everything*." She looked at him from under her brows. "For goodness sake, Deputy Teig. I am not the investigator."

Pressure tightened his collar and burned his neck. "You best remember that!" He narrowed his eyes at the four, clenched his teeth, and marched away to do real police work.

"Wait! I'm sorry." Mizz Walsh sprinted ahead and got in front of him. "Please, Billy. I mean, Deputy Teig. I'm only trying to help, and we found an important clue. You must listen."

Stepping on her was out of the question. Maybe, just maybe, the busybody did have something. He took advantage of his dark sunglasses and closed his eyes before he capitulated. "What did you find, Mizz Walsh?"

She covered her victory with a sweet smile and held up a scrap of paper. He wasn't fooled.

"Marilyn found . . ." A squeak from behind him stopped her. "I mean, *we* found a torn identification card in the wastebasket next to Court Eight."

He took the proffered card and held it by its edges. It was heavy paper; the type of card to fit into a luggage tag, maybe on a tennis bag. "It doesn't say much."

Mizz Walsh pulled down his hands to bring the card to her eye level. She hung onto his wrist as she pointed. "That's half a last name, and that KS means Kansas, right?"

She challenged him with her eyebrows and waited, but he refused to agree, refused to give her the satisfaction.

The pesky woman blinked first and stepped back. "We'll keep looking for the other half," she said.

"No." Teig dropped the card into a plastic baggie and put it inside the cover of his notebook. "Go home."

The garbage truck two blocks away groaned and belched. He wondered if she was right about a missing bag. "If you really want to help, get those people to go play their tennis games. And don't go starting any rumors." He huffed. *Like that's going to happen.*

"Sure, Billy. We're glad to help." She motioned for the other three women to urge the crowd to go on with their activities. "But there's something else I want to show you."

He ground his teeth. Try as he might, he couldn't be rude to the little lady. Nor could he ignore that Mizz Walsh had good intuitions. For a fact, she helped him score points with the sheriff in the real estate murder investigation months ago.

Not gonna happen again. Keep her out, he warned himself, but Mizz Walsh scurried like a field mouse around the backside of the tennis court. She stopped near a metal shed and beckoned to him. "Come on. Take a look at these." She ducked inside a row of hedges.

"Now what?" He hiked up his belt and quickened his pace.

4

Even the most persistent gawkers gave way as Deputy Teig ordered them back to make room for the EMTs to cart the body away. From a distance, Packi marveled at his commanding presence. He said little. Head and shoulders above most of the Paradise Palms residents, he herded them out of the way merely by stepping in their direction. His size and uniform gave him all the authority he needed.

An idling ambulance waited at the nearest curb with its red and blue lights flashing. EMTs heaved the wheeled gurney through heavy, wet grass and loaded the shrouded body into the back. The procession of concerned citizens followed the gurney's progress, then broke into small groups to whisper and speculate. Cell phones were out to spread fact, rumor, and misinformation.

To sort out her thoughts, Packi retreated to the relative quiet of the bleachers on Court Eight. From there, she surveyed her community. Except for two young auxiliary cops stringing additional crime scene tape around Court Nine, life began to settle into normalcy: two old guys in polo shirts and wide-brimmed hats wheeled their golf cart back to their fairway; the new tennis pro barked instructions for the 3.5 team on Court Six to form two lines; and bicyclists with beach totes pedaled toward the pool.

Packi's teammates found her under the canopy, deep in thought. They flopped themselves onto the cool metal bleachers, disrupting the scenarios running through her head.

"So what did he say?" Kay pointed casually toward Deputy Teig huddled with detectives near the metal storage shed. Her eagerness and heightened color belied her nonchalance.

Packi finished a thought and tucked it away before focusing on Kay's question. "He didn't say much, but he listened. I'm sure of it." Through the fencing, she caught Teig's eye as he pulled aside the windscreen. He ignored her wave and turned back to the detectives.

Beth rolled her eyes and waited for Packi to continue.

"I showed him the footprints you found near the maintenance shed, Beth."

"Really?" asked Marilyn. "So tell us what he said."

Packi set aside her worry about the victim and let a grin slip onto her face. "Well, mostly he growled, but I'm sure he's glad we found the prints."

"Yeah, right," Beth said.

Still under the pall of the murder, the women laughed only to themselves. The murder had shaken them, but Packi's little joke eased the tension. Kay was right—this sort of thing didn't happen in Paradise Palm. No one would feel comfortable until the murderer was in jail. Packi vowed to find what evidence she could, and Billy Teig *should* appreciate the help. Brainstorming with the team would bring out their best ideas.

"I suggested a killer might have aimed a through the flap in the windscreen," Packi told the group. "He agreed that the shooter might have hidden near the shed and gotten a good shot from over there."

Kay lowered her head and sighed. "So Deputy Teig confirms the man was shot."

"More or less,"said Packi. "He was studying powder residue on the screen."

"Shooting a man is hard to do." Beth bit at her lower lip and frowned toward the crime scene. "Hitting a stationary paper target takes skill, but shooting a human being takes something different."

"Especially if he's running back and forth playing tennis." Kay grimaced as if her beloved tennis game had been besmirched by the incident.

"This craziness drives me nuts," Beth said, gathering her gear. "I'd better go join the drill. The team captain has to set a good example, you know. Get things back to normal." The bleacher clanged beneath her heavy foot as she stepped down. "I know you're going to help Teig with the investigation, Packi. I want in on it, but right now, I have to join the rest of the team. Let me know when you need me."

"Me too," Marilyn said. "I mean, not that I'd be much help, but I want to work on the case with you. I could do something." She twiddled with the zipper on her tennis bag. "But I should go practice too."

Packi had hoped for team solidarity, a joint effort. "Sure," she said, though her confidence began to slide. "You girls go practice. The new pro barely knows me anyway. He won't miss me, and I want to see what the investigators find."

"You mean you're going to bribe Teig with your special cookies so he'll tell you about the case." Beth wagged her finger at Packi, snorted a laugh, and headed for Court Six.

"Well?" Kay's rump was still planted on the bleacher. Her eyes darkened with worry, but mischief played with her grin as she leaned toward Packi. "What's the plan?"

Heartened by Kay's presence, Packi knitted her fingers together and circled her thumbs against each other. It steadied her and helped to smooth the wrinkles in her thoughts. "I don't know. I'm afraid Deputy Teig's too busy here, and he'll forget about the tennis bag in the garbage truck."

"You don't really think the dead guy's bag is in the truck? And if it is, it's mashed up with garbage." Kay's nose crinkled, as if odors from the decaying mess had wafted her way.

Kay's not ready for this, Packi thought. "But what if it *is* there," she said, "and we don't try to find it?" Disappointed, Packi swung her legs off the side of the bleachers. "You can go to practice. I'm going to check out the truck."

She didn't begrudge the others for wanting to put the nasty death business behind them or for playing tennis as if lives hadn't changed. She was certain they were sincere about eventually helping. Tennis drills sounded attractive to her right now too, but she felt duty-bound to help the investigation and to find that tennis bag. *After all didn't I find the poor man?* She aimed her footsteps toward the parking lot, averting her eyes from Court Six and the team who expected her to be ready for the next match.

In the parking lot, the sun's glare bounced off the asphalt, reminding her of the dermatologist's standard admonishments. She pulled the bill of her cap down to protect her face and hoisted her bike off the rack.

"I'm right behind you, partner." Kay trotted toward Packi and gave an impish grin before retrieving her own bicycle. "You're not going to have all the fun without me."

A weight lifted off Packi's shoulders as she rode her Schwinn under the clubhouse portico and past the golf cart garage with her friend pedaling at her side.

* * *

They caught up to the garbage truck on Manatee Lane. The driver looked at them quizzically as Kay and Packi dismounted from their bikes five feet from his front bumper. A bronzed young man at the back of the truck bobbed his head to the beat of music playing through earbuds. He didn't see the women and went through his routine of dumping cans into the compactor.

Packi held her fingers beneath her nose to block the smell, hoping her reaction didn't offend the workers. *How do they stand the stench?* She and Kay walked their bikes upwind to the side of the truck.

The young man turned the trash can upside down on the grass and leaned the lid against its side. He removed his cap and brushed his long, sandy-blond hair away from his forehead with a glistening forearm. He turned to hop onto the truck's back platform but stopped, startled by the two women. He pulled his earbuds out and stood, cap in hand, waiting for them to speak.

Very polite, thought Packi, wondering if the disposal company trained employees to be respectful. "Hello." She gave him a small but amiable wave. "May I ask you a question?"

The young man peeled off large leather gloves and tucked them under a well-muscled arm. Packi hoped he didn't mean to shake hands and held firmly to her handlebars. He kept his distance and nodded, looking like he'd rather be anywhere else.

Embarrassed by his discomfort, Packi lost what she was about to say. Her partner came to her rescue.

"We're looking for a tennis bag—a gym bag," said Kay. "We thought it might have been in the clubhouse dumpster. Have you seen it?"

"Uhh." The young man tugged at the frayed collar of his thin T-shirt and looked toward the driver's door for help.

The driver opened his door and stepped down to street level. He bobbed his head in greeting. "Ma'am?"

Mesmerized by his wild beard, sharp eyes, and red-leather skin, Packi repeated Kay's inquiry and kept babbling. "If you did see a bag—but you probably didn't—it would help a lot if we found it." She stopped rambling when the driver climbed back on the truck and stretched across to the passenger side.

"This what ya lookin' for?" When his boots hit the ground again, he held up a black gym bag with a yellow stripe along the sides.

Packi leaned her bicycle on its kickstand and stepped forward until an odorous cloud stopped her, still several feet from her prize. "It appears to be." Her nose twitched, giving away her distress. "Where did you find it?" She wished he'd move out of the fumes, but he seemed to enjoy her struggle with the odor he worked in every day.

"Big dumpster. Right on top." He relented and stepped toward her. "Figured to bring it home, maybe sell it at the flea market." He sized her up from under a cocked brow. "Ain't nobody care if we take things that's been throwed out."

"No, no," stammered Packi. "I'm sure you're right, but it belonged to a friend of ours who threw it away by mistake. May I have it?"

The man sucked saliva through his teeth. "I earn extree money at the flea market."

"Of course!" Packi stepped back and smiled into his sunburnt face. "That's a wonderful way to recycle. Must be amazing, the things people throw out." She wished the men would give her the darn bag, get back in their truck, and end the encounter.

They didn't.

"Oh, wait," said Kay. She rooted around in the saddlebag of her bike and came up with a few dollar bills. She held the cash out to the driver.

He handed Packi the bag, removed the glove from his right hand, finger by finger, and took the money. The bills disappeared into his hip pocket. The driver then lifted his bearded chin to bid them farewell and hauled himself into his seat. When the younger man climbed aboard and thumped the side wall, the truck lumbered off, leaving a cloud of stink in its wake.

"Thank you." Packi tugged a tissue from her pocket and held it to her nose. "I didn't know what to do."

"Should've thought of the cash sooner." Kay laughed. "You know, that one on back could be Mr. February on my calendar any day."

"Kay! He can't be more than nineteen years old."

"Legal age in Florida."

"Oh, my God." Packi hid her blush behind the tissue but laughed in spite of herself.

Kay sobered up first. "Should we?" she asked, nodding at the tennis bag.

"I suppose so." Packi hesitated, afraid she held important evidence—or maybe nothing. Maybe they had only embarrassed themselves by chasing after garbage men.

The women hauled their bikes across the sidewalk to a bench overlooking the water hazard on the fourteenth hole. Packi put the tennis bag between them and scrutinized its outside: good quality, average weight, standard length, no garbage smell. She tapped the edge of a clear plastic rectangle where an identification card would be. Empty.

"You were right," said Kay, impressed. "Go ahead. Open it."

Packi produced another tissue from her tennis skirt pocket and glanced up and down the street to make sure they were alone. Across the pond, a foursome on the green paid them no mind. She grasped the zipper slide, pulling it to its full length until the bag gaped open. They leaned in close to peer inside.

Kay kept her hands on her knees as if afraid of contaminating the evidence—if that's what was in the bag. She squinted at the contents and tsked in disappointment. "Nothing unusual—a can of balls, towel, clothes."

"Deodorant, grip wrap," Packi added. "And . . ." Tucked along the side was a sheet of glossy, photo-type paper.

"Maybe someone we know?" suggested Kay with heightened interest.

Packi reached in with her tissue to grasp a corner of the photo.

"Uh-oh." Kay poked Packi in her ribs. "Company."

A white Lee County Sheriff's squad car slid to a stop at the curb. The women froze as if they were shoplifters caught on camera. Kay then jumped up from the bench to block Teig's view of the gym bag.

Packi recovered from her guilt while Deputy Teig hauled himself from behind his steering wheel. *Look now, or you'll never see it*, she told herself. Packi kept one eye on the deputy as he slammed his car door and hiked up his pants. With a magician's sleight of hand, she pulled out the photo and glanced down.

"Oh!" She dropped the picture as if the image burned her fingers right through the tissue.

Deputy Teig stopped in front of Kay, folded his arms above his belly, and looked over her head.

"From the garbage truck?"

Both women nodded. Kay moved aside.

"Touch anything?"

"No," Packi stammered, as she tried to shut the gaping bag. "Of course not."

Teig eyed the tissue in her hand and raised his eyebrows over the rim of his mirrored sunglasses.

"At least," Packi corrected herself, "not without protecting it from my fingerprints." She waved the tissue like a white flag and smiled up at his grim face. "Sorry, Billy. We were excited to find the bag." She stood up and offered it to him. "All the ordinary stuff in there, except . . ." She nodded into the bag.

Teig flexed his fist and took the bag without looking inside. Tension radiated from his shoulders and back as he asked about their conversation with the truck driver. His aggravation seemed restrained only by his badge, bulletproof vest, and professional courtesy.

Packi wished he'd remove his sunglasses. She needed to see if anger reached his eyes; if her actions had ruined their friendship.

"I want to help, Billy. You were so busy, and the truck would go to the dump."

Teig ignored her explanation.

"How about I bake brownies for you and Mikey? With pecans?"

The deputy set his jaw, making ropey muscles stand out in his neck. "No brownies, no cookies, no nothin'!" He stomped to his car. Climbing in, he said, "Stay away from this investigation."

Packi watched the squad car drive to the end of the street and turn in the direction the garbage truck had taken. *The photo is his problem now,* she thought. She wondered why she couldn't talk to Teig about the image. It was a clue, maybe a picture of the murderer, so why had she chickened out?

I'd make a lousy detective. She bumped her bike over the curb and pedaled after Kay. *Maybe I* should *stay out of the investigation.* She tightened her grip on the bike's handlebars and imagined her fingers closing around the throat of the man in the photograph.

5

H*ow can people go on with their lives?* Packi waited for her turn to volley with the tennis instructor. She and Kay had returned to the tennis courts to catch the last half of practice. Beth and Marilyn gave her questioning glances but accepted her shrug as a promise to divulge information after practice.

"Stay out of it," Teig had warned.

The ambulance was gone, but crime scene officials scurried like a brigade of ants to and from Court Nine with cameras, cell phones, and evidence bags. Golfers golfed. Zumba music drifted in from the pool area. Tennis players made their shots, kept score, and played their games—with occasional glances at the police activity.

Packi tried to play through the distractions but ruminated over the terrible event, Billy's anger, the gym bag—and the photo. She hit the ball into the net.

"Follow through," Sam commanded. "Swing low to high, Packi. Make contact below your skirt!"

Her second shot went into the net; the third, out of bounds. She looked to the sky and groaned. As she trotted to the end of the line, she spotted Deputy Teig watching her through the windscreens at the far end of the practice court. Embarrassed by her poor play, she pretended not to see him. He probably figured she'd forgotten the crime and gotten back to her simple life. *But how could I?*

Kay's tennis skills suffered too. Mopping sweat from her forehead, she joined Packi at the back of the line. "I can't play with him watching us." She masked her face with a towel and inclined her head toward the deputy. "He wants to talk to you."

"I doubt it." When the women glanced Teig's way, he turned his back to them. "Probably amazed at our agility and tennis prowess." Packi snickered at her foolish humor. "Or making sure we're not meddling with the investigation."

Packi focused on her shots when it was her turn, but while in line, five-deep with women intent on practice or chatting about their plans for the day, her mind wandered back to the murder. It wasn't yet official, of course, but certainly it was a murder. Others had died from heart attacks on the tennis courts but never had the aftermath been so intense. Any announcement of a homicide would be a formality.

The crime-scene specialists—and Billy too—had the experience, but Packi feared they were too focused on minutia. She had to do her part. She vowed to stay under the radar and out of Billy's way and keep her eyes open. That was the plan anyway.

Even as she made her decision to stay in the background, the photo invaded her mind and rolled a wave of nausea through her body. She beat back the sickness with a wicked backhand, an overhead smash, and a put-away drive. Her friends hooted their encouragement.

When tennis practice finally ended, she collected her gear and paid her fee to Sam.

"Good play today, Packi." Zinc oxide, slathered across the pro's burnt nose, shimmered in the sun. "Aggression gives you power. Keep it up."

Packi couldn't smile—not at his comical nose, nor into his kind eyes—but accepted his compliment with a nod. She sidestepped the gathering of players who muttered about the police still disrupting their world.

No gossip. She had promised Teig. Beth waved her over to the relative quiet of the bleachers where Marilyn, Kay, and Grace, the team's unofficial mother hen, had their heads together.

"Kay told us about the gym bag." Beth muffled her words behind her hand. "Anything good in it? What did Teig say?"

"Nothing good." Packi sagged onto a metal seat. "And I don't think he looked inside." Maybe it was the humidity or the intense practice, but the burden of the investigation made her wish for a nap.

"Well, what should we do?" asked Grace, her cherub face pink with anticipation. "What's your plan?"

Their presence bolstered Packi's resolve. She straightened her spine, shook off her weariness, and welcomed their enthusiasm. "No plan yet, but let's talk about what we know so far." The tennis players drew closer. "The garbage men found a gym bag, and Marilyn fished a torn identification card out of the trash. Probably taken from the bag."

"So what was in the bag?" Beth asked. "Anything worth getting killed over?"

"The usual stuff." Kay said, glancing at Packi for confirmation.

Not quite, thought Packi, glad Kay didn't know she'd seen the photo. She busied herself with the folds of her tennis skirt. "It seems certain the man was shot."

"Mizz Walsh!"

Packi jerked up to see Deputy Teig at the corner of Court Nine, a stalwart guard of the crime scene. He summoned her with a crook of his index finger.

Kay rolled her eyes. "The long arm of the law requests the honor of your presence," she said, though she barely moved her lips.

"Be right with you, Billy!" Packi unfolded her stiff knees and pushed herself off the bleacher. "I don't know if I'm in trouble or what," she whispered. "Can you wait for me?"

"If he drags you off to jail, we'll bail you out."

"Beth, be quiet!" scolded Grace. "He can hear you." She turned her motherly concern on Packi. "I'm sure you didn't break any laws, so don't let him bully you."

"Don't worry, ladies," Packi said. "He probably wants to confer on the clues we turned up earlier." But she wasn't so certain. She gathered her courage and walked toward Deputy Teig.

"I didn't touch anything else, Billy. Honest." She held up her right hand to swear to the truth.

"Humph." Deputy Teig pulled the brim of his hat lower. "You did good out there."

In shock, Packi stopped and peered up at him, shading her eyes from the sun. "You mean one of my clues helped the investigation?" Delighted, she wanted to hear more. "Was it the footprints? The bag? The scrap of paper?"

Teig humphed again. "I mean your tennis. You play good for a woman your age."

"Oh." Disappointment blew a hole in her vision of herself. Anger surged into the gap. "A woman my age, Billy? What kind of a crack is that?" She advanced on him with her finger pointed at his bulletproof vest. "You are such a curmudgeon, Deputy Teig. A grouch and a crab." She poked him in the chest to underscore each word. "I'm cordial to you. I bake for you. I help with your investigations, and all I get is a 'humph!' You better drop this antisocial stuff, or you'll be one unhappy old man."

He backed up into the fence and looked over her head at the women in the bleachers as if for help. Packi glanced back at their panicked faces too, and realized her small, bony finger was a mistake. Her anger fizzled. She clamped her mouth shut and clenched her shaky fist. *Momentary insanity—that's what I'll tell the judge.*

Deputy Teig caught her fist between his two huge paws. "Sorry, Mizz Walsh." His Southern drawl sounded like honey. "I apologize if I offended you. I didn't mean . . ."

Strength drained away with the adrenaline, leaving her knees weak. "Oh, Billy. I'm sorry." She closed her eyes and took comfort from his warm hands enveloping her cold one. "It's not the age thing. I wanted to help, to find . . ." She pulled her hand back from Teig's and hugged her ribs. "I've been upset since . . ." She paused a long second. "Did you look in the gym bag?"

His chest, already padded by protective gear, expanded even further as he drew in a slow, deep breath. "That's what I wanted to talk to you about." He took her by the elbow and led her along the path between two courts, away from her friends. "Did you recognize anyone in the pictures?"

"There was more than one picture?" Packi processed that thought and shook her head. "I don't know . . . I mean, he looked Asian. No, I didn't recognize anyone in the picture." The world suddenly seemed foreign and malignant, and she wanted no part of it. She shivered in spite of the late-morning sun burning her skin.

"I'm sorry you saw the photo." Teig's gruffness turned soft—the side of him she knew hid beneath his bluster. "So you let me handle everything," he said. "If Detective Leland questions you about the bag or finding the victim, I'll be with you."

"Thank you, Billy," she murmured, "but I'm fine. Really." She lifted her chin and rubbed her hands together to reenergize herself. "I admit I was upset. I feel like choking that man in the photo, but I can't. What I can do is help find him—be your eyes and ears."

"No, Mizz Walsh." His leather holster creaked as he pulled himself up to his full height and squared his shoulders. "You're done."

"But, Billy, I've also been thinking about the victim, thinking about the blood."

"Don't think, Mizz Walsh." He pulled out a cell phone and began to peck out a message with a stylus. "Just let it be."

She maneuvered into his line of sight and smiled, making a silent request to continue. "He was shot with a rifle, wasn't he?"

"A rifle?" Deputy Teig looked at her like she had two heads. "At that range, a rifle bullet would have done a lot more damage."

"But you confirm he was shot, right?"

"I didn't say that." He clamped his lips tighter and punched letters into the text.

"Even with a handgun, there should've been more blood," Packi said. "Think about it. These are clay tennis courts, Billy. The surface is designed to absorb rain. There are several layers down there to drain away water—or blood. That's where it went."

The deputy stopped pecking at the phone, the stylus poised above the screen. He listened.

"And did you notice that before the crime scene officials got here, there were almost no footprints on that court? Only mine, Kay's, and yours. None from the victim and none from his killer."

Deputy Teig slid the stylus into its holder. "Go on."

"The courts are watered each night, say at nine o'clock. That means he was killed sometime before that. His clothes didn't seem damp. They had time to dry. I could ask Dave about the watering schedule for you, or Sam would know."

Teig pulled the stylus out again. "Who's this Dave?"

"The groundskeeper." She waved in the general direction of Court One. "He was grooming the first court when I arrived this morning—before Kay and I found the body."

"And Sam?" The stylus all but disappeared within Teig's fat fingers as it hit letters in quick succession. "Who's he? Was he here this morning?"

"Sam Vickroy, our new tennis pro. He's the one in the floppy hat over there giving lessons. I didn't see him before our team practice."

Packi didn't mind the rapid-fire questions. Billy finally seemed to need her ideas and respected her answers. She scrutinized the deputy as he made his notes and waited until he paused.

"There's something different about you, Billy." She stepped back to get a wider view as he tapped out a few more words. He didn't look up.

"Ah-ha!" Packi pointed an accusatory finger at the deputy. "You've lost weight. You took my advice!"

"Humph." The big man slid the stylus into his pocket, flipped the cover over the phone, and turned away. "What I did was stop taking your bakery bribes." He nodded a good-bye to an investigator at the gate of Court Nine and kept walking.

Packi trotted after him. "Oh, come on! My cupcakes and cookies didn't do all that."

He stopped and slid a glance back at her.

She put her hand over her mouth. "Sorry, Billy, that came out wrong."

"No offense taken, Mizz Walsh. I'm telling you so you don't try to worm information about this case out of me with your desserts. Never worked, you know."

"Of course not, and that was never my intention." She looked away so her face wouldn't betray the fib. "I share because I love baking and can't eat it all myself."

She almost felt bad about derailing his diet when they first met. He had obviously lost weight since then, though he wasn't yet ready for before-and-after-pictures. Less flesh overflowed his collar, and his shirt strained less across his belly. She estimated twenty pounds were missing. "You look healthier, happier even." She came to a quick stop. "That's it. Billy, you have a girlfriend."

One eyebrow arched over the rim of his sunglasses, and he blew a frustrated breath from his still-fleshy cheeks.

"No?" She ran ahead to get in front of him. "Well then, something good is happening with your son? How is he?"

A hint of a smile threatened to surface at the corner of the deputy's mouth. "He's doin' good." Teig rounded the front bumper of his cruiser. "I'll tell Mikey you said hello."

Packi remembered the boy from a picture: a happy seven-year old, maybe eight now, with owl glasses, dressed in camouflage and holding a huge fish on the end of a line. The absence of grandchildren in her own life wounded her still.

Teig slammed the car door, and she stopped at the curb as he pulled away.

"I can at least bake for Mikey!" she shouted after the retreating vehicle.

6

Packi's teammates, still clustered on the bleachers, perked up as she headed for the court-side canopy. She broke eye-contact with Kay and hid a grin as she approached. Packi wondered how a stranger might view them: women in their fifties, sixties, and up; dressed in flirty, little tennis outfits; faces lined by experience; bodies held together with braces and therapeutic tape; thinning, dyed hair; toned muscles masked by sagging skin. *Life isn't fair.*

Yet, vitality radiated from these ladies. They beat back time with exercise, humor, and positive outlooks. They ignored the years and shrugged off skin cancers, lumpectomies, and a wide variety of medical issues. She loved that they accepted themselves, and each other, no matter their stage in life, their bank account, their past. A warmth, unrelated to hormones, flashed through her.

"So, no jail sentence?"

Beth guffawed at Kay's little joke. "She's trying to get arrested—poking him in the chest like that. What were you hounding him about?"

"That might have been a mistake." Packi groaned and climbed onto the second tier of the bleachers, grateful for the shade and to be off her feet. "He's our only conduit for information about this case, and now I have to work harder to stay in his good graces."

"You seemed unusually intense," Marilyn said, her soft, South Carolina voice wandering away. She frowned at some annoyance over Packi's shoulder and pursed her lips. "That man has no shirt."

"You can see why," Kay said, sitting up taller. "Now there's a bod to get intense about."

Packi twisted around to see what had offended Marilyn's Southern sensibilities. The affront was easy to spot. He stood at the edge of the crowd in cargo pants and heavy boots. His arms crossed over a gleaming, bare chest as if ready to command the troops.

"That's Jungle Jim," hissed Beth. "He's a fixture at the gym. Every morning I go to yoga, he's lifting weights, working on those pecs."

Kay patted her hair and did her best Mae West impression. "I may change my yoga schedule."

Packi ignored Kay's suggestive leer and watched the commanding figure in combat boots. He seemed to have an unusual interest in the crime-scene technicians—more so than the gossiping crowd. "I've never seen him before. Why *Jungle Jim*?"

"He loves to plant." Beth threw up her hands to illustrate an explosion of growth. "His yard is wild with vegetation from around the world, and he battles with the homeowner association about invasive species every month. There are rumors of machine gun nests and sniper blinds in his jungle."

"Now I know who he is." Marilyn shook off her prim silence. "That's no gentleman. He had a shouting match with Vince Pearce at the last board meeting, and his neighbors detest him."

"I heard that too," said Kay, now more interested in the rumors than the athletic specimen. "He gets right in their faces and doesn't back down."

"Interesting." Packi tried to envision his jungle in the middle of their uniform community. That could certainly affect home values and create hostility. Had it led to violence?

"Anyone up for coffee?" Kay asked, forgetting the body builder and sliding off the bleacher. "Let's go over to the patio. There's still time to get the free stuff."

"You mean the $37,000 coffee?" Beth huffed and slung her bag over her shoulder. "That little item in the annual budget is what Jungle Jim shouted at Pearce about. Called the manager a crooked fraud."

Marilyn gracefully stepped from the bleachers, shaking her head. "Well, I agree. I don't understand how the club spends so much on coffee."

"Don't know," said Kay, "but if our dues pay for it, I'm going to take advantage of it."

Hot coffee sounded pretty good, so Packi hoisted her tennis gear to her shoulder and stood on the lowest bleacher to take a last look at the crime scene.

Small, numbered signs marked where the body had been and where bloodstained tennis balls had rolled. Additional yellow tape cordoned off the maintenance shed. The robot ball thrower stood alone on Court Nine, mechanically aloof, as if it played no part in the recent murder. Technicians, fewer now, conferred, and Deputy Teig had returned. He marched along the fence, as if on a mission.

Wondering what had caused Teig to quicken his steps, Packi searched the gaggle of curiosity seekers for his target. She spotted Jungle Jim's broad shoulders among the onlookers. The shirtless man had also caught sight of the deputy's approach and melted into the crowd, behind the vehicles, and into the park across the street. By the time Billy got through the crowd, Jungle Jim had marched across the boardwalk into the woods. Teig stopped at the curb, wiping sweat from his brow, and stared after the retreating figure.

Packi hopped down from the bleachers and hurried to question Billy Teig about the troublemaker. Maybe he saw her coming, maybe he didn't. The deputy climbed into his squad car and sped away. *What was that about?*

* * *

Over coffee in the small, open-air snack shop next to the courts, the tennis friends chatted about the theatre, sick neighbors, grandchildren. They seemed to have forgotten the crime. Packi did not. She listened to their banter on the periphery of her mind.

"How many balls does the practice machine hold?" Packi's question stopped the conversations.

"A hundred?" Beth shrugged. "I'm guessing."

"Max," countered Kay. "And it changes. Sam tosses out the dead balls as he finds them. Why?"

Packi closed her eyes to envision the crime scene: the victim sprawled at the base line, red-stained tennis balls clustered around the body, and other balls scattered around the court.

"I counted about sixty balls behind the machine, meaning he returned that many. Twenty or so were behind the deuce side of his court, and another fifteen or so were around the body, stained with his blood. More than half were behind the machine."

"I'm sure that means something," said Kay, "but what?"

"It tells us about the time of death," answered Packi. "How long does it take for the machine to shoot out ninety balls? Ten minutes?"

"That depends on the speed setting." Beth took off her visor and ran her fingers through her damp, bluntly chopped hair. "At medium speed, I hit all the balls in about fifteen minutes." She held up her index finger to underscore a point. "Then, I pick up the balls, dump them back into the machine, and start over."

Packi's enthusiasm for her own theory faltered. "So he could have been on his third refill." Disappointed in the dead end, she rose to collect her gear. "I hoped to use our tennis knowledge to help the detectives."

"I think . . ." Marilyn's delicate drawl was impossible to hear in a crowd. As if years of habit taught them to cock their ears when she spoke, the women went silent.

Marilyn wilted in the face of the team's attention but continued. "We could check with Sam." Her voice lost momentum. "To see if someone signed out the machine last night."

Struck by the simplicity of the suggestion, Packi drew in a long breath.

"Let's do it." Kay jumped to her feet, startling Marilyn, and then plopped down again. "Except he's busy right now." She pointed across Court Eight where the tennis pro stood with a tall officially dressed detective. The woman was almost indistinguishable from her male counterparts but for the suit jacket straining to hide a buxom chest.

Detective Cheryl Leland, thought Packi. While teamed with Deputy Teig in last summer's investigation into the death of the real estate developer, Leland had been thorough, yet compassionate. Packi wondered if the detective remembered her and her part in identifying the killer.

The conversation between the tennis pro and the detective wound down. Packi tried to read their body language, his response to the questioning. *Was he overanxious?* Packi watched, as Sam hurried to his teaching court where men waited for their weekly tennis clinic. Detective Leland watched him too, as he gathered the men, loudly assured them nothing more was wrong, and regained control of at least one of his tennis courts.

Beth interrupted Packi's line of thinking. "It'll be more than an hour before we can ask him who was on the ball machine list."

"Maybe she asked him already." Kay eyed the detective making notes as she returned to the crime scene.

"Maybe," mused Packi. "No one's at the pro shop. Let's take a look for ourselves."

"Count me out, girls," said Grace. "My shift starts in an hour. I gotta run. Text me if anything exciting happens."

Packi watched Grace bustle off to her job driving a limo to and from the airport. Whether the job was for extra money or to give structure to her day, Packi didn't know. Grace's happy face was probably a welcoming sight for vacationers and snowbirds arriving for the winter season.

As the rest of the team trooped along the shaded paths, Packi dropped back to walk with Marilyn. "Do you remember anything else about the ID card you found . . . besides the Kansas part?"

Marilyn touched her fingertips together as if it helped her focus. "Half the name was torn away. ' . . . chard', it said, and ' . . . berg, KS' and then the zip code." Distress clouded her face. "I'm really sorry, Packi. I can't remember the zip code."

"You remembered more than I did." Packi patted Marilyn's thin shoulder. "That half a name might match one on the sign-out list and prove our theory."

"Theory?"

"That the shooter removed the tag, so the police couldn't identify the victim and tie the contents of the tennis bag to the killer."

Marilyn laughed in her soft, Southern way. "And he threw the bag into the dumpster, figuring it would be mashed up."

"Exactly."

The two women caught up to Beth and Kay at the entrance to the pro shop. All was quiet. The sun glared off the perfectly groomed, but vacant, bocci ball courts. Two kitchen workers sat on a bench at the rear of the restaurant smoking cigarettes. In the distance, beyond a row of royal palms, golf carts cruised down the first fairway. The pro shop door was unlocked.

"Hello!" Beth's voice was the perfect tool for waking the dead, but no one answered.

"I thought they hired an assistant for Sam," said Packi.

"They did," said Kay. "She hasn't started yet."

The women stepped around and over boxes of new merchandise and made their way to the counter. Beth continued toward the offices at the back of the shop.

"Boy." Kay whistled through her teeth. "If a kleptomaniac wandered in here, they'd have a field day."

"No, that wouldn't happen," said Marilyn. "Everyone at the club is honest."

"Sweetie," Kay said. "We found a body on the tennis court two hours ago."

Marilyn winced, her delicate pink cheeks turning a shocked white. She conceded with a nod and then bent to pick up a stack of visors, arranging them on the shelf as if her busy hands could put her world back in order.

"Nobody here," Beth said from behind the counter. "We'll have to find the sign-up sheets ourselves." She moved a pile of merchandise from the desk to a chair. "It's got to be here somewhere."

"There it is," Packi reached over to pull a clipboard from under several binders. While the others looked on, she flipped back the first page and then several more. "Yesterday's gone. Here's today, and two days ago, and the day before."

Beth took the clipboard. "I know there was a sheet for yesterday. My name was on it for late morning." She shrugged and handed the clipboard back to Packi.

"Well, it was here," said Packi. "Look at the torn paper under the clip." She plucked out a few scraps.

"What are you doing behind the desk!"

The clipboard clattered to the floor. The four women spun around to find the club manager in the hallway which led to the main clubhouse. He bristled like a red rooster defending his territory.

"Sorry, Vince," Packi stammered, not knowing whether to pick up the clipboard or kick it under the desk.

Beth took charge. "We're looking for the sign-up sheet for the ball machine."

"Yeah," said Kay. "We want to reserve the machine for later today."

"At two thirty," added Beth. She squared her shoulders and stepped into the manager's comfort zone.

Vincent Pearce glared up at her but inched back into the hallway. "All right then," he said from a safer distance. "Make sure you don't take any club property. There's too much going on for me to worry about thievery."

"What!" Beth's anger filled the shop.

Packi recognized her friend's rage and caught Beth's fist before it arced toward the man's jaw. Vince recoiled and fell against the door jamb.

"Easy now, Beth." Packi looked to the others for assistance, but Kay was locked in a fierce, dagger-like stare directed at the club manager, and Marilyn camouflaged herself behind a rack of tennis skirts.

"Kay?" Packi sent a plea to her tennis partner and tugged on Beth's arm until she felt her muscles relax.

"Mr. Pearce." Packi let go of Beth and approached the man. "You know, of course, that we'll guard the club's property from any thief that wanders in." She watched his eyes. "Do you happen to know what happened to the tennis sign-up sheet?"

His red, power tie seemed too tight to allow steam to escape from his dampened dress shirt. Thin, white fabric clung to his collar bones. *Why is he so tense?*

"Were you on duty last night, Mr. Pearce?" Packi asked. "Did you see or hear any disturbance down at the tennis courts?"

"Who are you to ask me questions, Mrs. Walsh? I've already spoken to the police." He clamped his mouth shut and looked over his shoulder for a way out.

"Do you know the name of the murdered man?"

The manager's skin quivered. "This is ridiculous. I'm too busy. I have too much to do—important things!" He threw up his hands and scuttled down the hallway toward the main dining room.

"That pigheaded wart!" Kay fumed. "Doesn't he know he works for us?"

"Not for long," said Beth.

"Maybe he's overwhelmed . . . dumbfounded," said Marilyn as she replaced the hangers that had been knocked to the floor. "He gets pressure from the board, from the members, and now this."

"*Dumb*-founded is right!" Kay's fierceness still had control of her face. She stooped for the clipboard and tossed it onto the desk, upsetting the pencil holder. "This got us nowhere. What now, Packi?"

"Let's ask around," said Packi. "If Mr. Pearce won't give up information, maybe other employees will. Marilyn and Kay, would you mind going upstairs to Member Services? Ask about recent guests or renters."

"Good idea." Kay straightened the clipboard on the desk. "I know Nicole up there. Mike and I had our new ID pictures taken last week." She collected pencils and put them in their holder.

"Let's meet at the pool patio in fifteen or twenty minutes," Packi said.

Marilyn nodded and stuffed paper trash into the garbage. "We'll ask about new members too."

"Stop cleaning." Kay took Marilyn's arm and hurried her down the hallway to the main club house.

"Good. Good," Packi muttered as she wove her fingers together and squeezed. It helped her focus. "Beth, how about you go to the gatehouse? The newsletter said we hired a new guard."

"Yep. For the day shift." Beth stopped halfway to the door. "You know, if a member drove in with guests as passengers, there was no reason for them to stop at the gate."

"True." Packi's temples throbbed. "But ask if he remembers anyone from Kansas or anything odd."

"Yes, Boss." Beth hopped over boxed merchandise. "And I'll check cars in the parking lot for Kansas plates." She let the heavy door slam and left a buzzing silence behind her.

Uncertain of her next move, Packi scanned the shop. Notices on the bulletin board announced upcoming events. Racquets waited to be restrung. Golf shoes peeked from their tissue in an opened box. *Ron would have liked these.* She ran her fingers over the mesh vamp and glanced at the price tag before a thought hit her. *Why are golf shoes in the tennis shop?* She answered her own question. *Because some golfers also play tennis.* With her new inspiration, she slipped out of the shop, pulled the door shut, and hoped thieves didn't wander in after all.

The parking lot outside the golf pro shop hummed with activity. Packi took Beth's advice and checked license plates. None from Kansas. She parked her bike near the gym and wove her way on foot through a bevy of golf carts. Her short-skirted tennis outfit was not acceptable golf attire and drew a few surprised glances. She recognized none of the men. Most were intent on their scorecards, getting to the next tee, or refreshing their beer.

The door to the pro shop was blocked by a hearty group of guys guffawing over their day. Big bellies were plentiful. Bowed, painful-looking legs too—as if they'd played football in their previous lives. She pondered how to get through the group until she spotted a little guy, wearing wire-rimmed glasses, holding court in the midst of the giants. Jeff Allair, the club's golf pro, explained one of a thousand golf rules as the men listened. What Jeff lacked in volume, he made up for with Italian-style hand gestures.

"Good afternoon, Mrs. Walsh," Jeff said when he noticed her. He hurried to open the door, and the wall of men moved aside.

How does he do that, she wondered? She played golf only once a week, one of a hundred golfers, yet he remembered her name.

"Hello, Jeff." She met his eyes and smiled, aware that several of the men exchanged looks over her head. "You're the very man I came to see."

"Have a good game, fellas." He waved to the golfers and followed her into the shop. "Haven't seen you in a while, Mrs. Walsh. Come for a lesson? I can fix your grip and your swing to get you more distance."

She waved away the idea. "I'm afraid I'm beyond hope."

"Oh no." He laughed. "It's never too late." He guided her to a quiet corner of the shop surrounded by the alluring scent of leather golf bags and silky shirts. "Now what can I do for you?"

"You heard about the incident on the tennis courts?"

Jocularity slid from Jeff's face, replaced with defensive blandness. "I did."

Her connection with him broke, but she pushed on. "Mrs. Chandler and I found the victim but didn't recognize him. I suspect he was a guest here and maybe played a round of golf."

Jeff glanced around the shop as if hoping some emergency would call him away.

"Do you remember anyone on the tee sheet with a guest in the last few days?" She tried to hold his attention. "Maybe from Kansas?"

The golf pro pushed his rimless glasses back up his nose. "Even if I remembered a guest, Mrs. Walsh, club policy forbids me to give out information." His tone had become flat and official.

"There was no identification on the victim. This could help the police."

"Vince Pearce would have my head if I gave out our records." Jeff gave her a sad smile. "Ask *him*. As club manager, *he* can break the rules."

The shop door opened, admitting a tottering gentleman and a blast of hot air.

"Mr. Hospodar!" Jeff glad-handed the old golfer and led him deeper into the shop. "Heard about your birdie on twelve yesterday. Congratulations!"

The rebuff irritated her. Was it a ruse to escape her questions, or did the pro have to kowtow to male golfers? *No so fast, Mr. Jeff.* Waiting for another chance to quiz him, Packi meandered through well-stocked displays and flipped through the sales rack. A lime-green skort called to her, but the price tag made her put it back. Glancing up from the bargain rack, Packi spotted the golf pro through the window as he hopped into a cart headed in the direction of the practice range. Miffed with herself for letting Jeff escape, she retreated to the exit. *Now what?*

Blinded by the sun, she shaded her eyes with her hand until she could find her sunglasses. A silent golf cart pulled up beside her.

"Heard what you said in there." The man seemed too large for the cart and dangled one leg outside, skimming the pavement with his shoe as he drove. His Wilford Brimley mustache twitched into a warm smile. "I was inside when you asked Jeff about guests."

"Oh?" Packi glanced in the direction the golf pro had fled. So much for a covert investigation. She felt eyes upon her and walked to the windowless side of the building, while the man stayed abreast of her in the cart. "Who are you?"

"Robert McCracken." He doffed his cap. "Call me Duffer. Earned that moniker years back."

"Pleased to meet you, Duffer." Packi liked him immediately and loved his slight Scottish burr. He was the type of person welcomed at any party. He'd be the one dressed as a jolly leprechaun or Santa Claus. "So, are you a member here?"

"Unofficially." He chuckled. "I'm the oldest, fattest bag boy at Paradise Palms, but Jeff keeps me around 'cause I taught him the game." The golf cart rocked as he shifted his weight to massage his knee. "Used to be good. Now I haul golf bags and clean clubs. In return, I get free golf." He grinned like the leprechaun but then turned serious. "I heard about the man killed on the tennis court. Why is a pretty lass like you nosing around in that?"

Packi looked out over the serene eighteenth fairway and wondered the same thing. "Because I can't stand having such evil in our community, and I have to get to the bottom of it." She closed off the world with a long blink and sighed. "You mentioned guests. Do any from the past several days stand out in your memory?"

"Aye. It's been a busy week." His brogue thickened. "Yesterday a group of memorable young ladies signed in. New member, a Ms. Stinson. Canadian, from the sound of it. They had the lads here falling all over themselves to help with their clubs."

His twinkling eyes teased her and heat rose to Packi's cheeks. "Anyone else?"

Duffer sat back against the seat and lost the twinkle. "Mr Graham played in a foursome about the same time. Didn't recognize the other old codgers. Already in their pints when they showed up for their ten o'clock tee time."

"Drunk?"

"They were by the end of the day. Pure sacrilege to play golf in that condition." Duffer shook his head in sorrow. "Two dollar tip from the whole bunch."

Great, thought Packi. *Canadian Barbie dolls and elderly tightwads. Another dead end.* She thanked Duffer for his help and dodged several golf carts on her way to the pool patio. She hoped her teammates had better success.

7

At the gate to the pool area, a woman juggled a beach bag, noodles, and an infant.

A five-year-old girl in a little pink bikini danced at her side. "Hurry, Mom. Hurry."

The lock proved too complicated for the encumbered woman.

"Let me help." Packi reached up to unlatch the tricky gate. The little girl ducked under her elbow and dashed across the patio.

"Emma, wait!" The woman clutched her baby and ran after the heedless girl. "Emma!"

The girl launched herself from the pool deck into the water. In seconds, she popped to the surface, all smiles, with her arms flung skyward in joy. "Come on, Mom!"

Shaken by the little one's escape, Packi scooped up fallen beach toys and rushed after the young family. While the mother admonished the girl, Packi deposited their beach paraphernalia on a nearby chaise lounge. She meant to apologize for her culpability in the girl's mad dash, but the mother was engrossed with settling the situation.

Children and grandchildren here on vacation, Packi mused. She watched the family scene for a moment and then scanned the patio for her friends.

"What was that about?" asked Beth as Packi mounted the steps to the shaded deck overlooking the pool.

"Just me trying to drown the poor child," Packi said, unsettled by her thoughtlessness. "Good thing I didn't have children." Her statement startled her friends, and she realized she'd shared too much. "So, any luck?"

"Not really." Kay protected her eyes from the glare of the sun with her hand and squinted up at Packi. "Though you have a fan in Members Services."

In the shade of a market umbrella, Marilyn sat with her feet tucked under her chair. She nodded in serious agreement.

"Nicole is quite impressed that you saved that alligator last April," Kay said. "She and her little girl visit Big Joe's pond every weekend and have taken your tours of Hammock Preserve."

"Sure. I remember them." Packi edged a chair under the umbrella, hoping Kay didn't take offense that she chose Marilyn's shade to Kay's baking sun. "They were on the night hike a month or so ago."

Kay pulled herself forward and leaned her elbows on the glass table as if to draw her friends into her confidences. "As we suspected," she said, "Nicole can't share member information." Kay looked over her shoulder to make sure no one was in hearing range. "She couldn't say what was in the registration files, but for you, she'd say what was *not* in the record."

Caught by Kay's enthusiasm for intrigue, Packi lowered her voice. "Okay. What was *not* in the file?'

"Well," Kay smoothed the air in front of her with her hands. "Nicole couldn't say where renters and guests came from, but she did say *none* were from Kansas."

"That's something, I guess." A disruption at the entrance gate cut short Packi's disappointment. Beth had arrived, returned from her assigned task and obviously uninterested in covert movements.

"Hey, all!" She balanced a tray on her hand, carhop style, as she let herself in the gate. "Thought we could do with a cold beer." She strode across the pool deck with the ease of one who might have spent years in the service industry. Sunbathers glanced up from their books, perhaps hoping the frosted mugs were for them.

Beth slid the tray onto the table and placed a beer in front of each of the women. "Here ya go. This is a perfect day for a cold one." She plopped herself in an open chair and took a slug. "Ahh!"

To be polite, Packi sipped from the heavy, plastic mug. To her surprise, she liked the feel of the icy liquid sliding down her dry throat. "Not bad." She licked her lips and took a longer drink. "Thank you, Beth. Are we celebrating something?"

"We're toasting to my report." Beth grinned and raised her glass again before settling in to make a story of her findings.

As the others had discovered, club policy restricted the flow of information. However, the gate guard had seemed enamored of police work.

She'd boasted of providing a list of registered guests to the sheriff's department. "A female investigator," Beth said.

"Detective Leland." Packi sighed. "They're one step ahead of us." She watched a drop of condensation slide down her mug and then flicked it off before it could puddle on the table. "I had hoped we could help with the investigation and think of things they wouldn't."

"We still might," said Beth. "The new guard wants to help. She gushed about us—well, about *you.* She heard about you solving the case with the real estate guy last spring."

Packi ignored the mention of her recent notoriety and slid her half-empty mug through its little puddle. "Can she tell us anything about recent visitors? Anyone stick out as odd?"

"Nah," said Beth. "Delivery people and the usual service providers. You know, landscapers, appliance repair, pool cleaners. There was another tennis team two days ago, and several couples with kids. Nobody that seemed like they'd get themselves murdered."

Marilyn flinched.

"That's not much, but let's stay in touch with the guards." Packi absentmindedly took a sip of her beer, but it was no longer icy. She pushed it aside. "I had a little better luck when I asked about visitors at the golf pro shop." She filled her friends in on her conversation with Duffer McCracken. "The only guests that stuck out in his mind were a foursome of Canadian women." She rolled her eyes to let them know the gist of that part of the discussion. "And three men playing with a club member named Graham. Apparently, he doesn't tip well."

Kay gave one of her intense scowls, lowered her chin to her chest, and whispered. "You mean like Oliver Graham?" When Packi nodded, Kay leaned in close. "He's right over there in his usual chair, next to the wading pool."

Surprised at the coincidence, Packi eyed the man propped in a chaise lounge from under the brim of her cap. About eighty years old, big sunglasses, a straw hat pulled low, and a beer belly that took decades to grow. Packi was relieved he had opted for baggy Bermuda shorts, a golf shirt, and long socks rather than a bathing suit. Her insides squirmed with the thought of him in a Speedo. "Those his grandkids?"

"I don't think they have any." Marilyn had no need to whisper; her normal voice never carried more than three feet. "But he's good with kids and is here almost every day."

"I've never met his wife," said Kay.

"Ursula." Marilyn leaned forward as if that was a secret. "She used to be a Mahjong player. When she hosted, he'd lock himself in his office while we were there. He does computer work of some sort."

"So, does being a bad tipper and a computer geek make him a murder suspect?" Beth guzzled the last of her beer and set the glass down with a bang. "I mean, really?"

"No." Packi laughed. "We're brainstorming. How else are we going to find out the victim's identity and who killed him?"

"We could let the police worry about it," said Marilyn.

"May I clear your table for you?" One of the veteran servers leaned over an empty chair to reach for their glasses. "Sorry you had to serve yourself. I just now came on duty."

"No problem," said Beth, smiling up at the young woman. "I did my time as a server back in my college days."

Packi watched as Beth and the girl talked and laughed together. The server had a way of making everyone feel special. She remembered names and sometimes even their member numbers. Packi checked the name tag on the young woman's shirt.

"Brittany," she read.

"Yes, Mrs. Walsh?" The server's ponytail swung over her shoulder as she turned.

The girl either had a genuine interest in each of them, or her acting was worthy of an award. Packi chose to believe the former. "I was wondering if you noticed any members here with a guest in the last few days. A man, about sixty, shaved head, tall, athletic build."

Brittany gasped. "Does this have anything to do with the man who died on the tennis court? Are you investigating?"

Thoughts of keeping the investigation under the radar vanished as sunbathers looked over their sunglasses at them or paused with their cold drinks halfway to their lips. Packi motioned for the girl to lower her voice. "We're not really investigating. I'm trying to think of things the police might not."

The girl's face colored in excitement. "I get it." She stroked her ponytail and stared out across the pool for a moment. "Not too many guests this time of year."

Packi thought she'd met another dead end until Brittany held up an index finger. "Now let me think." She raised both eyebrows and grinned, very pleased with herself. "Mrs. LaRue came in for lunch yesterday with a man."

"Helen?"

Packi's disbelief caused the girl to muffle a giggle. Beth wasn't so kind. Her guffaw rattled the glasses on Brittany's tray.

"I think he's her brother," the girl whispered. "He's old and bald and kind of in good shape, just like you said."

"I see," said Packi but dismissed Helen's brother as the victim. Helen had been at practice this morning and would have noticed if the man being carried out to the ambulance was her brother. "Anyone else?"

Brittany closed her eyes to think. "Well, three days ago, Mr. Graham was at the bar with three men."

"Were they dressed for golf or tennis?" asked Beth.

Kay poked Beth in the shoulder. "Look at him. How could Graham play tennis?"

The girl stepped back from the table and apologized as if she had given the wrong answer. "Golf, I think."

"You're probably right, Brittany," said Packi. "That fits with what Mr. McCracken said. Were any of the guests younger and athletic?"

"I suppose so. One." Two women at the next table waved, trying to get the server's attention. "I'll be right there, Mrs. Coleman." Brittany smiled but didn't move. "From the way they held their cards, I think they're not supposed to gamble."

Packi glanced at the next table but saw no cards. "Do you mean . . ." She motioned to the nearby women.

"Oh, no," said the girl. "I mean Mr. Graham and his friends. They like hid their playing cards when I brought their meals. I think they play poker or something and don't want their wives to know." Brittany shrugged and tugged her order pad from her apron pocket. "Excuse me. I'd better get to work."

The tennis team ladies turned back to their own conversation and scooted their chairs closer. "So where does this leave us?" asked Beth.

Almost nowhere, thought Packi. She glanced at the old man snoozing in his chair. "He couldn't hurt anyone."

8

Spears of late afternoon sun poked from the edges of the window shades meant to darken the room. Serenity was the goal. Packi followed the instructor's fluid movements, but her mind went off in other, less serene directions. She'd hoped the weekly Tai Chi lesson would help focus her thoughts, open some way to move forward in the investigation. *I should have stayed home.*

The mindfulness needed for Tai Chi was more than Packi could master. In the floor-to-ceiling mirror, she compared her own stilted movements to Marilyn's graceful poses. Packi slid her gaze around the room. Every woman there seemed to be in nirvana, even Diane, a tall, rawboned Kentuckian who was a bundle of static electricity from dawn to midnight.

Packi sighed at her own disquiet and tried to concentrate on the instructor's soothing cadence. *Impossible.* Too many questions whirled in her brain, the clock ticked, and the exit door beckoned. After the final cool down posture, she grabbed her purse.

"I'm so pleased you came, Packi." Chris, the instructor, caught her before she could follow Marilyn out the door. "You moved beautifully through the sun salutation."

Her father had admonished her to accept a compliment with grace, so Packi bit a contradiction off at the tip of her tongue. "Thank you, Chris. You're an excellent teacher."

A benign smile touched the instructor's face as she talked about Tai Chi. With each sentence, her hands floated and came together as if a lotus bloomed in her palms. Packi wondered what it was like to exist in such a tranquil place.

"Hey, Packi." A shrill voice split the hushed tones of the Tai Chi studio. "I got blankets for you," said Diane, making her way around several women with her rolled exercise mat under her arm. "What are you collecting for anyway?"

Energy bristled through the broomstick of a woman, and laugh lines repeated themselves around her wide mouth. Packi liked her immensely. "Thanks, Diane. A friend of mine distributes them to a group of homeless men living out in the woods."

"Homeless? Around here?" Obviously stunned, Diane worked her jaw in thought. "Well, that's truly amazing, Packi, and you're doing a good thing. I can get more blankets. You just tell me how many you need, and I'll collect them and bring 'em right to your door."

"That would be wonderful," Packi said. "I hope to collect thirty before I deliver them."

"Thirty it is." True to her word, Diane began her collection efforts by stopping each of the Tai Chi students as they prepared to leave.

Packi slipped out the door, away from Diane's cajoling and away from the allure of Chris's softened world. She pedaled her bike toward home. To take her mind off her aching quads, she thought of Mark. She hoped the blanket collection pleased him.

What pleased *her* was Mark Hebron's honest, blue eyes. The kindness in them balanced ambition and nonstop work, though she admired those characteristics too. With a frown, she recalled his vehemence when he vowed never to be homeless again. She wished him the best and tried to be generous, but technically, he still didn't have a permanent home. Mark slept in the basement of an elegant high-rise on the river for which he maintained the mechanical systems. He also waited tables at the fanciest restaurant in downtown Fort Myers and invested his earnings in the repair of an old house. He planned to flip the rehab and buy another and another.

Packi mulled over what she knew about Mark and pedaled robotically. She called upon her logical mind to analyze her feelings for the man. *Yes, I like him, but he's so different from Ron. How could he fit in here?* She felt her dead husband's disapproval. *Or is that my own misgivings? Mark is so busy. He has no car.*

She sighed and pedaled faster. *At least I can help him with this blanket project.*

Packi wheeled into her own driveway, propped her bike on its kickstand near the garage, and walked around to the front door, still examining her feelings. She broke off those thoughts to marvel at new blooms of pink, plate-sized hibiscus along the walkway. Then, a stack of three or four blankets on the bench caught her eye.

"Ah, good."

Packi thumped the blankets to frighten away little lizards that might have taken up residence. No lizards, so she looked for a note from whomever left the blankets. As she bent to lift the stack, the toe of her shoe kicked a tennis ball. It rolled from beneath the bench, bounced against the wall, and joined several other balls scattered on either side of her welcome mat.

When did I drop those? She wondered—until she saw the blood.

She jumped and ran. Halfway down the driveway, she chanced a look back. With blankets clutched to her chest, she stared at the bloodstained tennis balls. Identical to those surrounding the body on the tennis court.

Packi hid behind the massive trunk of a royal palm and pecked at numbers on her phone. She whispered to the dispatcher but kept her eyes on the windows of her home. With a gasp of fear, she realized the probability of a blind-side attack. She whirled around.

The street in both directions was quiet. No one skulked between the houses. Nothing moved, except two white ibis stalking through the grass four doors down. Peace and tranquility.

Packi squinted at the tennis balls at her front door and regretted making the hasty call for help. The red was too bright for real blood. This is a joke, she thought. A sick joke. Who would do this? Kay? Beth? No way!

Angry and determined, Packi vowed to take back her home. Uncertainty kept her from marching in the front door in case the joker was inside. Instead, she tiptoed to the back of the house, cracked open the screen door, and slipped into the lanai. Water cascaded from the hot tub into the pool, just like normal. Soothing, peaceful. She lay the blankets on a chaise lounge and bent low to get past the windows.

Packi flattened herself against the stucco wall and slid open the patio doors. She stood to the side and listened for sounds inside the house. The air conditioner whirred. Ice dropped from the ice maker into its tray. Sounds she knew.

"If anyone is in there, you better get out!" For good measure, she shouted, "I called the police!"

She heard no running footsteps, no heavy breathing, nothing. Still wary, she peered into the coolness of her home. Nothing disturbed the quiet familiarity. She relaxed and took a deep cleansing breath as the Tai Chi instructor had taught. The breath stopped in her throat.

Tennis balls littered her living room. Blood-red, stark against her clean white tile. *Inside my own home!* Sweat broke out across her shoulder blades and slid into her waistband. This was no sick joke. A lump of dread fell into her stomach. *It's a warning. A warning from somebody who knows where I live.*

9

Packi paced and waited. She counted the bricks in her driveway, multiplying width times length. Math comforted her. Calculations arranged her brain in linear formation and blocked emotion. She looked for patterns in the bricks and in the facts. *How do tennis balls make sense? Who violated my home?* She was ticked.

Deputy Teig's squad car, an older model Ford, turned onto Hibiscus Lane and lurched to a stop at the end of the driveway. He extricated himself from the car faster than she'd ever seen and descended upon her, red faced. "Tell me what happened."

"I'm all right, Billy," she assured him, laying her hands flat on his heated chest to stop his forward momentum. An instant surge of energy bolstered her courage. She wondered whether it was his size, his concern, or his bulletproof vest that soothed her.

Packi regretted that her call to Teig sounded needy. She had intended to cancel the emergency and merely report the bloodstained tennis balls, but their presence in her living room rattled her. The case had become personal.

"Did you go in?" He patted her hands and curled his fingers around hers as he scanned the front of the house, staring at the shuttered windows.

"No." Embarrassed by her lack of courage, she stepped back and frowned at her pink hibiscus. "But I doubt anyone . . ."

"Stay here."

Teig stepped over tennis balls at the front entrance, nudged the door open, and entered. Packi followed. Determined not to foul the new crime scene, she thrust her sweaty fists deep into the pockets of her loose-fitting yoga pants. Teig disappeared down the hallway to the guest bedroom.

The alien feel of her home unsettled Packi. Her living room was still neat and clean but contaminated by the intruder. Foreign fingerprints lurked. She could almost smell the invader. Red-stained tennis balls left the impression of general disarray. Five tennis balls. She noted one beneath the kitchen's archway. One stopped at the ottoman. Others didn't make it that far.

"I thought I told you to stay put." Teig's exasperation lacked anger. He stepped over the tennis ball near the hallway and gave her the universal signal to stay.

Packi gripped the lining of her pockets. "No one is here."

"I know, but I have to check."

She bowed her head as he passed her on his way to the master bedroom. He made her compact home feel even smaller. Her Ron had not been a big man, never filled the hallways like that.

Sorry, Ron. She sighed, questioning her need to apologize. Was it because another man was in their bedroom? She clucked her tongue. Or was it because her bullheaded *crime solving* brought wickedness into the quiet home they'd shared for five years?

"All clear," said Teig as he ambled back into the living room. Dust, highlighted in the day's last sunbeams, swirled in his wake. He stopped before her with his arms crossed and used his height to gain authority. "So tell me what you saw and did when you got home." The kindness in his voice belied the severity of his stance.

Floating dust ruffled her confidence in her housekeeping abilities. Tennis balls mocked her. "Can we sit in the kitchen?" She didn't trust her quivering smile. "I'll pour tea. Do you want hot or iced? I have cookies."

He massaged his forehead as if he, too, needed to pause and put the day on hold. "Iced tea suits me fine."

The routine of her kitchen cleared her mind. Activity calmed her. Packi set a plate of oatmeal cookies on the table and motioned Teig to sit. The rattan chair creaked beneath his weight. Ice cracked as she poured tea into his glass.

"Talk," he said, ignoring the cookies and accepting the tea.

Packi perched on the edge of her chair, wrapped her fingers around a mug of hot tea, and told Billy about her day. Details spilled from her. She talked about the gym bag, Duffer McCracken, her clues and her suspicions. By the time she finished her monologue, the room had darkened and she got up to switch on a light. Her tea had grown cold. "The tennis balls are a warning, aren't they?"

"Looks that way." He gave her an I-told-you-so kind of smirk. "We have to take it seriously." He motioned a chubby thumb toward the front door and patio sliders. "There's no sign of forced entry."

Packi stared into her mug and shook her head, reluctant to admit her naiveté. She shrugged. *The truth is the truth.* "I left the door unlocked."

Billy's chair complained and the air conditioner clicked on. He arched one eyebrow.

"I know—not smart, but I didn't want to carry a key when I rode my bike to Tai Chi class. Thought I might lose it." Packi dismissed her error and wiped a water ring from the glass tabletop. "I was only gone an hour." She slid a napkin beneath her mug. "Maybe ninety minutes."

"Who knew you'd be gone?"

She wondered that herself. Certainly Marilyn, Diane; maybe other teammates. Packi's gaze met his. "Maybe the neighbors?"

He blew air from his puffed cheeks as if he'd just blown away a decision to keep information to himself. "The fingerprints from the victim came back as Lawrence Pritzle, Ohio. Prior arrests." He pointed to a tennis ball in the kitchen doorway. "Don't know if this is connected, but you stay out of it and watch yourself. Lock your doors."

"Oh." That wasn't the name on the tennis bag. She had been so sure the victim would be from Kansas. Her grip tightened on the mug as her mind wrapped around the idea. "So he was a criminal. What did he do?"

Teig stood to take his empty glass to the sink. His back was to her when he answered. "Rape."

Tea sloshed out of Packi's mug. She watched the spill spread across the table. Guilt stabbed at her for having seen the man, for having sympathy, for praying for him. "Rape," she murmured but then scrubbed the filthy word from her lips with her napkin.

"You stay alert." Billy's hand weighed down her shoulder but reassured her as he gave a gentle squeeze.

"The evidence unit must be busy on another call," he said. "Let's take a look outside before it gets too dark."

Teig offered his hand as she rose from the chair, and she didn't hesitate to take the support. He led her to the front door, taking a long, careful stride over two balls in their path. "That's paint, you know."

"Too bright to be blood," she said. Tempera paint, a child's paint, had a distinct smell and color. "Any chance this is a joke?"

"You got friends with that kind of humor?" He didn't wait for an answer and continued outside where he bent to get a closer look at the brick pavers. He squatted on his heels and shined a flashlight over the mulch and sandy soil surrounding the bushes.

Packi walked the length of the walkway and back, taking her own survey, trying to help. She stopped at the bench under the protected entryway.

"This is where the blankets were."

When the deputy didn't acknowledge her statement, she turned toward him. Still on his knees, Teig frowned, staring through the growing dusk toward the road. Packi followed his gaze to a gangly black kid shuffling down the street, a gray hoodie pulled low, covering his face. As he slumped into the glow of the street light, Teig grunted and narrowed his eyes.

Packi jumped to reassure him. "That's Dr. Grant's grandson." She put her hand on his forearm to forestall any instinctive police action. "He lives at the end of this street."

"I know." The deputy hauled his belly up with him as he stood to his full height. He groaned and adjusted his leather holster. "Wonder if he saw anything." He raised his arm and motioned for the kid to come. "Curtis!"

The boy peered from the depths of his hood, shrugged, and sauntered up the drive way. "What's up, Mr. T?"

The deputy thumped the boy's shoulder. "Coach let you play yet?"

"Still on the bench," Curtis mumbled. He eyed the toes of his purple Nikes, but a dimple deepened on his smooth, well-scrubbed cheek.

Packi had seen the skinny kid on the streets of Paradise Palms almost every day for several months. Eventually, gossip about him stopped. Everyone knew he'd been sent to his grandparents to get him away from a school in the suburbs of Akron where his father had his practice.

"Your grades good?"

"I guess."

"C's or B's?" Teig lifted the edge of the boy's hood with one finger and peered into his face.

"B's." Curtis pushed the hood off his head and grinned up at the deputy. "And an A in English."

Teig humphed and crossed his arms. "Bring me your grades, and I'll write that letter."

The boy pulled a worn paper from his hip pocket, smoothed out the worst of the creases, and handed it to Teig. He ducked his head and waited.

"So you came prepared." Teig's flashlight hovered over the paper as he studied the printing. "Okay." He clicked off the light. "I'll send the letter."

Curtis's eyes lit up and his limbs shivered with excitement inside his baggy sweatshirt.

"No promises now." Teig's hand on the teen's shoulder kept Curtis in place. "We won't know until a month before spring training, but I think we can get you in the program—at least evening and weekend games."

"Thanks, Mr. T." Curtis did a flashy move which rivaled an end zone celebration.

Deputy Teig ignored the exuberant dance. "Show me another good report card next semester, or we're done." He shook the tattered paper. "Your granddad see this?"

"Yeah."

"You mean, 'Yes, sir.'" The deputy folded the paper. "Can I keep it?"

"Yes, sir."

The boy's firm response seemed to please Teig who refolded the report and slid it into his breast pocket. "You see anyone here today, Curtis? At Mizz Walsh's door?"

The young man shook his head. "Nope. Just a lady with blankets."

"What'd she look like?"

"White." Curtis's eyes slid to Packi and then down to the pavement. "Old, like my Granny but skinny." He glanced up at Teig as if for approval. "Big hat. Shades. Ain't nobody I ever seen."

Teig raised his eyebrows.

Curtis corrected himself word by word. "I have never seen the woman, I mean, the lady, before."

Packi and the deputy suppressed their smiles. After a few more questions, Teig and Curtis bumped each other's knuckles, and the boy trotted toward home.

"What was that about?" asked Packi.

A bland expression replaced the deputy's pride and pleasure. "He wants to be a bat boy for the Twins at the stadium. Maybe get to know the players and someday play major league baseball."

Teig directed another county vehicle into the driveway. "My buddy runs the program."

Packi stepped out of the way of the evidence unit's SUV and contemplated Billy Teig from a new perspective. She stood at his side, watching the crew unpack their supplies. "Is he any good?"

"Curtis?" Billy looked down at her. "Don't know about baseball. He's too new to the school. And small for his age. But he's a good kid and doesn't need to find trouble here."

* * *

After Deputy Teig and the evidence team left, Packi locked the doors and turned on every light. She had assured Billy she was used to being alone. Determined to forget that some twisted person had invaded her home with red tennis balls, she pulled a book from the shelf in the den. With a cup of hot tea on the side table, she settled into her favorite chair and covered her legs with an afghan. Reading always relaxed her. The stories transported her out of her own problems and into a new world. Words brought companionship. Several pages into the novel, she realized Stephen King had not been the best choice. Dark shadows now lurked in every corner of her home.

"Enough of that," Packi said, plunking the book on the table. The teacup clattered against its saucer. She steadied the tottering cup and heard a faint sound not coming from the dainty china. Her hand went rigid over the cup.

From the den, she could see half the living room and into the brightly lit kitchen. Nothing moved. Still holding her breath, she rolled out of the cushioned chair and tiptoed to the den's door. She listened and heard a scrape against concrete.

Outside! She sprinted, ninja-style, across the living room to peek through the blinds. The dark lanai leered back at her, ominous and empty. She flipped on the lights. *Nobody.*

Packi heaved a sigh. *You're letting your imagination run wild.* She clucked her tongue and then noticed the stack of blankets she had left on the chaise lounge. *Might as well bring them in.* She unlocked the patio doors and got halfway around the pool before she felt a presence.

Nanosecond images flashed in her mind. *An alligator breaking through the screen. A burglar. The killer.* Ready to bolt, she clenched her fists and whirled around.

Shrouded in shadow, a young man yelped and flattened himself against the wall. He stared at her with wide, frightened eyes. "It's me, Mrs. Walsh!"

A tremor shook Packi. She squinted into the shadow until moonlight caught the gray of his sweatshirt and the curve of his chin. "Curtis? What are you doing here?"

"Sorry, Mrs. Walsh." He held out an open hand in a gesture meant to reassure or to guard against attack. "Didn't mean to scare you. Just trying to be quiet." He bent his knees and reached for a thick bundle. "My granny sent me down. Said you needed blankets."

"Blankets," she repeated. The word felt foreign on her tongue. Its meaning took several second to travel to her brain. "Oh. Blankets." Her mind cleared, and she took the bundle he offered. "Of course. Tell your grandma thank you. These will come in handy."

"Mrs. Walsh?" Curtis lingered at the screened door, torn between staying or darting into the night. His words were muffled from within his hood. "I need service hours. My granny says I should ask you."

"Is that a school program?" Great idea, she thought. Young people learning to volunteer. Or was it a punishment ordered by the court? His slumped shoulders and monotone voice gave no clue.

"We gotta have a hundred hours, or we don't graduate." He shoved both hands into the front pocket of his sweatshirt. "Helping old people counts, but you gotta sign a paper."

Old? Packi ran a hand through her disheveled hair and straightened her posture to counter the image. "That sounds fine, Curtis," she said, though she didn't know what work she could give him. "At some point, I'll deliver these blankets to the homeless. Maybe you can help me with that."

"Teachers like that stuff." He gave her a wave and headed toward home.

Packi watched the skinny kid disappear into the darkness, back to his grandparents. *Was he in trouble?* She hoped it wasn't gangs or drugs that got him shipped down to Florida from the town up north. Deputy Teig trusted him, maybe she should too.

10

The next morning, the team agreed to meet early to warm up before their match against Hideaway Bay. Packi rode her bike to the tennis courts to awaken her leg muscles. The wind ruffled her short hair, cooled her scalp, and made her feel free, safe, and alive. Her speed disturbed ibis grazing in the grass. The birds lifted, squawked, and then resettled to resume their search for insects.

She secured her bike in the rack near Court Six and tugged at her compression shorts that had ridden up her thighs. As she ended the unladylike, but necessary, task, Beth rode in from the opposite direction.

"Hey." Beth braked to a sudden stop and jumped from her bike. "What went on at your house last night?"

The team captain's gruffness agitated Packi and backed her into the bike rack in self-defense. Still shaken by yesterday's scare, she held her bike between them as a safe zone, a barricade. From her limbo of uncertainty, she recognized her mistake—Beth was worried, not angry. Packi's foolish overreaction colored her cheeks, and she released her grip on the handlebars.

"How did you know?"

"No secrets around here, girlfriend. Your neighbor told me a squad car was parked in your driveway for a long time." Beth shoved damp bangs back from her forehead and put her fists on her hips. "What happened? Why didn't you call?"

The question disturbed her. Why hadn't she thought to call any one of her tennis friends? She'd been alone too long, she decided. Too independent. "Sorry, Beth, I should have. I could've used the company."

Beth dismissed the apology with a wave and listened to Packi's story about the red-stained tennis balls. When the tale ended, Beth whistled. "Things are heating up, my friend." She put on her best *Inspector Clouseau* impression, tweaked an invisible mustache, and produced a paper torn from a spiral notebook. “This,” she said with a flourish, “is a list of guests who requested dining privileges.”

Packi sucked air through her clenched teeth and grabbed the crumpled paper. “You’re kidding! Where did you get this?”

“Let’s just say you owe Brittany a big tip the next time she serves you lunch.”

Packi unfolded and smoothed the sheet and scanned the half-dozen, handwritten names and addresses. “Kansas,” she mumbled to herself. There it was, second from the bottom. “Leonard Pritchard, Strausberg, KS.” She muffled an uncharacteristic squeal. “The tennis bag ID was right after all. Did you call the sheriff’s department?”

“Pfft, no,” Beth said. “That deputy is your friend, not mine. Besides, what makes you so sure? And of what?”

“Don’t you see? Billy said the victim’s name was Lawrence Pritzle. This is Leonard Pritchard. Same initials. It’s an alibi!”

“Alias.”

“What’d I say?” Packi waved away the slip. “You know what I mean. I’ve got to tell Billy.” Packi pulled her phone from the bike’s saddlebag and stepped to the side of the walkway while Beth sauntered ahead and pretended not to listen.

* * *

“So, was he impressed?” Beth asked when Packi caught up to her.

“Think so. He might even agree. I’m happy we figured it out before the detectives.” Packi tried to rein in her exuberance but felt like skipping. “Billy said he’d follow up on the names on the list. I suspect he’s pleased.”

“How can you *tell* when he’s pleased?”

“Well, he said ‘humph’ in a lighter tone, if I’m not mistaken.”

The two women laughed more than the joke warranted as they jostled each other to the practice court. Teammates arrived. “Let’s keep these names to ourselves,” suggested Beth, “so Brittany doesn’t lose her job.”

After Kay and Marilyn deposited their gear on the bleachers, Beth announced that Packi had news. To the rapt audience, Packi told of her shock at finding the red-stained balls and her fright at catching Curtis on her lanai with the blankets. She left out the names Leonard Pritchard and Lawrence Pritzle.

“You need a burglar alarm with cameras,” suggested Marilyn when Packi finished.

"Yeah." Kay frowned and nudged Packi's shoulder. "A couple over on Conch Shell Way got a system that texts them every time anyone opens the door. Amazing. You'd get video of anyone on your lanai."

"And would've caught the joker who threw in the balls." Beth pounded her racquet strings against the palm of her hand.

Packi surveyed the three women perched on the tiers of metal bleachers. The team always had an answer. She marveled at their collective wisdom. No matter the issue, one of them came up with a solution. She warmed to the idea of protection for her home and promised to ask Mark to install a security system. *Although*, she argued with her thoughts, *now the police have the victim's name, maybe I won't follow up on the murder. They'll track down the killer, and I won't have to worry.*

"Good morning, everybody!" Grace bustled up the sidewalk with a few more team members following in matching white and lime-green team uniforms. Helen dawdled behind, looking as though her breakfast didn't agree with her.

The eight uniformed players buzzed about, caught up on gossip, joked, and fussed with hats and shoelaces. When the clock ticked toward nine thirty, Beth clapped her hands on her knees and stood up to take control. "Listen up, people." She drowned out the chatter with a ringmaster's gusto."We have a new team member. Kimberly Stinson. She'll warm up with us today and probably play next week."

Packi wondered if this was how she'd been introduced to the team not long ago. She swiveled slightly in her seat to watch the team's reaction.

"That's wonderful." Marilyn said in her typical gentile politeness."Is she a full-time resident?"

"Don't know." Beth paced in front of the group. "Our pro is gaga over her. He didn't know which team to put her on, so he asked us to take her under our wing."

"Is she a decent player?" Kay's question mixed curiosity with hope. The Paradise Palms team won a fair share of games but could use a boost in fourth court.

Beth donned a diplomatic expression and gave her racquet a twirl. "Let's just say she's self-rated."

"Oh, great!" Helen grunted and banged her gear bag onto the bleacher.

"I saw Sam giving lessons to a woman yesterday." Grace's face lit up. "I bet it's her. Oodles of hair, cute face. Lots of curves, and none of them from donuts."

"Probably bought and paid for." Kay groaned and massaged her forehead as if a headache threatened. "Can she at least play?"

"She'll be fine," Beth assured them. "I hear she's from Toronto where she was a big-deal news anchor." The team captain raised her chin and squinted toward the parking lot. "Maybe that's her."

All eyes pivoted to stare the length of several tennis courts. Outside the pro shop, a woman with a glittering tennis bag strapped over her shoulder, swung her long, bronzed leg over the seat of her bicycle. She parked her bike, adjusted her little skirt, and fluffed her waves of chestnut hair. Then she posed in the sunlight.

"That's the one I saw." Grace chirped as if she'd spotted a celebrity.

Like birds of a feather, the team sat up straighter and adjusted their shirts or visors. Several patted their hair into place.

"Oh. My. God. She's beautiful," Kay groused. "I hate her already." She received a friendly clout to the shoulder from Beth and doubled over, feigning grievous injury. As her amusement faded, Kay straightened her spine and sucked in her little belly.

"Looks too young to be on this team." Marilyn studied the woman striding with confidence toward them.

"Old enough—over fifty. I checked," Beth said. "I heard she got booted off her TV show because she got too old but, officially, because her ratings dropped."

The team murmured sympathy and solidarity until four men, including Beth's husband, on Court Three, put their tennis game on pause to ogle Kimberly. She tossed her curls, swung her hips, and ignored her fans.

Some primal instinct alerted the team to the encroachment on their territory. As one, the women tensed to guard their own. A wary distrust set them on edge and narrowed their view of the newcomer. Even Packi, who had no husband to protect, saw the danger.

"Be nice," growled Beth, as much to herself as to her friends. "She's okay. We talked when I called to invite her to hit with us this morning."

The group lowered their hackles, relieved the attack had been canceled, but their excitement over welcoming a new team member had dampened.

"Sort of bossy though," Beth muttered.

"Bossy?" Kay's snigger eased the tension. "Can't have a bossy woman on this team."

Beth ignored the statement until she recognized Kay's sarcasm. Her brows shot up. "You mean me?" Offended, she scanned the team for support but was met with noncommittal grins. Her raucous laugh broke the standoff. "Okay. So, I'm bossy. You love me anyway, right?"

There's no shaking that woman's confidence, Packi thought.

Without waiting for a reply, and as if it didn't matter, Beth marched out to meet Kimberly. They shook hands like two Titans of womanhood, and the captain guided the television celebrity back to meet the team.

"Everybody, this is Kim." Beth clapped the new member's shoulder. "She'll warm up with us for a while. Let's go."

Kimberly Stinson's long eye lashes, highlighted by smoky green shadow, blinked in surprise, perhaps at the brevity of the introduction. She stood like a model with her hand poised on the strap of her tennis bag. "Pleased to meet you," she said with a practiced smile, showing even, pearly teeth contrasted against precise, luminescent red lipstick.

Team members scrambled off the bleachers and grabbed their racquets to follow their captain. Everyone, except Helen, smiled as they passed Kimberly. Each patted the newcomer's shoulder or touched her arm. "Welcome to Paradise Palms!" "Glad you're on the team." "Pleased to meet you." And then they were gone.

At the side of the empty bleachers, Packi pretended to fuss with her cap and wristband and studied the ex-anchorwoman. *Is this the Canadian beauty Duffer McCracken mentioned? No wonder the men stumbled over themselves.* But it wasn't Kimberly Stinson's beauty and celebrity that interested Packi. She wondered if the woman was connected to the dead man. *Was she his rape victim? Had he been a celebrity stalker? Just a coincidence she arrived in Paradise Palms at the same time. Right?*

Kimberly did not follow the team. They had already forgot her celebrity, expected her to be one of them, and paired off to begin their warm up routines. The newcomer hesitated beneath the canopy, her shoulders twitched as if tension held them rigid.

Packi spotted the crack in the woman's facade and took pity. She remembered being on the edge of belonging. *Heck, some days I still feel that way.* She quieted her suspicious mind and went to the woman. "Welcome to the team. I'm Packi Walsh." She extended her hand.

The woman took her hand but cocked her head as if to listen more carefully. "Packi?"

Packi shrugged. "My baby sister couldn't say Patty, and the name stuck."

"Well, thank you for the welcome." Kimberly's professional grip held on longer than expected. She sighed with a dramatic huff.

"I'm all wrong, aren't I?" She stepped back like a soldier for inspection and gestured with splayed fingers to her face, hair, and outfit and then let her hands fall in surrender.

"You look beautiful." Packi surprised herself with the simple statement.

The woman's miserable expression softened her mask of perfect make-up. "But?"

Loath to hurt Kimberly's feelings, Packi regretted not being out on the courts with the team. *How to phrase this?* She resolved to be truthful but kind. "You'll get sweaty during practice. Maybe you'll be more comfortable without . . ." She drew a circle in the air in front of her own bare face. "Most of us wear only sunscreen."

Kimberly clenched her teeth and stared at the underside of the canopy over their heads. "I know. I know." She drummed two fingers against Botoxed lips. "I feel so naked without the makeup. I'm so afraid everyone will figure out I'm old and starting to wrinkle."

"No one cares," whispered Packi. "Look at us. We're all there with you. Maybe you remind us that we once cared too much about looks, too. Here, if you're a good person and can win a game now and then, you're in." Packi waited for tears, or belligerence, or anger.

Kimberly watched the older women on the courts for a moment and then blew a long breath of capitulation from her ruby lips. She fished a towel from her rhinestone-studded tennis bag and scrubbed at her face. She threw the makeup streaked cloth onto the bleachers and presented her naked face to Packi. "Better?"

Packi couldn't help but smile. "Maybe the . . ." She motioned to the woman's wrists.

"Oh," said the ex-Barbie doll. She stripped off glittering jewelry, tossed the bling into her bag, and followed Packi onto the court.

11

After the Hideaway Bay match, as they did every week, win or lose, the team celebrated with lunch on the outdoor patio. Several players had invited Kimberly to ride along to watch the match and join the camaraderie of the carpool, but she had begged off, claiming a golf lesson.

They were in high spirits. Though Helen and Marilyn lost a tiebreaker on Court Four, points won on the first three courts moved the team ahead in the rankings. While Beth toasted the team with a glass of iced tea, Helen groused about her loss.

"Their asphalt courts shouldn't be allowed in this league," Helen complained. "Too hard on the knees, and it ruined Marilyn's game."

A frown twitched across Marilyn's forehead, but she ignored her partner and replaced irritation with serenity. "Congratulations, everybody." She clinked her glass against Packi's.

"Don't worry about it, Helen," a jovial Beth said from across the table. "You won't have to play hard courts next time. I'll schedule Kimberly." The team captain's pointed stare ended Helen's griping.

"Yeah! Our new team member hit the snot out of the ball in warm-up," Kay exclaimed. "And did you see that crazy serve?" She raised her glass to Marilyn. "I like her."

Though the tennis players poked fun at the absent woman's unorthodox serve, they heartily agreed Kimberly was an asset to the team. While they celebrated, Helen pouted, pushing her food around her plate with her fork.

Packi joined in the merriment but finished her salad quickly and excused herself early. "Gotta run. I asked Mark to install that security system."

Kay's eyebrows shot up. "Well, that was quick. You snap your fingers and there he is."

Too late, Packi realized she revealed more that she wanted to. "I called him," she stammered. "He has the afternoon open."

"Relax," Kay said. Her sly grin did nothing to alleviate Packi's discomfort.

"Good for you," Beth called over the din. "Great job today."

Eager to get away from her friends' speculations about her relationship with Mark, Packi pushed her chair in and gave a general good-bye. She hurried away through clustered diners, umbrella stands, and energetic servers. As a shortcut to the parking lot, Packi left the sun-drenched patio through the pub.

Inside the clubhouse, the contrast in light blinded her. While her irises adjusted, she maneuvered around crowded tables and focused on the light at the exit.

"Packi Walsh!"

She waved to the female voice emanating from a table to her right. "Hi!" Packi called, smiling into the dimness, almost able to make out four seated women. Golfers, she thought.

"Did you get the blankets we left at your front door?" A broad-shouldered silhouette raised a plump arm in greeting.

Packi paused for a moment, flustered and unable to identify the shadow. "I did. Thank you very much." She covered embarrassment with enthusiasm and moved on.

A thought hit her at the exit door and she turned back to survey the sea of people. *Which table was that? Is it possible one of those women delivered blankets and threw 'bloodstained' tennis balls into my home as a joke? Would they be so bold to call out to me?*

Packi stood on the edge of the crowd as her eyes adjusted to the indoor lighting. She scanned the room again, but the faces melded together. She couldn't be sure who had called out and none looked her way. She recognized no one.

With her heart pounding, she pushed open the heavy door, relieved to be in sunshine and out of the noise and air conditioning.

You're too suspicious, Patricia.

Packi convinced herself that neither killers nor practical jokers would call attention to themselves in a crowded pub. She pedaled away from the clubhouse and calmed her mind by counting her blessings. Life is good, she thought. The blanket collection had turned into a popular project; she'd given Teig several clues; she and Kay won their games against a stronger team; and in an hour Mark would arrive. Her bike picked up speed. Pedaling seemed effortless.

Seven minutes later, Packi stopped at the end of Hibiscus Way. Sensing a change in her neighborhood, she dismounted her bike to observe the street. Houses in various shades of beige still lined up like soldiers. Royal palms stood tall, on guard.

Halfway down the street, a black pickup truck disrupted the order. Dusty and dented, the imposing truck took up too much room. It overpowered the blue periwinkle lining her driveway. She wondered what Leonard Pritchard's murderer drove.

She approached the black vehicle at a slow roll, wary, prepared to pedal past her own home. Metal clanged as a ladder slid from the truck bed. She recognized the shoulders first. A firm, strong back. A snug polo shirt.

Intent on hoisting the unwieldy ladder, Mark didn't see her, so she waited and watched. In the month since she'd last seen him, a deeper tan had burned into his plain face. Rugged, she thought, like a scrubbed-clean sailor or a cowhand ready for Saturday night. She imagined the smell of his soap.

The palm of her hand tingled where it had once brushed over his close-cut hair. She had been brazen. As he had bent to test the air pressure in her car tires, she dared to skim her hand over his buzz cut.

He caught her in that awkward memory. "Hey, stranger!" The ladder on his shoulder swung toward her, missing his truck and a cabbage palm. A parentheses of laugh lines framed his white grin and dug a single dimple into his cheek. His sea-blue eyes took her in.

"Hello, Mark. You're early." She wiped her hands on her clothes, suddenly aware of her skirt's scant length and her perspiring cleavage. "But it's good to see you. Thanks for helping me with this."

Overheated from her long ride, blood rose to her face. She focused on her handlebars as she rolled up the driveway and leaned the bike on its kickstand. A grip on the seat stabilized her, while he set the ladder against the house. Packi faced him. The tip of her tongue involuntarily wetted her lower lip. *Should I shake his hand? Hug him?* She glanced down the street where Dr. Perez walked his beagle, and Libby Smith retrieved her mail. *Would they notice?*

"Got through Home Depot fast, so here I am." Mark reached for both her hands and guided her forward until they stood toe to toe. "Hello, Packi. I'm glad you called." He caressed her fingers with his carpenter's thumbs as if memorizing a rose petal.

A zinger flashed from his skin to hers, a heated current to weaken her bones and almost set her hair on fire. Blood cells quickened. His candid, blue eyes stared down at her like waypoints, guiding her home. *Neighbors be damned!* Packi locked onto the homing beacon and squeezed his fingers like a wanton hussy. She reveled in every detail: his raspy callouses and bold gaze; her racing pulse, and even Libby's bemused curiosity. The moment delighted her but shook her foundation.

Packi fought to steady her feet on the shifting sands. "Who lent you the truck?" She released the moment but not his hands.

"That's all you can say?" A surprised blink changed Mark's eyes from laser beam to mischievous. He gave her fingers a little shake. "I'll have you know, Mrs. Walsh, that I own this fine vehicle."

"Congratulations, Mr. Hebron." Pleased that his financial position had improved, Packi stepped back to give the dented truck its due attention. A Dodge. She recognized the shiny ram logo on the hood. Spotless interior. Tool boxes lined the bed.

"It's perfect for you," she cooed just because he stood in her driveway with pride almost popping his buttons.

"The exterior is beat up, but the engine is strong." Mark pulled a rag from some hidden place among the tools and swept dust from the bumper. "Your friend, Deputy Teig, got me a deal from a mechanic on Metro. Cheap and with five years to pay." He rubbed at a spot beginning to rust. "Did you have anything to do with that?"

"Me? I don't have those kind of connections." Packi knew to tread lightly on his pride. It had been battered worse than the old truck, after his home, construction business, and marriage disappeared in the housing bust. "Besides, Billy Teig is spitting mad at me. In his bullheaded thinking, I'm a pesky old woman sent to earth to bedevil him." She grinned, knowing that part wasn't true.

"You're sure you didn't arrange this?"

"I am," Packi said. The deputy hadn't mentioned anything about the truck. He, too, must have recognized Mark's stubborn independence.

Mark's crooked smile chased away his suspicions. "Teig said I'd do the mechanic a favor by taking it off his hands." Mark gave the fender a last buffing and reached into the cab. "Here's your security system," he announced, holding up a pile of small boxes. "I'll have the wire run and these devices installed in several hours."

The electronics didn't yet generate a sense of security, but having Mark near did. "Lunch first?"

"I never turn down an invitation from a beautiful woman.

* * *

Feeding a man again felt right.

The night before, Packi had made a big crock pot of soup. Her husband had loved her chicken vegetable recipe and expected it during Sunday football games. She ladled the steaming soup into Mark's bowl. *Sorry, Ron.* She squelched a bit of guilt and piled extra turkey onto thick bread, man-sized. Ron would have to understand.

Packi called Mark away from his work, waited for him to wash up, and served lunch on the lanai next to the pool. She knew the meal was perfect. Even so, she couldn't take a bite until Mark pronounced the soup delicious. Then, she was content. They ate to the sound of water spilling into the pool; watched a small alligator cruise across the pond; and talked about their lives.

"The blanket project is going well," she said, leaning back in her chair, unable to finish her sandwich. "How many will you need?"

As if he'd done it a thousand times, Mark stood to collect silverware, glasses, and bowls. "As many as you can get. What the men's camp doesn't use, the mission downtown will take."

Packi gathered the remaining dishes and followed him into the kitchen. "Women I've never met have asked about donating, and Diane is collection central. She washes the blankets and even sews loose bindings."

Mark paused with a plate suspended over the dishwasher and looked at her through soft eyes. "You're an amazing woman, Packi."

A wet plate slipped through her fingers and splashed into the water. "Not me." She hid a grin and fished the elusive dish from the suds. "Diane's doing the sewing."

A little laugh came from deep in his chest. A homey, safe sound. He bent to arrange dishes on the rack, and she snuck a peek. Stubby, workman fingers. A bronze forearm. Prominent muscles. His bicep flexed and pushed back his sleeve, revealing a neatly scripted name in blue ink. She cocked her head to read. *Gwendolyn.*

Mark caught her studying the tattoo and yanked down the sleeve. "My ex-wife." A squall raged in his sea-blue eyes. " When I have money again, I'm getting that thing lasered off."

"Sorry." She hated that the air in the room had changed—that a hostile ghost now swirled around her kitchen. "I didn't mean to pry."

"No." He breathed out as if trying to expel his demons. "I'm sorry. I apologize for letting her get to me like that. I'm happy here with my new life, with my new friends." He reached for Packi's hand and tried to grin, but an old weight pulled at his smile.

She squeezed his hand and waited for his eyes to brighten. "Too bad her name wasn't Sue."

Mark closed one eye and squinted at her through the other. "What?"

"Less ink to remove."

He rubbed his face and chuckled, or perhaps sobbed, into his hands. "I'm a piece of work." His fingers plowed through his buzz cut, and he wagged his head. "Your alarm system won't get installed if I don't get started." He closed the dishwasher and straightened a dish towel on the counter but didn't look up.

"Thank you, Mark." Packi said, searching for the usual easiness between them. "While you're busy with that electronic stuff, I'll wash the blankets my neighbor's grandson brought. We have more than thirty to deliver tomorrow."

"That's good." Mark left the kitchen muttering almost to himself. "Might get chilly over the next few nights." He stopped halfway through the living room and traced the floral pattern on the headrest of Ron's favorite chair.

"Thank you, Packi." His eyes found hers and locked on. "For everything."

12

Outside her window, dawn arrived. Mark came to her then, floating above ocean waves like the promise of spring. His scent reached her, as hot and fragrant as a beach breeze. Sensations quickened her skin. Images wafted beyond her reach and faded.

Packi struggled to remain in her dream world. She curled her body around his image but found a poor surrogate in her feather pillow. Her hand searched for warmth and slid over the sheets where he could have been. Disappointed, she flopped onto her back to sort dream from reality.

No tennis today. New security system. Call Beth. Pick up Curtis. See Mark. In spite of lingering dream fragments, the prospect of an exciting day urged her from bed. She crawled from beneath the quilt and slipped her feet into woolen slippers.

Minutes later, with a steaming mug of tea held to her chest, she stood at her patio doors watching a flotilla of brown pelicans glide across the pond. Captivated by the majesty of the big birds emerging from the mist, she slid open the door.

"Back door is open!" The female voice came from deep within her own home.

Packi spilled tea down the front of her pajamas. The alarm system! Though she remembered she had two minutes to get to the control unit, she sloshed hot tea over her hand as she rushed to the front door to silence the recorded voice.

What's the code? What's the code?

She imagined sirens awakening her neighbors as she scanned Mark's written instructions. They had chosen an easy code. *What was it? Her birthday, 0-9-2-3.* She punched in the numbers.

"System disarmed," the digital woman finally said.

Packi groaned, mopped up the trail of spilled tea, and hoped security was worth the bother.

* * *

Tai Chi will restart your day, she thought. Intent on giving the morning another try, Packi changed into her yoga clothes and positioned herself on the chilly lanai with a full view of the pond and green fairway beyond. She moved through the sequences, counting repetitions, as the sun rose over the cypress trees in the distance. After fifteen minutes, she bowed from the waist to offer the traditional thanks to nature.

Only then she noticed folded blankets on the chaise lounge in the far corner. "Uh." She searched her memory and realized she'd dropped them there to sneak up on the invader who threw tennis balls into her home. She'd apparently forgotten them when Curtis frightened her two nights ago.

"You're losing it, girl."

Packi shook dew from the blankets and sent a brown anole flying from within the fabric. The lizard righted itself on its tiny splayed feet and skittered into a crack in the cement. Ugh. But she had learned to appreciate the bug-eating little critters.

Packi gave the bundle another vigorous shake and marched into the laundry room. The bottom blanket had the feel of wool. Good quality. She dumped the armful on the dryer and searched for a care tag. Her fingers ran over a crusty spot.

"Hope that comes out." She flipped on the light and examined the stain more closely. As she picked at the thin smear, red flecks stuck to her fingernail. Paint. Red tempera paint.

She dropped the blanket as if it crawled with lizards. *Is this another warning?* Her first impulse was to shove the blanket into hot water and wash away the issue. Instead, she set the stained blanket aside as evidence.

Did I transfer damp paint from the balls to the blankets? No, I never touched the balls. She ran through her memory. *Had Billy? Curtis? Did a thrown ball graze the pile of blankets?*

Could the person who delivered the blankets be the one who delivered the warning? A skinny, white woman, Curtis had said. Four blankets, more than one delivery? A man? Maybe the woman had seen him.

Her mind reeled as she searched for her cell phone and then tapped on a saved number. "Beth?"

"Hey, I was about to call you." The team captain's loud voice crashed through Packi's thoughts.

"Went through my camping gear to find something to give your homeless guys. Found a tent and lantern. They'll be useful, right? And we got an extra ticket for the Florida Rep theatre tonight. It's a comedy. You in?"

Packi tried to break into her friend's stream of enthusiasm. "Beth!"

Her rebuke was answered by silence at the other end. She softened her tone. "Beth?"

"Sorry, Packi. I'm here. What's going on?"

Packi organized her thoughts before she spoke. "Someone who donated blankets might have also tossed in the tennis ball warning. Could've been a woman."

Beth whistled.

"I have to find her," Packi said. A silhouette image of the plump woman in the pub flashed through her memory. She tried to remember the others at the table. "Maybe a golfer. Old, skinny, and white." Curtis' description still amused her. "Know anyone like that?"

"Ha. Half of Paradise Palms."

"I know, but one who donated a blanket or two."

"Sorry." A heavy sigh carried Beth's disappointment, but she brightened. "I can't help, but Kay knows more golfers than me. We can talk about it tonight on the way to the theatre. How about it? Marilyn's brother is visiting, so she's giving away her ticket."

Packi resigned to Beth's persistence. "Yes, I'll go, but I pay for the ticket."

While Beth talked on about a carpool for the evening, Packi again sifted through her memory for the plump golfer in the pub. *Who was she? Who was with her? Would the waitstaff agree to review receipts from that day?* She'd ask Brittany. A plan formed.

Find the golfers; find the one who warned her; find the murderer.

* * *

Within the hour, Beth arrived at Packi's door with her arms full. "Here's the stuff. This is a forty-degree sleeping bag. That's a decent two-man tent, but it's too big for my kayak camping. The lantern works and has fuel." She deposited the gear on the outside bench. "Gotta go. Rex is taking me four-wheeling in the Everglades. Good luck. You're meeting Mark at the camp, right? Be careful."

Whirlwind Beth trotted down the driveway and hopped into the open-sided Jeep next to burly Rex. He waved from the driver's seat, looking every bit a match for Beth.

"Bye," said Packi as an afterthought. She shook her head at the disappearing Jeep and marveled at the growing pile of donations for the homeless camp. *How had word traveled so fast to so many willing donors?*

She checked the time. Iris Grant had agreed Curtis could accompany Packi to the homeless camp as part of his community service. Packi hurried inside to bag blankets fresh from the dryer but was waylaid by a beep from the answering machine. She dashed to the phone and pushed *Play*.

Mark's voice came through faint and garbled. "Rush job . . . park on Shoemaker Road . . . before noon." The rest was scratchy.

She played the message a second and third time to get what she could. Mark's messages were always short because free minutes were limited. The city's phones-for-the-homeless program gave only basic communication, but it was more than he'd had before.

We'll find the place, she thought as she returned to the laundry room.

The doorbell rang. "Shoot. Curtis is early." She shoved the last blanket into a plastic bag and hurried through the living room. She put on a smile for the boy and threw open the door.

"Oh!"

A massive, bare-chested man filled her doorway, eclipsing the sunlight beyond. A halo of white hair glowed. Heat radiated from his body.

Involuntarily, her nostrils flared and caught the close smell of hot tanning oil. Transfixed by the gleaming, bronze chest eight inches from her nose, she couldn't move. He flexed his chiseled pecs as if to call attention to his nipples standing at attention.

"Mornin', ma'am." It was a command, not a simple greeting. "I heard you're collecting camping gear. Got some here." He motioned to the bench where new items had been added to the pile.

Packi blinked, still mesmerized by fine, golden hairs sprinkled across his chest. "Yes. Put them there." Inane and robotic words were all she could manage as she marveled that a man of his age could look so virile.

"My campin' days are done, I'm 'fraid." He looked over her head, into her living room, as if scanning the territory or surveying her situation.

His invasive curiosity roused Packi from her stupor. Her aloneness had been detected. Refusing to allow this intimidating stranger access to her privacy, she pulled the door shut behind her. The move put her closer to him, to his golden chest, but he stepped back, giving her room to breathe.

He wasn't a complete stranger, she realized. She recognized the close-cropped beard and now detected an angular scar neatly camouflaged by white whiskers. She'd seen him at the crime scene and marching down the streets in his cargo shorts and boots. Jungle Jim, Kay and Beth had called him. Tarzan came to mind.

Packi resisted the urge to fan herself. "Thank you," she said. "Camping equipment is always appreciated." She put out her hand in greeting, extending her arm uncomfortably far to push him back. This magnetic man was the kind of trouble her mother should have warned her about. "I'm Packi Walsh."

"Jim Voss." He cradled her hand as if it were a sparrow and seemed to peer into her mind.

She broke the connection and nodded over her shoulder to the inside of the house. "My friends and I will deliver these things late this morning."

Not fooled, he apologized with a patient smile and backed out of her comfort zone before getting back to business. "Got a propane stove here and two big tarps." His well-used fingers traveled over the blue nylon as if remembering long ago adventures. "Somebody should use 'em."

He huffed, as if banishing the memories, and took his bronze body down her walkway.

Packi sighed in relief but eyed him all the way—straight, confident back and shoulders as sculpted as his chest. He's a retired marine, she recalled.

He turned back to point to the pile of equipment. "Those canisters are fuel for the . . . " He caught her staring.

Startled, she gasped and backed into the door.

Jungle Jim winked as if a secret had passed between them. "At your service, Packi Walsh."

Mortified, she ducked into her empty house and locked the door.

13

Packi busied herself with blankets and camping gear, packing them into the Audi's small trunk.

"How embarrassing," she muttered, shoving the last bulky bag into the backseat. "That man."

She worked in a hot, airless garage, because an open door would have been an invitation to any other shirtless, dangerously flirtatious men marching down her street. She slammed the car door and then, for good measure, the trunk.

Time to leave, Packi thought. She pushed the door opener and watched daylight stream in as the clanking chains hauled the garage door higher. She bent low to scan for lurking hiking boots on her street. Only a pair of purple Nike high-tops waited. The neighborhood was clear of shirtless men.

The door cranked into position, revealing more and more of Curtis. When the noise stopped, they exchanged greetings. Hers a pleasant "Good morning" and his a quick nod from behind the cardboard box in his arms. He seemed to want to disappear into his hooded sweatshirt. "My granny sent food. Fruit and bread and stuff."

The box contained oranges, apples, wrapped carrot sticks, and loaves of bread. Packi hadn't considered that fresh food would be welcomed in the camp. Iris Grant had even thought to include a dozen or more small baggies of homemade oatmeal cookies.

Curtis loaded the box into the back and slouched into the passenger seat. Having no experience with teenager communications, Packi bumbled through questions about school and his baseball aspirations and got only vague, single-word responses.

As the Audi idled at a long light at Daniels Parkway and Metro, she became desperate in the silence and handed him her cell phone and a scrap of paper. "See if you can find that address on the GPS. I don't quite know where we're going."

"I know where they're at."

"Really?" Keep him talking, she thought. She hoped her expression of deep, personal interest didn't convey the utter terror she felt whenever talking with a teenager.

"All the kids know." He shrugged, oblivious to her discomfort or trying to ignore it. "People say stay away from there and warn us and stuff, so we check it out."

"So you've been in the camp?"

"Not into the woods." Curtis shook his head emphatically. "There's some bad dudes around."

Packi tapped her brakes in spite of the green light. *Bad dudes? Is this place going to be safe?* She reviewed her contact with homeless people. Most were shy and quiet, just beaten down by life.

"My friend, Mark, will meet us there," she reassured the boy.

Bad dudes already dismissed, Curtis flipped through screens on her phone, as intrigued as if she'd handed him an abacus. "This is old."

"It's a smartphone," she said in the device's defense.

"Turn here." Curtis waved to the right without looking up from her phone. "You got a camera at your front door. Cool."

"How'd you find that?" She tried to watch the road and see the screen beneath the boy's thumbs at the same time. The camera app eluded her ever since Mark showed her how to use it. "I thought it disappeared."

"Naw. Icon on the main screen. Up ahead."

She glanced to the phone and back to the road. "What?"

"Turn in past the sign."

The small parking lot was not the tourist-friendly site she'd come to expect in the Sunshine State. Ruts ran through the sand and coquina surface. Three loaded dumpsters guarded the left end. On the right, a lonely portable latrine leaned against a chain-link fence. Lifeless, brown palm fronds hung from tired trees at the edge of deeper woods tangled with undergrowth. No other cars waited in the lot.

"Are you sure this is the right place?"

"What it says." Curtis held up her GPS screen. "School's on the other side of these trees. We tried to watch from there."

"You spied on the homeless men?"

The boy shrugged to absolve himself. "Never saw nothin'."

Packi let it go at that and maneuvered the car into the most welcoming section of parking lot, facing the woods, away from the dumpster and latrine. There were no painted lines, only dust and ruts.

A live oak with long horizontal limbs dropped dry leaves onto the Audi as they waited for Mark. After ten minutes, Packi drummed her fingers on the door handle. *Where is he?* Curtis had abandoned her phone and was engrossed in his own screen, bobbing his head to whatever music came through those things in his ears.

Movement in the rearview mirror caught her attention. She twisted in her seat, hoping to see Mark's battered pickup truck. Instead, a windblown man on a bicycle rolled into the lot, his unbuttoned tropical shirt flapping behind him. A plastic grocery bag swung from the handle bars. The bike bumped over the eroded ground until a rut grabbed at his front tire. He made a clumsy dismount and pushed forward until he spotted the Audi. He eyed the car with frank curiosity.

Packi raised her hand in a friendly wave, but humanity slipped from the man's craggy face. Suspicion hooded his eyes, squashing any bond she might have felt for him as another human being. Her greeting had somehow crossed a line. She dropped her hand into her lap as he rolled the bicycle through a thin spot in the bushes at the far end of the lot.

Well, she thought, as the vegetation swallowed him up, *he'll like us better when he sees what we've come to deliver.* A twinge of doubt made her look again for Mark's truck. She became impatient to get back to her own sunny community.

"Do you know how to find numbers on my phone?" Packi asked.

Duh, Curtis's stare seemed to say.

She put her phone into his hands again. "Please find Mark's number. I can't see the little print and want to tell him we're here."

"You want me to send a text?"

"He doesn't have text, just voice mail."

The boy raised one eyebrow but kept his disbelief to himself and swiped his index finger across a few screens. "This him? Mark H.?"

Packi nodded, though she couldn't see the name. He tapped the screen, handed her the device, and went back to his music. Mark's recorded greeting irked her again, but she left a message and resigned herself to another wait.

A cold night, the forecasters had said, at least by Florida standards. The breeze coming through the open windows was cooler than it'd been in weeks, but the sun fought back. As the car's interior heated up, digital minutes clicked by as sluggish as an old dog in Alabama.

She looked for the twentieth time for an incoming message and sighed. "Let's go ourselves." Packi opened her door and was gratified by cool air rushing against her bare legs.

Ready to go, Curtis pulled out his earbuds and hopped from the car to retrieve the food box from the back seat. They filled their arms with donated goods and walked away from the safety of her car.

14

At the edge of the parking lot, about where the bicyclist disappeared, Curtis found a half-hidden path in bushes. Packi and he pushed back branches and picked their way along the dirt trail into woods thick with ragged palms and tangled underbrush. Vegetation closed in behind them, blocking the view of the parking lot and her car. Road noises became muffled and seemed to be part of a different world.

This doesn't feel right.

She adjusted the weight of the plastic bags on her shoulder and stole a glance back at Curtis. The boy seemed okay. His expression betrayed no fear, but his eyes darted from side to side, and he hugged the box he carried tight to his chest.

Let's get this done and get out of here.

For Curtis's sake, Packi pushed aside her own trepidation and marched forward as if she knew where she was going. *Dang Mark. He should be here.*

A hundred feet further along, the bushes thinned out. Sharp-edged palmetto palms rasped against each other. Metal clinked somewhere in the distance and punctuated an undertone of human voices. The smell of cooked oatmeal wafted through live oaks and slash pines. *Civilization,* she thought.

Up ahead, a flash of bright blue showed through the shrubs, and the scenery changed. A sagging, blue pup tent sat in a trampled clearing. Beyond, other tents in various colors and conditions were scattered about. Ropes, strung between trees, supported tarps in angular configurations. Hammocks swayed, heavy with belongings.

Jumpy men turned their backs to them or slipped away. The bicycle rider they'd seen in the parking lot grabbed his bike and rolled it out of camp.

"Get the hell out of here!" a bearded man yelled from the far side of the clearing. He waved like a maniac and ducked away.

Packi sucked in her breath and stopped. Some homeless people are mentally ill, she reminded herself. She slid an anxious look at Curtis, but the boy held up well in the face of the man's anger. She shifted the bulky weight in her arms and dismissed the hostile greeting.

Thirteen ragged campsites squatted in amongst the palms and live oaks. Surely, these people would appreciate new blankets and camping gear. She looked for a leader, an unofficial mayor of the village of tents, tarps, and grocery carts.

A tousle-haired, unshaven man in flip-flops and a once-white, sleeveless undershirt flicked a glance their way. He stood at a propane stove propped in a three-wheeled shopping cart and continued to stir a steaming pot. Oatmeal, from the smell of it. His space, delineated by a yellow tent and a woven hammock, appeared more organized, more prosperous than the others. Beneath a shock of wavy blond hair, his eyes showed no welcome but darted to a cabbage palm on the other side of the path.

Packi understood the signal, grateful for a place to deposit the donations but was peeved they had been otherwise ignored. *Patience*, she warned herself. She dropped her heavy burden and groaned as she straightened her aching back. Curtis placed the box of food near the base of the tree and swung a bag from his shoulder.

"You want me to run to the car for more?" the boy asked in a low whisper. He, too, seemed befuddled by the lack of welcome but less annoyed.

"Not yet. Let's see if anyone wants this much." The foolishness of their mission crept in on her. Mark must have been wrong about the need. That miffed her. Determined to see it through for Curtis' sake, she knelt to open a bag and pulled out blankets. Maybe if she displayed the items, the men would understand their intentions.

Satisfied with the quick arrangement of goods, Packi stood and brushed sand from her knees. She opened her arms over the array as if to announce 'Come and get it.' No one came. Eyes were upon them, she knew, but even the oatmeal man had disappeared. The sound of a zipper told her he'd retreated into his tent.

"We have camping gear and blankets here," she said to the yellow nylon tent. She waited.

"Leave it and go," the man finally growled. Packi detected a hint of something beneath the gravel in his voice. Fear? Despair? A warning?

"Okay." She shrugged her disappointment to Curtis.

The boy shrugged back, but Packi was heartened to see that while his innocent face held sadness, there was no defeat or apprehension. Suddenly, his expression changed. His muscles tensed as if adrenaline shot through his veins. He pressed his lips into a tight line and narrowed his eyes at something behind her.

Forewarned, Packi turned. Beyond the yellow tent at the far end of the encampment, three young men swaggered into the clearing. They wore menacing black. Chains swung from their belt loops threatening to pull down their low-slung pants. Black caps sat askew, shadowing fiendish sneers. "Whatcha got for me today, you . . ."

Shouted obscenities shocked Packi. Words she'd never heard in person ran from their mouths. She gripped Curtis's arm to pull him behind her, to protect him, but he held his position. Anger twisted his smooth face. She realized he'd seen this scenario before.

The leader's long dreadlocks swung against his back as he surveyed his conquered domain. His two teenaged goons rousted a frail man from beneath his tarp, grabbed his flask, and flung it into the sand. The poor victim scrambled after the leaking container as they tossed through his grocery cart. Finding nothing of value, they moved on to plunder the next campsite while the occupant looked on in helpless resignation.

"Dis'bility checks came yest'day. Who got somethin'?" The lead pirate turned a languid circle in the clearing. He eyed every inhabitant as they were pulled from hiding by his henchmen. "Don't make me burn this shit hole."

The thought of torching the camp seemed to entertain him. He chortled and danced hip-hop style—until his leering gaze fell on the yellow tent and on Curtis behind it.

"What you doin' here, man?" He marched at Curtis and got into his face, his dreadlocks shaking in anger. "This be my territory. Don't you see the sign?" He flashed a hand signal and stood back as if his performance had proved his dominance. Curtis had sense enough to lower his eyes.

The invaders' violation of the quiet camp and her fear for the boy raised Packi's hackles. "How dare you!" She got between Curtis and the punk and shook her finger into the leader's face. "These men have nothing. Leave their stuff alone and leave this boy alone. Your mother would be ashamed of you! I'm ashamed of you!" She trembled with rage while Curtis grabbed at her arm to pull her out of danger.

The invader's dead eyes bore into hers. He worked his ample lips as if curbing his response and reliving old arguments. "Get yo grandma out my sight." He turned his back on them and strode over to the display of donations. A kick smashed the lantern against a live oak, spewing shattered glass over the donations, the yellow tent, and him.

Surprised, the gang leader rubbed at a cut on his cheek. The blood on his fingers angered him, and he rounded on Packi as if she had caused the injury. She could have ducked behind the tent and made a run for it but, instead, gritted her teeth and put her hands on her hips. Her defiance didn't stop his advance.

Curtis jumped in front of the man, geared up for violence. "She's old, man. She didn't mean nothin'."

The thug clouted the boy to the ground and turned blazing eyes on Packi. Curtis sprang to his feet but into the grip of the other two gang members. She froze and braced herself for a blow.

"Hold it."

The gang leader's retribution was distracted by a boozy voice coming from the yellow tent.

"Hold on now." The blond man mumbled and tumbled from his tent on his hands and knees. He struggled to his feet with a bottle clutched in his fist and scratched at his undershirt. "Youze guys want a cell phone?" He swayed and looked through one eye at the intruder. A mighty burp nearly knocked him off balance, but he grabbed his knees and waved a loose thumb toward a tattered box on his hammock. "Found one yest'day."

The bully's nostrils flared in disgust at the drunk. "Yeah." He spat. "And I want what else you got." He ordered his cohorts to search the box.

The thugs dumped the contents onto the ground, kicking aside hardcover books and trampling papers and a photo into the gritty soil. With sufficient damage done, they picked up the device.

The leader grabbed the old flip-phone and shook it at the drunk like a weapon. "Piece a junk!" Even so, he slipped the phone into his pocket and shoved the unsteady man to the ground. "Where's yo cash?"

The drunk rolled onto his hip and raised a trembling hand in surrender. "S'okay." He brushed sand from his bottle and ran a thick tongue over his lips. "Drank it." He swirled dregs of liquor in the bottom of his precious bottle and crawled forward. He offered up the last swig.

Within feet of the bully's shiny, high-top shoes, the poor man's florid face distorted. His eyes bulged and his cheeks distended as if vomit threatened to explode from his lips. The invader jumped back in disgust, out of the danger zone. He loosed a string of obscenities and signaled his fellow thieves to move onto a less troublesome victim. The drunk fell back onto his rump.

With the thieves' attention diverted, Packi felt for the phone in her pocket. At her side, Curtis bounced on the balls of his feet, itching to get into the fight. She warned him to stay put and stepped behind the yellow tent to call for help. Sunlight obliterated the screen, but she aimed at nine, one, one. She had no idea how she'd give directions to the dispatcher without drawing the gang's attention again.

15

The gang leader strutted about the clearing like a barnyard rooster, demanding respect. Behind his back, several campers retreated to the woods. Other unlucky, or perhaps braver, residents defended their belongings, but the hoodlums shoved the campers aside, searched their pockets, and rifled through old suitcases, crates, and plastic bags.

Packi kept her eye on the punks and felt her bones clacking together. Fearing the 911 dispatcher's voice would alert the thieves, she buried the phone against her stomach. A muffled voice broke through the silence.

The gang leader stopped short and swiveled toward the yellow tent, listening.

"Yo!" he shouted. He leaped over boxes and logs, his dreadlocks flying behind him, and sprinted for the trees at the far end of the clearing. The other two thieves jerked up, grabbed bags of loot, and hurtled after him.

Packi whirled around at the sound of commotion bearing down on them from behind. Something was coming. Adrenaline urged her to run, to flee with the villains. She tensed for an escape until she spotted a familiar figure running through the trees. Mark! A cop's uniform hustled along twenty feet behind him on the path leading from the parking lot.

Breathless with relief, Packi smiled a welcome as Mark made a beeline for her with Deputy Teig as his back-up.

"What the hell are you doing here?" Mark panted to a stop in front of her, dripping in sweat, his eyes ablaze. "I told you to stay in your car."

Shocked, she stiffened and balled up her fists. "You told me no such thing!" Packi trapped her indignation behind clenched teeth. "Your said you'd meet us . . ." She stopped, remembering the scratchy, incomplete voice message, but didn't want to admit her part in the misunderstanding. "Where were you! You said you'd be here."

"I said not before noon." He raked his stubby fingers across his buzz cut. "Thank God I got your message. I left the job half finished. Two campers out in the parking lot told me about the raid."

"You okay, Mizz Walsh?" Teig offered himself as a buffer between the two combatants.

"Yes, Billy. Thank you." Packi blinked as if seeing him for the first time. "How'd you get here so fast?"

The deputy clamped his beefy hand on the nape of Curtis's neck. "Got your text. Next time I might not be close enough. What'd I tell you about this place?"

"Community service," the boy said in his own defense.

Teig pulled down his dark sunglasses and looked over the rims. "But *not* here."

Curtis heaved a heavy sigh and stared out over the camp where the residents picked through the mess to retrieve their valuables.

"Why not here?" asked Packi. "He shouldn't be afraid of homeless people." She glared directly at Mark, daring him to dispute that. "We didn't need to be rescued."

"Packi," Mark said with too much patience. "It's not *you* or Curtis in danger here. It's them."

He turned away, leaving Packi with her mouth agape. He shook hands with the blond drunkard who was now clear-eyed and erect. "Can you give me a few hours this afternoon?"

"Ready when you are," the scruffy blond man said. "Need any others?" While they talked, he gathered papers, pens, and other small items and packed them with steady hands into his box. He retrieved the damaged photo from beneath his hammock, smoothed the new creases, and slid it into a book.

Amazed at the blond man's transformation, Packi strained to listen to the conversation between him and Mark. She needed to make sense of the last half hour, but the two men lowered their voices. They glanced more than once in her direction. Somehow bringing donations to the homeless camp was wrong, she figured, but she couldn't wrap her head around that.

Packi wanted answers from Mark, but Deputy Teig took her elbow. "Let's get you two out of here." He herded Curtis and Packi down the path toward the parking lot.

Teig and the boy talked about baseball and school but not about the ransacking of the homeless camp. Packi wandered behind, the outsider. She wondered if the irrelevant chatter was Billy's attempt to calm Curtis, to reassure him that normalcy would return. *Maybe theft and bullying were normal here. Would the sheriff's department even bother to investigate?*

The deputy's attention was on Curtis who talked with far more animation than Packi had gotten from the boy. *Billy must be a wonderful father,* she thought.

Through the trees, Packi spotted several camp residents trudging back toward the encampment. Teig either didn't see them or chose to ignore that the men stood still as sticks, obviously trying to avoid his attention. *Why did they act so guilty?* She wondered about damage to her car in the isolated parking lot and strained to see it as they neared the end of the path. The deputy's squad car and Mark's pickup blocked her view of the Audi.

"Mizz Walsh." Teig stopped at the edge of the dismal parking lot and pulled out his notepad. "Can you describe the three who trashed the camp?"

"I suppose so," she murmured, sidestepping the deputy's bulk to confirm her car was safe. "I remember the leader well but not the other two." She ticked off the details of the dreadlocked young man but could not dredge up images of his accomplices.

Curtis, apparently unfazed by the incident, recalled the bullies vividly: their T-shirts, gang symbols, types of shoes, a snake tattoo over one eyebrow, their swag, as he called their bling.

"You ever see them before?" Teig asked the boy.

Curtis shrugged. The deputy waited.

"Maybe I seen them after school."

"OK." Teig put his hand on the boy's shoulder and let the discussion drop. The moment Packi activated the key fob, Teig opened her car door and motioned her inside.

Packi almost complied, ready to get back to her own world, but felt a last bit of commitment to her volunteer project. "I'll run these other donations back to Mark."

"No." Teig glanced into the backseat. "I'll take them. Mark should have known better than to let you go in there."

Resigned to letting Billy complete her mission, Packi flipped the front seat forward to get at the backseat. "To be fair," she said, "I misunderstood Mark's message." Still confused about the lack of welcome at the camp, she handed out the last two plastic bags. "What was going on back there, Billy? I mean besides the thieves harassing the residents? What did Mark mean . . . he wasn't worried about us but about them?"

Billy Teig hiked up his utility belt and shifted to put his body between Curtis and their conversation. "Mizz Walsh, most those men in camp are under court orders to stay away from children." He removed his sunglasses to see if she understood.

"You mean . . ." She thought of the skittish campers, the frail ones, the blond man who had intervened.

Teig nodded. "They break parole if they get caught within a thousand feet of kids, schools, and playgrounds. All kids." He rolled his eyes toward Curtis who pretended not to listen. "No apartments or shelters in the county fit that criteria, so they live here or go back to prison."

"But there must be somewhere for them," Packi countered. "There are retirement communities with no kids everywhere in this county."

Teig sniffed. "And who can afford to live there?"

Packi held up her hand to acknowledge her gaffe.

"Nobody wants them." Teig motioned back to the camp. "Some are predators, so we allow them to stay where we can find them. If certain crimes occur, we start our investigations here."

"But the school?" Packi pointed in the direction Curtis had indicated.

"Just beyond the limit. Officially, this place doesn't exist," Billy said, as if he'd had the discussion before. "Most want to be left alone and get on with their lives. Murphy, the one Mark came to hire, has been on the sex-offender list since he was nineteen and dating a sixteen-year-old. Her father had him arrested, and now he can't get a job."

Packi pictured the blond man. Murphy. "I think he tried to save us from the bullies."

"We all try to do the decent thing." Teig lifted the plastic bags to prove his point. "Now you two get out of here and forget about this place." He frowned at Curtis and removed a folded paper from his shirt pocket to shake at the boy. "Make sure Mizz Walsh gets home okay."

"I get it, Mr. T." Curtis pulled his hood over his head and slumped into the passenger seat.

Packi recognized the paper as Curtis's report card and Teig's promise to get the boy into the batboy program at the stadium. She also recognized the opportunity to take advantage of Teig's softer side. "Before I forget, Billy, what's new in the murder investigation? Any clues? Did you follow up on that name we found?"

Deputy Teig ignored her questions. "Back out slow. Watch out for the stump there." He tapped on her fender when she cleared the stump and stood guard over the parking lot until she turned onto the road. In her rearview mirror, she saw him gather the plastic bags and head for the homeless camp.

16

Miffed that Teig never valued her insights, Packi drove with an internal dialogue playing in her head. *I could help the investigation. Be their eyes and ears. Age gives a body wisdom. Well, maybe not today.* She regretted exposing the boy to the dangers of the camp and stole a glance at the teen in the passenger seat.

Traffic on I-75 seemed to hold the boy in a trance. No music blared into his ears. His phone and earbud wires lay in his lap.

"Curtis, are you okay?" At a loss for how to talk to a teenager, Packi's palms began to sweat. She pushed forward. "Are you upset about what happened back there?"

The trance released him. "No, ma'am." He plugged his music back into his ears and set his jaw. His face hardened, less like the boy with dreams of playing baseball, and more like the punks trashing the homeless camp.

Her heartbeat quickened. Others were trying to save this boy: his grandparents, Teig. A tour bus trundled past them as Packi wrestled with what to say. "Curtis . . ."

A sudden noise startled her. She gripped the wheel as a terrifying whine closed in on them. As she prepared for the unknown disaster, a motorcycle zipped between her car and the bus in the next lane and spurted out in front of the bus.

"OMG!" The biker's flapping shirt mesmerized Packi as he darted through traffic. Brake lights lit up the lanes ahead as far as she could see. She listened for a crash.

"Dumb ass." Curtis released his grip on the dashboard and swiped the wet sheen from his upper lip.

"Agreed!" Packi shook off her scare and concentrated on her driving until she could escape the interstate at the Colonial exit. At the red light at the end of the long ramp, she closed her eyes to recuperate with a moment of meditation.

"Mrs. Walsh?"

Packi opened her eyes to see Curtis staring at her. His dark brows met over the bridge of his nose.

"Did you say OMG?"

Uh oh. Had she stepped into teen territory by using text lingo? A nervous giggle escaped her. "Maybe."

His dimple deepened and highlighted a beautiful set of teeth. "That's cool."

She laughed with relief. Her ladylike twitter quickly morphed into a raucous horse laugh, unfettered by good manners. She lost it. Anxiety pent up after a day of fears and unknowns turned funny.

The boy caught the joke. He fought against the first chuckle, but laughter soon shook him.

Tears blurred her vision as the light turned green. She dared not drive. Cars honked, and that was funny too. She waved to the impatient drivers and covered her mouth to suck sobering air through her fingers.

Curtis remembered his cool and pulled up his hood. Packi wiped at her eyes and regained enough control to pull into traffic. She slid a glance at her passenger. His phone and earbuds lay unused between his knees. He hid under his hood with pursed lips, but a dimple betrayed him.

As Packi drove toward Metro, happy endorphins bubbled beneath her skin, fueling new confidence. The sky turned bluer. Birds soared. All was well.

"Curtis, I'm sorry I brought you into the camp. I didn't know . . ." She paused to choose delicate words. He filled in the blanks.

"Everybody knows about the pervs."

Startled by the boy's directness, her confidence drained. "Not all of them are, uh, perverts."

He looked at her. His cheek twitched and something flashed through his eyes and disappeared.

What was that? Disappointment? Accusation? Packi pretended driving needed her attention and groped for words. *I'm terrible at this.*

At the next red light, she hazarded another peek at the boy. Sun glinted off clean, black curls escaping his hood. Such innocence. He fingered his electronics but hadn't yet retreated.

"Curtis," she said, hoping she read the signs right. "Did any of those men say or do anything to make you uncomfortable?"

He shrugged and gave a quick negative jerk his head. "Those men don't bother me."

Packi felt thin ice breaking beneath her feet. "Someone else bothers you?"

He stared at the delivery truck in the next lane. "There's this creeper," Curtis said.

"You mean back home." She nodded and urged to boy to continue. "In Ohio?"

Curtis shook his head. "Here. At the park."

Packi reeled. *Help!* She floundered in inadequacy but pressed on. "Our park? When?"

The boy twisted his mouth in uncertainty but bobbed his head once. "Couple days last week."

Packi no longer trusted her driving and took a quick right turn into a gas station. She took the car out of gear and turned toward Curtis.

"What did he do?" She hoped her tone was open and non-threatening, but he sealed his lips and squirmed in his seat. Packi leaned forward to lock onto his eyes and waited. The teen finally gave in but ducked his head.

"Watched me shootin' hoops," he murmured. "Jus' made me feel dirty like."

"Can you describe the man?"

Curtis had a ready answer, as if he'd been waiting for someone to ask. "Old white dude. Cowboy like. In a golf cart." Curtis pressed his full lips together and narrowed his eyes. "Said he was visiting. Askin' me the way to the gym."

Not awful, Packi thought. Maybe the cowboy merely enjoyed basketball. *No.* She stopped herself from giving the man a pass. *Trust the boy's instincts.* She sent a silent prayer through the sunroof to keep Curtis safe. "Did you tell your grandparents?"

The teen rolled his big eyes before hiding his troubles behind man-sized hands. "They don't know about stuff like this."

Packi stifled a smile. "Deputy Teig?"

"I can't tell no pig." He gaped at her in disbelief.

"Curtis!" His use of the old hippy term shocked her, but she softened her response. "Let's call them police, or cops, or officers. Not pigs."

His thin shoulders twitched. "I guess T's different."

"He is." Packi gripped the steering wheel as much to steady herself as to hold onto her belief in the good in people. "Do you mind if I mention this to him? He'll track down the man and warn him away from you."

Curtis gave a brief nod and blinked as if he trusted her to fix the adult problem. She got a quick flashback to the five-year-old he might have been—a little guy with a worn, flop-eared stuffed bunny in his lap. Her heart lurched with a sudden fear for that child and the need to protect him.

Packi found a warm smile to give the boy, but he'd apparently had enough and plugged his music into his ears. The teenage barrier was up again. She was left alone to stew in the realization that not all "pervs," as the kids called them, camped in the woods.

17

With Curtis safely returned to his grandparents' home, Packi left a message for Billy at the sheriff's office. She wished for the comfort of her easy chair and a cup of hot tea, but sordid thoughts of the camp and Curtis's creeper refused to let her relax. What to do? She rolled out of the fat cushions and called Marilyn.

"I can't hear you," Marilyn shouted. "I'm at the beach with my niece and her kids."

"I said, I delivered the blankets. The camp is full of sex offenders. Did you know that?"

"It was in the newspaper, Packi." Squawking gulls and the roar of the surf tumbling ashore drowned out half her words. "They plan to shut down the camp because it's too close to the school."

"Where will the men go?"

"That's the shame of it," yelled Marilyn. "Form another camp, I suppose. Listen, Packi, it's too hard to hear. I'll talk to you later. Have fun at the theatre."

The theatre. Packi moaned and dropped the phone into its cradle. Exhausted by the day, the trip downtown seemed like a burden rather than a pleasure. On the other hand, maybe Beth and Kay could help identify that cowboy dude in a golf cart. With the prospect of their moral support, she relaxed and curled under a blanket on the sofa, hoping to get some rest before her friends picked her up at six.

A whirl of thoughts interrupted her nap. She wished Mark were there to discuss the events and alleviate her worries. He would comfort her. They could talk, sit together, maybe even . . .

The image of a broad, bronze chest with fine golden hair came to mind, rather than Mark. She indulged herself for a moment. Then she pushed away the memory of the man at her door earlier that day, certain that Mark also had an acceptable chest.

Mark wasn't a Tarzan. He was a gentleman: clean, fully clothed, and thoughtful—the type of guy to change the oil in her car and clean the dryer vent. In return, she cooked dinner and bought steaks for him to grill. The manly smell of sizzling steak and the swirling smoke in the lanai had pleased her.

His work took most of his time, but she loved the few days when he'd arrived at her house in a borrowed car to ask for her to-do list. Once, they played hooky and drove to Bunche Beach. They strolled along the shore collecting shells, watching dolphins, and waving to the gambling boat as it sailed out of the protected harbor.

Her house seemed more like a home when Mark visited, yet he never put his feet up or stayed too long. She wondered when he would. Perhaps when his finances improved.

Call him. The thought niggled at her until she kicked off the blanket and left it in a heap on the couch.

As she rummaged in the drawer for Mark's number, she readied her excuse for phoning. She'd apologize for going into the homeless encampment. "That will work." She dialed and waited, but the call rejected her and went to voice mail. His curt request to leave a message irked her.

She hung up with a bang. *That's it then,* she thought. *I tried. Let him call to apologize for his harsh words at the camp.*

Packi detoured around resentment at Mark and set her mind in another direction. Grace could get information. The woman was a whiz at the computer and could save Packi an hour of frustration.

Thanks to the miracle of caller ID, Packi didn't have to identify herself. The moment she picked up, Grace asked, "Do you want to hit some balls? I have the machine reserved for three o'clock."

Grace's enthusiasm was contagious, but Packi shuddered. The eerie image of the machine lobbing balls at the dead body hadn't left her. "No, thanks, Grace. I need to get cleaned up for the theatre this evening, but I wonder if you have a minute to do a search."

"Sure. I'm at my computer now. Whatcha need?"

"A newspaper article about a homeless camp on Shoemaker Road."

"I remember that one. Fort Myers Gazette." Grace hummed an Irish ditty while her fingernails clicked against the keys. "Here it is. Last week. Let's see

. . . Neighbors complained. Contacting the land owner. Closing it down. I don't find much of a history on the subject."

Disappointed there wasn't more, she thanked Grace. "You're a Google guru."

"No problem. I emailed a copy to you. Anything else?"

Packi hesitated, embarrassed and afraid to offend Grace's Catholic sensibilities. "Deputy Teig mentioned a sex offender list."

"That's easy. I'll email you a link to the county's website." Grace clicked and hummed a few more bars. "We have one in Paradise Palms, you know, and another over in Deep Harbor."

"You're kidding?" Shocked, Packi sputtered. *Could that be Curtis's creeper?* "But we have children here."

"I don't know how the rules work. They gotta live somewhere."

Unwilling to betray Curtis's confidences, Packi moved the conversation to safer territory with a mention of tennis. Grace jumped on the subject and recounted her last third-set tiebreaker. Packi let her crow about the well-deserved win last week, but her own heartbreaking loss wasn't worth reliving.

After the tennis diversion, Packi said good-bye and hurried to her computer to read Grace's emails. The article contained little Grace hadn't already mentioned. She scanned the facts, looking for hope for the homeless men but found none.

Her fingertips itched as she clicked on the link to the county's website. Her eagerness to view the list felt dirty. Was it wrong to want to know about a sex offender in the neighborhood?

Packi quelled her reluctance for the sake of Curtis and community safety but dreaded finding a familiar name on the list. She navigated to the page and scanned for her zip code, shocked to see so many faces staring back at her. Different races and ages. All male. One address stood out on the long list. Paradise Palms did indeed have their very own sex offender.

She pressed print, slipped the offensive papers into a folder, and drummed her fingers on the outside. Did Deputy Teig know about the offender in Paradise Palms? Had he gotten the message she'd left at his office? Did he follow up on the pictures or the name she found in the bag?

She pretended Billy Teig would be glad to hear from her again and picked up the phone.

* * *

Promptly at six, Kay's green Prius pulled into the driveway with Beth filling the passenger seat. Packi activated the alarm, grabbed her purse and jacket, and ran out the door. She climbed into the backseat, taking a quick glance at her friends to make sure she was dressed appropriately. Dress slacks and blouses. Perfect.

"You two clean up well," Packi said as she searched for the seatbelt. She had learned from these women that humor was appreciated. They liked gentle teasing, but Packi knew there was a line somewhere between fun and hurt feelings. She wanted no part of that line.

Kay was up for the challenge. "We're ready for a night on the town." She struck a model's pose and fluffed her hair. "As long as we're home by nine." Her wide smile contrasted with her glowing tan and was highlighted by the shimmer of her silky, beige top.

Beth snorted a laugh and adjusted the seat to accommodate her long legs. That morning she had been dressed for mudding in the Everglades. Now, her transformation was remarkable: a touch of mascara and lipstick, an elegant blouse, even an artsy necklace. She seemed uncomfortable in the costume. "Hey. Did you and Mark get that pile of gear and blankets to the homeless camp?"

"He came later."

"What do you mean?" Beth twisted in the seat to face Packi. "You went by yourself? Why didn't you tell me? It's not the best neighborhood. If he wouldn't go, any one of us could have gone with you."

Packi held up her hands to stop the onslaught. Beth meant well, but Packi decided to keep her tiff with Mark to herself. Besides, it was settled. He had finally called with sweet apologies for the miscommunication at the camp and made it easy to admit her naiveté. Mark had even asked to pick her up Monday evening for a surprise. She was thrilled but not prepared to share that news with the team. To cover her secret she told the rest of the story.

"Doctor Grant's grandson came with me."

"What?" Kay squeaked from the driver's seat. "Didn't you read the newspaper?"

"I know. I know." Packi defended herself as much as her guilt and foolishness would allow. "I missed that part and thought I'd help Curtis get his community service hours." She sank into the seat and kneaded her fingertips into her forehead.

"So what happened?" Kay's eyes bore into her from the rearview mirror

By the time Packi told her story about the homeless camp, the wary residents, and the thieving bullies, they came to the stoplight at Fowler and Colonial. Her confession gave no absolution.

"Something else," Packi said, pausing to gain their full attention. "Dr. Grant's grandson mentioned that a creepy dude parked at the basketball court to watch him play. Curtis called the guy a pervert. Do you know anyone with a golf cart who looks like a cowboy?"

"Boots? Spurs? What?" Beth screwed up her face in an intense scowl.

"I don't know." Packi gave a helpless shrug. "I did well to get that much out of Curtis. I wonder if the sex offender in Paradise Palms fits the description."

"What?" Kay's surprise nearly ran her off the road.

"I thought that was a false rumor," Beth said. "Who is it?"

"The name on the list is Spiro Kristos," answered Packi. "On Osprey Lane. One of the townhomes, I guess."

"Never heard of him," said Beth. "What'd he do?"

"Don't know." Packi wanted to ditch the whole subject. "All it says is 'sex offender' which is apparently a lesser crime than 'predator.'"

Wide-eyed with disgust, Kay shook her head. "So we're to be relieved we don't have a full-blown sex maniac in our area?"

"Sorry I brought it up," said Packi. "The guy looks like he's eighty."

Unsettled by the news, the three women speculated and tested theories about the man at the basketball court until they arrived downtown. Parking became the issue. The theatre lot was already full, and the main streets were lined with cars and crowded with pedestrians.

"Down there," said Beth. "Turn here."

"But we're blocks from the theatre," Kay argued.

"Hey, we're tennis players, for cripes sake," Beth said. "We can walk."

"It'll be dark when we get out." Kay waved toward the tall live oaks, heavy with Spanish moss and already collecting shadows.

"Bah." Beth dismissed the worry. "The street lights will come on, and we'll be with the crowd leaving the theatre."

Packi's failures with Curtis and at the homeless camp stole her confidence to take sides in the debate. She obediently exited the vehicle on a narrow bricked street, amid closed stores and legal offices.

Beth and Kay seemed to forget the darker side of the city and walked side by side in the comfort of daylight, remarking on the old buildings and shuttered storefronts. Fort Myers was a beautifully restored city that needed more businesses and the visitors to support them. At least the restaurants had lively overflow crowds, thought Packi. Tourists filled the few short blocks of the historic area with life and adrenaline but left side streets deserted.

"So, finish telling us about the homeless place," Beth said. "Did anyone want the lantern?"

"Sorry. The punks trashed everything. They smashed your lantern against a tree." Responsibility for the waste weighed on Packi, and she quickly covered her guilt. "No doubt, the tent got snapped up. The tarps too."

For several seconds, Beth clucked her tongue in harmony with the staccato of their footsteps in an empty side street. "Huh. Who donated tarps?"

Hot blood rushed to Packi's face. "I forgot to tell you." That was a fib. She remembered well the man at her door but hoped to avoid the subject. "A man named Jim Voss stopped by with several items to donate."

Beth's guffaw echoed off the old walls. "You mean Jungle Jim? Did he have his shirt on?"

Kay stopped short to get the answer, but Packi turned aside, too embarrassed to admit she had a surge of attraction for the man. "Mmm. Let me think. I don't believe he had a shirt. No, I don't think so." Packi fanned herself. "Whoo. A hot flash."

Beth wasn't fooled. With the tip of her finger, she turned Packi around and chortled. "Ha! Hot flash, my eye. You're blushing. What did he say?"

"Leave her alone," Kay said, hiding a laugh behind her hand. "The man is a pain in the butt, but he does have a hot body."

"Virile," Beth agreed solemnly.

She and Kay amused themselves with stories of Jungle Jim's rants at board meetings, run-ins with his neighbors, and other women's bawdy comments on his physique. Packi let them talk. Jungle Jim may have started the rush of blood, but she easily replaced his image in her mind with Mark's.

"Look at you," teased Beth. "Is that a hot flash too? Another senior summer?"

Packi hid behind her hands, wishing her reaction could be blamed on menopause. "I'm too old to talk about men that way."

"You're never too old, baby, and if your man has a little blue pill, woohoo."

Packi didn't want to hear about anyone else's sex life. She huffed and walked ahead. Beth hurried behind her with a big, lurid grin.

"You mean you and Mark never did the sheet dance?"

"What?" Packi drew in a gasp and stopped short. "No. We . . ." She stood with her fists on her hips, stunned. Sure, Beth could talk like that. She had a husband—a healthy husband. Packi's Ron had been gone five years and had been sick for at least a year before his death. She sagged beneath the ache for him. Sadness washed the hot flash away.

"Oh, honey. I'm sorry." Beth's humor vanished. Her one-armed hug bolstered Packi, preventing her from sliding into self-pity. "I was joking."

Exposed emotions flustered Packi. "No, it's okay," she assured her friend. "I'm just tired." She slipped away from Beth's mothering and hurried toward the theatre, needing to be alone, needing to breathe. "It's been a long day."

Unperturbed by Packi's rebuff, Beth caught up and trotted beside her like an eager terrier. "Hey, consider the source." She elbowed Packi gently. "I'm an idiot, right? Ignore everything I say." She prodded and teased until Packi surrendered with a helpless laugh.

Satisfied she'd been forgiven, Beth hooked arms with Packi and Kay. "Yeah, baby. Let's have some fun tonight."

18

For Packi, part of the entertainment of attending plays at the hundred-year-old Arcade Theater was the building itself. Had Myna Edison ever walked through the elegant lobby? Had the red carpeted floors been as tilted then. Signs in the ladies' room now warned of ancient plumbing and, certainly, the peeling wallpaper was more recent. The flaws added historic ambiance and never deterred a flock of faithful season-ticket holders. Packi and her friends were no exception

After the last ovation for the night, the crowd spilled out onto quiet downtown streets, leaving the din of the theater behind. The group experience had ended, the connection broke. As the audience filtered away, some laughed, some held hands, but most stumped to their empty cars in groups of twos and fours.

"So what did you think?" asked Kay. "I thought it was well acted and fun."

"Yeah," said Beth. "The old aunt cracked me up."

Packi agreed. "She's in every play, you know. She's amazing."

The women walked away from stark parking lot lights, discussing bits of the play until their voices lowered, as if their comments needed privacy. The theater crowd was gone.

Muted music with a deep bass drifted from a rooftop bar where neon lights beckoned the younger set. The clink of glassware sharpened in contrast. Whatever nightlife was beginning to build hadn't reached the streets between Hendry and Broadway.

As they stepped from a curb at a cross street, a cool breeze, misted by warm river water, wafted from between tall brick buildings. Cooking oil. Damp foliage. A lamb's faint bleat. Packi stopped to listen.

Kay stepped on Packi's heels. "Oops. Sorry, I . . ."

"Shhh" Packi jerked her hand up to signal a stop. The women came to halt with an audible intake of breath.

"What's going on?"

Packi ignored Beth's question and cocked her ear, straining to find the source of the thin, plaintive cry. She peered down the narrow street, between the densely packed buildings. Shadows shifted at the far end of the block, accompanied by the rumble of male voices.

Passing headlights separated the scene from the murkiness.

With his back to a brick wall, an old man thrust his cane at two figures hunched into hooded sweatshirts. He poked and parried. Like an elderly Errol Flynn, he held his left arm back in defense of a small woman. The young men mocked the defender and danced away. They dodged the swipe of his cane, then batted the gallant weapon from the old man's hand. The cane clattered into the gutter, leaving the gentleman and his lady exposed.

"Hey!" Beth's yell exploded and drove the dark vignette into reality. As Beth charged into the crime scene, Packi followed.

Two shadowed faces turned toward the three women advancing on them. The shorter kid darted around the corner, while the lanky one rifled through the old man's wallet. He shoved the contents into his pocket and tossed the wallet into Beth's path. He took his time. He dismissed the rescuers with a snide half-grin before four long strides took him out of sight.

Beth chased the mugger as far as the corner, stopping in the blue glow of a halogen streetlight to scream curses after them. Kay hung back and whipped out her cell phone, while Packi ran in Beth's wake. She paused to scoop the cane from the gutter. Panting and hyped on adrenalin, Packi positioned herself between the threat and the elderly couple, brandishing the cane at the long-gone attackers. She agreed with Beth's curses, proud of their vehemence.

Still in the shadows, the elderly man clung to the woman as she snuffled against his chest. Kay gently guided them into the light and questioned them in soft professional tones.

"Thank you, girls. Thank you." The gentleman's slack face barely moved as he whispered. Kay urged him to sit on a stone wall, but he reached out to his wife with a shaky hand.

"Sit down, my dear."

"Harold!" The woman clutched her handbag in both hands. "Stop dithering. Let them take care of you."

Her tone defeated the man as the muggers could not.

"Don't you worry, sir." Kay patted the purple-mottled skin of his arm. "My friend will take good care of your wife. What's your name?"

His body sagged into the nurse's care. He closed his eyes and sighed. "Baskin. Harold Baskin. Please take care of Dora."

In spite of Dora's strident impatience, Packi put a protective arm around her frail shoulders. Sharp bones threatened to poke through the fabric of her stylish dress, and the woman's spine went rigid beneath the touch. Packi resisted the urge to pull her hand back. She lifted her chin toward Kay to ask a silent, "Is this one okay?"

Kay nodded and left the care of the relatively healthy Mrs. Baskin in Packi's amateur hands.

Packi did her best to emulate her friend's nurturing demeanor and led Dora to a bench several yards away. Packi watched Kay administer to the gentleman, take his pulse, and ask gentle, probing questions. She wracked her brain for something to distract the wife.

"My friends and I attended the Florida Repertoire this evening. Were you there?"

"We were." Dora sniffed, but her gaze never left her husband. "I've seen better."

Patience, Packi told herself. Squirrels or palm rats scurried through the branches above her head while dampness from the metal bench crept through her slacks. Packi banished the image of rats and pushed on. "Mr. Baskin seems to love you very much. Have you been married a long time?"

The halogen light at the end of the block glinted off Dora's hardened eyes. "Fifty-two years. What's with the questions?" Other than a downward tug of her eyebrows, her face didn't change. As if steel rebar held her erect, she turned back to watch her husband.

Chilled by the rebuke, Packi sputtered. Only willpower kept her on the bench. She clamped her mouth shut, reminding herself the sour woman had suffered a traumatic experience minutes before. *Cut her some slack.*

Packi busied her mind by reviewing details of the attack. *How did it happen? What street is this? Hadn't she seen the grinning mugger before? Perhaps they had loitered outside the theater.*

Heavy footsteps interrupted her questions.

Beth galloped toward them like a Clydesdale in pumps, returning from her guard duty at the intersection. She retrieved the discarded wallet from the middle of the street and presented it to the debilitated man. "I'm afraid they got your money."

Harold dismissed the worry with a weak wave and leaned to the side to keep his wife in view. "This was nothing. I have plenty of money." He slid the wallet into his sport coat's pocket and looked around Beth. "How's Dora?" It sounded more like a plea than a question.

Packi sent him a smile to let him know she and his wife enjoyed each other's company. Dora dabbed her nose with a handkerchief.

"Your wife is no worse for wear," Kay assured him, but from behind her patient's back, she gave Packi the universal signal for a phone call. "I want you to rest easy now, Mr. Baskin. I'm requesting an ambulance, so we can get you and Dora checked out. Okay?"

Relieved to have an excuse to leave the unpleasant woman alone on the bench, Packi moved a discreet distance away and searched her purse for her phone. She whispered to Beth to keep an eye on Mrs. Baskin.

"Didn't think of an ambulance," Beth said.

"I wasn't thinking at all," said Packi. "Kay called the police. Maybe they send an ambulance automatically. Maybe not." Packi punched numbers and gave the dispatcher the additional request as a siren whooped nearby.

Over the noise, Beth bent down to Packi's ear level. "Are they traumatized?"

"The woman's tough." Packi said, cupping her hand around her mouth to increase the volume. She glanced back at the victims. "Kay looks concerned about the man."

Blue and red light beams bounced along the street, and sirens howled through the canyon of buildings. In the chaos of noise, a quick panic seized Packi. *City cops,* she thought. *They'll want descriptions.* Her eyewitness responsibilities weighed on her. She closed her eyes to recall the muggers, but all she could see was that cocky grin.

19

Packi's fingernails drummed against the screen of her phone. *Too early to dial Billy*. Instead, she picked up her rainbow-decorated mug and put it to her lips. Ugh. She put the tepid tea into the microwave and watched the clock tick toward 6:50 AM.

Her sleep had been restless. Dreams of a mugger with a snake tattoo over his eyebrow and wearing cowboy boots woke her several times. She had chased the young punk from the homeless camp to the golf course. When she finally caught him, he morphed into Curtis. He dove into the pool, was unable to swim, and she couldn't save him. Packi lay awake for hours worrying about the boy.

The moment the clock hit seven, Packi dialed the number Deputy Teig had written on the back of his business card. His recorded message answered. She clicked the edge of the card against her granite counter top as she listened.

"Billy, please pick up. This is Packi Walsh. Sorry to call so early, but I'm worried about Curtis. He's okay, but I had a bad dream. And I have to tell you about a mugging. Please call me."

She knew she sounded frantic. *Heck, I am frantic.* Her anxiety and pent-up nervous energy spilled over into her message. She tried to envision soothing waterfalls and dialed the number on the front side of Billy's card.

"Sorry, Mrs. Walsh. Deputy Teig isn't on duty today," said the dispatcher. "May I take a message?"

Packi left her phone number with the sheriff's office but thought, *I'm on my own.* She dressed quickly and headed for the only place open that early.

* * *

There was a chill in the air as she pedaled her bicycle into the clubhouse parking lot. Golfers in long pants and jackets milled around rows of golf carts.

Some held steaming Styrofoam cups. Others gesticulated with their hands while they talked. None paid her any mind.

A line of cars idled at the curb, waiting to unload golf clubs. She dodged between them and propped her bike in the rack near the exercise room. She scanned the assembly of senior men until she spotted Duffer McCracken under the bag drop canopy, clipboard in hand.

"Golfin' today, are you, Mrs. Walsh?" He was teasing. It was men's league day and there were no women in sight. The Scotsman's impressive mustache hid his grin, but jolly cheeks gave him away.

"Mr. McCracken." *Two can play the flirtation game,* she thought. "You're the man I need." She tilted her head just so, smiled, and locked her gaze onto his.

He blinked first. "Ha!" He clapped his massive hands together and deepened his Scottish bur. "'Tis a fine morn when a bonnie wee woman comes to visit a fat, old bag boy. What can I do for yer, lass?"

Duffer won the game after all. His blunt admiration made her blush. *I stink at this flirting stuff.* Flustered, she searched her memory for the reason for her visit and forged ahead.

"Sorry to bother you on such a busy day." She stepped aside as a young bag boy trotted over to grab a bag of clubs. "Does the pro shop keep a list of golfers who drive personal carts?"

Duffer cocked his head to the left, as if he hadn't heard the odd question. "You still investigating that foul business on the tennis courts?"

"I've been ordered to stay out of that." She shrugged one shoulder. "Now I'm trying to protect a teenage boy. Do you know of a cowboy-like dude who drives a golf cart off the course?"

Duffer startled and lowered his ragged eyebrows. As if trying to tell her something, his Scottish eyes glowered down the row of beige golf carts. His stare pinpointed a green cart with a striped canopy. Inside, a lanky old man settled himself onto the seat and flipped a cap onto his bald head.

"We have a list," Duffer said with no trace of an accent. He glanced at the pro shop windows. "Nine or ten personal carts were grandfathered in before the rules changed. Not all those owners play golf though." He beckoned her to the check-in podium beneath a large umbrella. "My old back won't let me bend so much. See if there's a black binder on the bottom shelf."

She stooped to retrieve the binder and handed it to Duffer, not daring to hope he'd share the list with her. The big man put his back to the windows and flipped several pages, puffing air from beneath his mustache, as if trying to come to a decision. Finally, he tugged out a sheet and folded it in half and then in quarters.

"That's last month's copy," he said. "It should be the same." He slipped the paper into Packi's hand. "Now, bonnie lass, I must be about my duties." The burr returned. "I can't stand around blethering when there's work to be done." He hailed the driver of a Lexus at the curb and hustled to remove clubs from its open trunk.

Packi tucked the paper into her pocket and decided to take the long route back to her bicycle. Strolling behind the row of club-owned beige golf carts, she paused for a moment at the green cart and squinted at the bag tag. The engraved name jumped out at her.

The cart driver heard her gasp and turned with a questioning glare. She disguised her intrusion with a forced smile and feeble wave. Any courtesy he might have had dissolved as a dark scowl furrowed into his weathered cheeks. She backed away, loath to make the acquaintance of Curtis's *creeper.*

His stare burned into the back of her shirt, as she hurried to her bicycle. She pulled her bike from the rack, buckled her helmet as if haste didn't matter, and pedaled away.

With the golfers, the pro shop, and those angry eyes behind her, Packi stopped her bike at the corner of the tennis courts in the shade of a live oak. Spiro Kristos, she repeated. If he *was* Curtis's cowboy dude, she'd strangle the man herself. *What proof do I have?* She pulled Duffer's list from her pocket to confirm the name, to see it in writing. As if printed in bold italics, his name and address leaped off the page as it had done on the county's sex offender website.

A loud speaker suddenly blared and shook Packi back to the present. She glanced back at the pro shop to see a massive traffic jam. Golf carts scattered in every direction. Men waved and shouted.The shotgun-start had begun. She searched for Spiro Kristos amid the chaos, suddenly afraid he might chase her down to confront her.

If I need help, could I count on Duffer? Where is he?

Two golf carts broke from the pack and headed her way. They bore down on her, gaining speed. Too startled to think, she jumped onto the curb and pulled her bicycle up behind her as if it could shield her. Like a raccoon mesmerized by headlights, she braced for the coming assault.

Several seconds of panic passed before she realized she recognized neither driver. Spiro Kristos was not in the cart. Instead, two jovial golfers waved as they zoomed past and raced up the path to the tee box behind the tennis courts.

A shaky laugh restarted her breathing. "Get a grip," she muttered. "You're being ridiculous."

To calm herself and reorganize her thinking, she resorted to common sense. Logic told her that Kristos could do nothing to her, at least not in public, in the middle of the day. Did he even fit Curtis's description? Old, white dude. Yes. Skinny. Yes. Cowboy like. Maybe.

Duffer's list of names had absorbed the sweat from her palm. She spread the crumbled wad out on her bike seat and smoothed it out, but blurred ink made reading difficult. She squinted at the list of neighbors with personal golf carts. No cowboy names stood out. Oliver Graham was on the list. *Too fat. Harold Baskin? A familiar name.* She stared up into the quaking leaves of the live oak to roam through her memory. She found an image of a gallant man defending his wife with a cane. *Harold Baskin, pleasant old gentleman.*

Packi pedaled toward home, but her bike seemed to have a mind of its own. She found herself on a new route, one that went past the Baskin house. *What could it hurt to pay a visit to a mugging victim? If I happen to get a look at his golf cart . . . that's icing on the cake.*

The Baskin mailbox was missing one of its numbers, leaving only a faded image to confirm she'd found the address on the list. She parked her bike on the brick walkway and followed a line of brittle shrubs toward the front door. A welcome sign hung from a broken string on a royal palm. The sign's thin wood had warped and molded itself to the trunk.

The house seemed shrouded and lonely, but she rang the doorbell, just in case. Thirty seconds later, she rapped on the door. Spiderwebs, coated in dust, clung to the stucco walls. Defeated flower stems withered in a cracked pot. Sheer lace covered the side-panel window. *Would it be rude to peer inside?* Before she could decide, the curtain quivered. A moment later, locks clicked and the door opened a crack.

"Who are you?" Irritation edged Dora Baskin's soft voice. Mesh screening darkened her scowl.

"Hello, Mrs. Baskin." Packi inclined her head toward the older woman and clasped her hands together as if speaking to a nun. "I'm Packi Walsh. We met last night. Downtown. When those muggers attacked you."

"What do you want?"

Packi sputtered in the face of the woman's animosity. She didn't expect to be hailed as a hero for her part in stopping the muggers, but a little appreciation was in order.

"How is Mr. Baskin?" she asked. "My friend, the nurse, was worried about him. Is there anything I can do for you?"

"No. He's fine." Dora's face disappeared, the door closed, and the lock clicked into place.

"Well, there we are." Packi rolled her eyes upward and caught sight of a wasp nest the size of a softball tucked in the eaves of the entryway. *Yikes.* She backed away, keeping an eye out for flying insects. Her retreat was cut short by the sound of the lock. The screen-door creaked opened and Harold Baskin stepped out, using the door jamb to steady himself.

"My, my. If it isn't one of our heroines." He gained his balance and reached for her hand to clasp between his. "How are you, my dear?"

The soft coolness of the elderly gentleman's palms disarmed Packi's anger at his wife. "Hello, Mr. Baskin," she said. The charming old rogue deserved a smile. "A night's sleep did me good after our little excitement last evening, but my friends and I were worried about you—and Mrs. Baskin."

"Takes more than two hooligans to defeat Harold T. Baskin." He performed an elegant parry with an invisible sword but then accepted her arm to avoid a fall. He sighed. "A few extra aches and pains but one gets used to that."

His bravado ended in a weak puff of air. He waited in patient silence, as if he had many moments of life to squander. Mr. Baskin reminded Packi of her professor of psychology who listened more than he lectured. The type who wore knitted mufflers in the winter, had suede patches on his jacket elbows, and smoked a pipe while contemplating the universe.

Dive right in, she told herself. "Do you own a golf cart, Mr. Baskin?" She raised the list in her hand as if he could connect it to the question.

An indulgent smile vied with his long penetrating gaze. "An odd inquiry, my dear."

He seemed to see through her motives. Packi felt analyzed and found lacking, as though she stood in front of that professor with her late term paper in hand. She stumbled over her words.

"Oh, well, I . . ." She hung onto the list as if it could save her. "I'm thinking of buying a golf cart, and I'm going down this list of members who own one." The thin veil over her real motive threatened to slip away. Lying was not in her nature. But before she could confess her true mission, he took her by the elbow.

"So, you're in the market. Splendid. Simply splendid." His cool fingers tugged at her arm. "It so happens I have a golf cart in need of a buyer."

He led her to the garage, relying on her for stability, and punched a few numbers into the keypad at the side of the door. Her heart pounded as the door cranked up in its slow, grinding way. Dust swirled in the breeze sucked into the two-car garage.

A shiny beige Grand Marquis took up most of the space, but parked next to it was a boxy shape under a canvas tarp. Mr Baskin took hold of a corner of the tarp and tugged with little effect. His dress shoes slipped on the gritty floor, and Packi jumped forward to steady him. He leaned against the Grand Marquis as she grabbed an edge of the heavy canvas and dragged it away to reveal a green golf cart. Striped canopies must have been a fad a decade ago.

"I haven't golfed in years," said Baskin.

Nor had the cart been driven in years. Dust coated the seat, and the four dry-rotted tires were flat to the floor.

The old gentlemen spotted her eyeing the tires. "Florida heat devastates rubber. The battery needs replacement as well." He reached into the cart for a set of keys and pressed them into her hand. "But for fifty dollars, it's yours."

The cart wasn't the one driven by Curtis's creeper, but it was quite a find, and at fifty dollars, a giveaway. Packi almost wished she wanted a golf cart. "I couldn't . . ."

"Twenty-five."

The keys felt right. She envisioned herself tooling around in the little cart.

"Wonderful!" Baskin clapped his hands. "I'll get new tires and a battery installed and have it delivered to your house."

"What?" Realizing she must have nodded during her little daydream, Packi protested, "Mr. Baskin, I can't. You're too generous."

"Nonsense. You need a golf cart, and my garage is too cluttered." The old man gave a feeble wave at shelves lined with Christmas boxes, tarnished trophies, and garden tools. His red-rimmed eyes pleaded with her to accept his gift. "Please do me this kindness, Mrs. Walsh, I'm putting my affairs in order and wish to acknowledge your thoughtfulness last night."

Her conscience fought a battle with her practicality. *How can I tell him my true motive for visiting his home? Why do I need a golf cart?* "Please let me think about this, Mr. Baskin. This is happening too fast."

"Certainly, my dear." He smiled as if he'd won the negotiation and patted her hand.

Packi escaped to her bicycle and looked back as she pedaled away. In the shade of the sago palms framing his home, Harold Baskin seemed to wither like the spent flowers at his door. His shoulders stooped. The effort needed to hold himself erect during her visit had apparently taken its toll.

20

Dr. Perez, the neighbor from down the street, stooped to pick up his dog's droppings and wrapped them into a plastic bag. Packi echoed his cheery "Hola" and pedaled past him with a wave but shook her head. *The things people do for their pets.*

A musical ring tone interrupted her thoughts on pet ownership. She picked up speed to bump over the curb into her driveway, swung her leg over her seat, and rushed to unzip the nylon pouch on the handlebars.

"Hello?"

The phone rang a third time. She jabbed blindly at the sunlight-obscured screen.

"Hello?"

"Mizz Walsh." Deputy Teig didn't bother with social niceties. "Got your message. What's this about a mugging? You're not getting Curtis mixed up in your investigations, are you?"

"Now, calm down, Billy. Certainly not." His assertion that she'd intentionally lead the boy into trouble irked her, but she kept her composure.

"Curtis and I," she said in a modulated tone, "finally talked while we drove home from the . . . Well, never mind." She didn't want to remind the deputy of her poorly planned trip to the homeless camp.

"Anyway, Curtis confided that a man is hanging around making him feel uncomfortable. He called the guy a creeper. The man sits at the basketball court, watching him play."

"Why didn't Curtis tell me himself?" Hurt lurked at the edge of the deputy's gruff voice.

"I don't know, but he gave me permission to tell you." Packi struggled to keep the phone to her ear while she parked her bike in the garage. "As much as he respects you, you're still *the law* and there appears to be some sort of code against ratting anyone, even creepers, out to the cops."

Packi walked through the house as she relayed the rest of the conversation to Teig. In the kitchen, she propped herself in a straight-backed stool at the counter. Ready to concentrate, she broached the subject that had been under her skin for two days.

"Billy," she said, kneading the space between her eyebrows. "Grace showed me the county's sex offender website. Have you seen it? Did you know there's one right here in this community?"

Packi waited for his surprise but listened to a long pause instead.

"I got a look at him," she whispered. "Spiro Kristos. I think he's the same guy bothering Curtis."

"Mizz Walsh," Teig said, underlining her name with exaggerated patience. "I know about the list. Mr. Kristos is not under suspicion for anything. Give him his privacy."

"Privacy?" Packi took the phone from her ear and glared at it in disbelief before ready to speak to Teig again. "What if he's been stalking Curtis?"

"Mizz Walsh. Stop. He's not."

"But how do you know? He has a golf cart."

"What?"

In one long-running monologue, Packi ran through the club policy on personal carts, gave Curtis's description of the man's golf cart, and described the dirty looks she'd gotten from Spiro Kristos. She hated her own chattiness but had to get it out, had to get Deputy Teig to understand.

"Mizz Walsh. Stop," Teig said. "It's not his M.O." He took a huge breath. "Now tell me about the mugging. Where were you?"

He doesn't get it, Packi thought. She put aside her annoyance at Billy's lack of concern for Curtis and gave him a run-down of the mugging incident downtown. She highlighted Beth's braveness and Kay's nursing skills but glossed over her own ineffective presence.

"Remember how Curtis described the thieves at the homeless camp?" Packi asked, breathless from the long story. "The gang leader had a snake tattoo above his eyebrow. Right?"

Teig grunted.

"One of the muggers, the tall black guy, had the same tattoo," she said. "I forgot to tell the city police about that. Beth said she didn't notice any tattoo on the white kid she chased. Do you think it's a gang sign, or is it the same guy as in the camp? Please tell your buddy downtown. It might help solve both crimes."

"Thank you, Mizz Walsh. That's useful information," Teig said. "Now go play your tennis games and stay out of police business."

She had been dismissed. Their good-byes were cordial enough, but the conversation left Packi out of sorts. She tossed her phone into her purse and drummed her fingers on the granite countertop certain she hadn't gotten the importance of the clues across to Billy. He hadn't even asked to see the golf cart list. She grabbed the club's membership directory and her car keys.

If you're too busy to follow up on our local sex offender, Deputy Teig, I'll do it myself.

* * *

A plump, dark-haired woman wrapped in a beach towel answered the door at the first address on Duffer McCracken's golf cart list.

"Thank you for seeing me, Mrs. De Luca."

"I'm sorry." The woman tightened the towel. "I was out at the pool when you called." She waved Packi inside. "Come in. Come in. I haven't talked to anyone in days and have a pitcher of iced tea ready."

"I really can't stay." Packi held up the list to explain her urgency, but the woman padded away. Packi had no choice but to follow her through the tidy townhome and out to the lanai.

"So what can I do for you?" Mrs. De Luca filled a second tumbler with tea and listened to Packi's story about buying a golf cart.

"Do you or your husband still play golf, Mrs. De Luca?"

"Call me Rose." She sat back into the cushioned chair and sighed with contentment. "Beautiful, isn't it?" She opened her arms to the scenery: a rippling pond, a clearing, and a thicket of wild trees beyond. "I sit here every day and watch for deer and bobcats."

"You have a great view," Packi agreed and quelled her impatience by sipping the refreshing tea. She snuck a peek at her phone's clock. *Time to get to the point.* "Rose, do you still own a golf cart? I was wondering if it might be for sale."

Rose paused. Her amiable smile froze and then slid away. "I sold the cart after Jerry died." She leaned forward to slide a plate of lemon wedges toward Packi. "Kept his golf clubs though. Don't know why."

A familiar pang hit Packi. "Oh, I'm so sorry." She reached across the table for Rose's hand and felt a bond shimmer between them."Tell me about him."

Packi listened. She watched the sun creep through Mrs. De Luca's beautiful scenery, refilled both glasses, and understood. Rose reminded her of herself two years ago, when she, too, had been isolated after her husband's death. She had never been a joiner, but the tennis team shook her out of her loneliness. Rose needed the same sort of push to help her restart her life.

Later, after urging Rose to try tennis, tai chi, or even buncotini, Packi pulled herself away from the pleasant conversation. Rose waved from the front door, still wrapped in her beach towel.

Packi drove out of sight of the De Luca home and then pulled to the curb. She needed a moment to cover her exposed emotions. Rose's grief had rubbed Packi raw. Reliving her own grief and putting a positive spin on life for Rose's benefit had exhausted her.

Get me through this, Ron. She huffed a major sigh and checked the mirror to see what damage tears had done.

Okay, back to business. Packi mentally crossed Jerry De Luca off the list and drove to the next address.

* * *

George and Lydia Pope were easy to cross off the golf cart list. As Packi cruised the street of detached executive homes, she spotted a two-tone brown golf cart parked in their driveway. Wrong color and, according to the script across the front panel, it had been christened "Pope-mobile." Curtis would have noticed that.

Oliver Graham was next. Packi tapped the paper with the nib of her pen and almost ran a line through his name. The man was too fat to be described as a cowboy, but Packi reminded herself to follow every lead and wheeled around to the Eagle's Nest section of Paradise Palms.

She pulled the Audi to a stop at the curb and double-checked the address, 1324 Periwinkle. The house was the same style as those on either side but different. Like identical twins with opposite personalities. The Graham house was the stiff and surly twin while the other homes seemed airy and inviting.

Packi climbed out of the car but paused at the end of the walkway to read a small sign stuck in a row of meticulous shrubs. *Unless you're selling thin mints, GO AWAY.* She wondered if the Grahams were funny or obnoxious. Convincing herself the sign couldn't apply to friendly neighbors, she rang the bell. No one answered nor peeked from behind the heavy draperies. Packi waited. She thought it rude to open the screen door to knock, so she rang the bell again and got no response.

Rejected by the shuttered house, Packi wandered down the walkway to her car. At the curb, she stopped short when a golf cart nearly took her kneecaps off.

"What do you want?"

The fat man's look of hatred scared her off her questions about golf cart sales and tennis guests. "I'm collecting blankets for the homeless."

"I heard about that." Oliver Graham sniffed. "Those perverts won't get anything from me." He aimed his remote control at his garage like a gun. "Get off my property or I'll call the cops!" The house swallowed the offensive man and shut itself up like a fortress.

Infuriated, Packi escaped to her car, slammed the door, and gripped the roots of her hair. "Arrgh!" She yelled at the Audi's roof and beat the steering wheel. She dropped her head against the seat and closed her eyes, trying to stuff her anger back into its cage.

Moments later, knuckles rapped at her window and jolted Packi out of her attempt at serenity. She flinched, fearing Graham's retaliation. Outside her driver's side window, a man's naked abdomen filled the view. Definitely not Oliver Graham's. Her gaze travelled over rows of hardened bronzed muscles, upward to a golden chest. Her fear was replaced with another sort of adrenaline rush.

"May I help you?" Packi said before realizing she couldn't be heard. She fumbled for the buttons to open the windows. "May . . ."

"Sorry to scare you."

Jungle Jim's grin didn't seem at all repentant. Packi struggled to keep her eyes on his face, but from her low-slung seat, she could see only his lower half. His U.S. Marine buckle was at eye level, twelve inches from her nose.

She yanked the door handle and shoved, hoping to push him back. Instead, he caught the door frame and held it open like a gentleman. He offered his hand, but she climbed out on her own.

Packi tugged on the hem of her shirt and faced him from a safe distance. "Is there something you need?"

"No, ma'am." He cocked his head toward Graham's sullen house. "Looked to me like you could use my assistance."

"No, I'm fine. Thank you." She wondered how much of her temper tantrum he had witnessed. *Dang. Probably every second of it.*

"Why are you here?" Residual anger sharpened her tone.

Jungle Jim Voss eyed her but didn't lose the grin. "Oliver Graham is a maggot but also my neighbor." He motioned to a house across the street. "My humble abode."

Packi peered at the overgrown vegetation all but obscuring a beige house within. Jungle Jim was certainly an appropriate nickname, she thought. Unlike every other house in the community, his looked like a botanical garden gone wild. No wonder the homeowner association, the club manager, and his neighbors feuded with him. By all accounts, he fought back in rough leatherneck language.

He followed her gaze and paused to give her ample time to take in the scene. "Horticulture is my hobby," he said as if expecting her to be impressed. "Would you care for the ten-cent tour?"

Packi stammered. She shook her head and meant to say no, but the wild plantings intrigued her, and curiosity won out over common sense. "Yes, I would."

She matched her stride to the ex-marine's and marched across the street with him. Jungle Jim led Packi through a wooden arch covered with trailing vines of bright red flowers. *Mandevilla,* she thought. He ducked beneath low-hanging vines and held them aside for her to pass. A tunnel of greenery led to the front door, but Jim turned off onto a flagstone path to the side of the house.

"Most of these are Florida natives." He stood back, allowing her time to enjoy the planted beauty and variety. "Others, I've collected on my travels." He pointed to exotic flowers and named their origin: Hawaii, Thailand, Brazil, Cuba.

Packi recognized some of the plants from her volunteer work at the nearby Hammock Preserve, but for most she bent to read the tags affixed to stakes. Every plant and tree was identified with their common name and genus. As Packi walked the path and delighted in each recognition and discovery, Jim followed behind without a word.

At the back of the house, palms of several varieties defined an inviting sitting area and framed a long view of a sunlit pond. Packi sighed and faced the man who had created his own paradise. "This is lovely."

The retired marine's ruddy cheeks flushed. He turned aside and bent to snap off a spent flower. He plucked at the petals before tossing it to the ground. "Sit," he ordered.

Packi took pity on the man's momentary, but obvious, discomfort and stepped away, hiding a smile. Still a bit unsettled by her proximity to a half-naked man, she chose a sturdy chair nearest the sunlight.

"Made these myself." Jungle Jim thumped the back of an identical Adirondack-style chair. He sat in it, erect and in command, like Captain Kirk at the helm, but with sun glistening off his hairy calves.

Packi admired the chairs and ran her hand over the smooth surface. "Well done. Where did you . . ."

"Why were you visiting Graham?"

Startled by the abrupt question, she protested. "I wasn't *visiting*. It's none of your business, but I went there to see if he owned . . ." She stopped. *Why am I telling him this?*

Jungle Jim narrowed his eyes and gave her the same sly look he'd had when he slipped away from Deputy Teig at the tennis courts. She slid to the edge of her chair. *Why was Billy trying to track him down?*

"Oliver Graham is a jerk," she muttered to close the conversation.

Voss worked his fist open and closed as if exorcising unresolved anger. "A taste of power can make a little man a tyrant."

Packi nodded her agreement and wondered what went on between the two neighbors. The demeanors of both men seemed to confirm rumors of bitter debates. She arched her eyebrows, waiting for more information.

"You stay away from him." Jungle Jim accentuated his warning by bouncing his fist on the Adirondack's arm. "There's foul business going on in that house."

The level of the man's aggravation seemed more than homeowner issues would warrant. She hoped his anger would loosen his tongue. "What do you mean? Did something happen with the guests he had last week?"

Surprised, Jim's engraved frown deepened. "I see stuff," he said, more wary now. "Stick to your volunteer work and don't nose around Oliver Graham. I'll deal with him." The marine veteran squared his shoulders and clenched his teeth.

Fighting mode. Packi sat erect and gripped the chair arms. She wondered what mission he was on and why she sensed danger. The backyard jungle seemed to close in and darken. Packi didn't know whether a storm approached or her instincts warned her, but she jumped from her chair.

"I have to go," she said to cover her anxiety and sudden rudeness. "Thank you for the tour." She rushed to the stone path before Jim could rise from his seat. *Keep moving,* she told herself.

She fought through the clinging mandevilla and burst onto the street, making a beeline for her car. *Keep moving. Look normal.* She rehearsed an excuse for her sudden departure. *What if he catches up?*

Packi climbed in the car, slammed the door, and gunned the engine, no longer caring what he thought. She checked her rearview mirror, but no one emerged from the jungle. The Audi roared down two blocks of beige homes. At the next intersection, Packi considered blowing the stop sign, then jammed on the brakes. She put the car into neutral to catch her breath. The street was quiet. There were no ex-marines in her mirrors. She flipped the AC vents toward her heated face and closed her eyes.

What was that? Running away now seemed foolish. She could have pumped him for information about Oliver Graham. Could have asked him what he'd witnessed on his marches around the neighborhood. Should have asked why Deputy Teig wanted to question him.

Frustrated by her lack of detective instincts, Packi stared down a long row of bottlebrush trees and shook her head. *Why does he scare me? The man loves flowers*, she reasoned. *He donates to the homeless. He's . . . he's . . .* The word she avoided was *sexy*. She groaned. *But there's something else beneath that, something animal inside him—power, violence, virility.* She told herself she wanted no part of Jungle Jim Voss.

21

The further Packi drove away from the Voss house, the more Paradise Palms returned to the tranquil, beautiful place she knew. Jungle Jim's effect on her diminished. The dangerously sexy image of him was replaced in her mind with a picture of Oliver Graham's repulsive sneer.

A tyrant, Voss had called him. She could see that in Graham. Her disgust with the odious man rekindled. She forced her brain to recall the rest of his image: his wobbling jowls under a stupid "Old Fart" hat; a thick belt cinched across his bulging belly; two sets of golf clubs on the back of the green cart—with a striped canopy!

"Well, Mr. Nasty Graham, cowboy or not, you're still on my list."

Peeved, Packi stomped on the accelerator. She ignored the posted speed limit, almost hoping Deputy Teig was in the neighborhood to pull her over. She'd get answers about Voss. She'd report Graham. She'd get the jerk arrested. She'd . . . She'd look stupid and emotional. Packi sighed and slowed down.

Think, Patricia. Other than being grotesque and rude, what is Graham guilty of?

She thought of Duffer McCracken's remarks. He loved to gossip about the goings on at the club and the behavior of various members. *What else might the old bag boy know about Oliver Graham?*

The Audi seemed to be on autopilot and took her to the golf course. Packi cruised the lot looking for a parking spot and watching for Mr. McCracken at the same time. Bag boys toted golf clubs to and from cars and ferried carts around the busy staging area, but Duffer wasn't among them.

Packi hurried across the lot toward the pro shop and hailed a young bag boy to ask after Duffer. The teenager paused only a moment to direct her to the cart barn.

The cart barn was a mystery to her. After each weekly round of golf, Packi and the other league players were asked to drop off their carts outside the huge garage. She'd never gone inside but heard the barn had facilities to store clubs, wash carts, and to recharge batteries. It seemed an alien environment, not meant for club members.

No one greeted her at the open overhead doors where sunlight drew stark lines on cement floor. As she waited for her eyes to adjust, bag boys and carts scurried past. Water streamed into drains. Fans whirred in the rafters, barely moving heavy, damp air. From amid a din of mechanical noises, she picked out Duffer's voice off to the right and sidled between rows of parked carts toward the conversation.

McCracken, who had lost his Scottish burr, stood gabbing in a tight knot with two other men. He became more engrossed as a shorter man made a finger gun and pretended to aim and shoot. The big Scotsman listened, scratching at his white whiskers, then spotted Packi and pushed down the man's imaginary gun. The two others glanced her way and shut their mouths.

"Mr. McCracken?"

"Good afternoon to ye, Mrs. Walsh." Duffer's florid face brightened with a leprechaun smile. His companions gave her a nod, wandered off, and Duffer swung his big body into the golf cart nearest her. "I'm delighted to see ye, lass, but what brings ye to my humble domain?"

"Were your friends discussing the recent killing?" She formed her own fingers into a pretend gun. The man's pantomime had piqued her curiosity and seemed like an invitation to get involved in the murder again in spite of Deputy Teig's warning.

"Aye, bonnie lass. Sorry to say, we men are worse than old biddies when it comes to scandalous gossip." He rested his sun-damaged forearms on his belly.

"Is there news?" she asked. "Do they know anything about the incident?"

"Nothing ye wouldn't already know. They repeat what they hear, and the story grows." He huffed from behind his thick mustache, then held up one beefy finger.

"You asked me about guests. I've been thinking about that." The cart groaned and tilted as he leaned to the side and struggled to fit his hand into his pants pocket. He extracted a folded paper and spread it on his knee.

"This, wee lady, is the time sheet from the day before you found the victim." He thumped a chubby index finger on the morning time slots.

Packi picked up the paper and examined the blur. “I can’t read it.” She angled the sheet toward the sunlit doors.

“Try these.” Duffer offered her a pair of bifocals from his shirt pocket. “Mr. Oliver Graham and guests had an eight A.M. start time. The Canadian beauties were right behind them.”

Packi spotted Kimberly Stinson’s underlined name first, but the glasses slid from her nose before she could read the rest. She pushed the readers into place. There, clear as day, beneath Oliver Graham’s name were three others: M. Brainard, Tom Jordan, and L. Pritchard.

“Do you know any of the other players? His guests? Any of them look like cowboys?”

“Whoa, lassie. I dinna ken your meanin’. Cowboys?”

The brogue returned and Packi knew he was laughing at her excitement, but why shouldn’t she be excited? That L. Pritchard name could match the name on the tennis bag’s ID card. Could the tennis court victim be the same as Curtis’s creeper?

She opened her hands and smoothed them through the air to calm herself. “Yes. Cowboys. Could any of those men be described by a teenage boy as a cowboy?”

Duffer’s snicker ended as he stroked his mustache before answering. “Mr. Graham’s cart partner. Called him Lenny—arrogant bast . . .” He caught himself. “My apologies, lass.” The old bag boy cleared his throat and continued. “Lenny is tall and lanky. Younger. A gym rat, I’m guessing. Aye. I could imagine him roping cows.”

Packi’s mind strayed through bits of information. She looked at the list again to click an idea into place. “Were the Canadian women friendly to the men?”

Duffer dragged his cap from his head and rearranged the few hairs left on his pate. “No danger that.” He poked his finger at the underlined name. “That lady there, Ms. Stinson, wanted naw to do with them. Demanded a different time slot. The schedule was tight. Best I could do was push a foursome between them.”

“Did you tell the police about these names?” Almost breathless, Packi held the paper to her chest. “Do they know about Graham’s guests?”

He settled back against the cart seat. “Only the bonnie wee lass in front of me came askin’ about time sheets.”

Packi leaned into the cart and planted a kiss on Duffer’s cheek. “Thank you!”

"Aye. Friends call me Sherlock McCracken." He touched his cheek and called after her as she squeezed through the rows of golf carts. "You'll know, they named it *Scotland* Yard for a reason."

* * *

As if on a model's catwalk for the world to see, the woman ahead of Packi tossed her long chestnut curls and pranced along the path to the tennis courts. Her hips swayed side to side.

Nobody else walks like that. Packi jumped from her car and trotted across the clubhouse parking lot. "Kimberly!"

The news anchor turned with a beautiful, practiced smile and gave a celebrity wave, though she took a moment to focus on Packi, and another few seconds for recognition. "Hello, Patty," she called. "Playing tennis today?"

Packi slowed to a walk, dabbed perspiration from her upper lip, and didn't bother to correct her name. "Hi, Kimberly." She raised her hand to ask for a moment to catch her breath.

"No tennis for me until the round robin this evening." Packi sucked in air. "You have another lesson?"

"Yep. One of these days I'll be as good as the rest of you." Kimberly grinned and adjusted the thin strap of her form-fitting top. "Anyway, I'll keep trying." She glanced toward the teaching courts where three women were packing away their racquets and paying Sam Vickroy for their lesson.

"You'll fit in, Kim. Don't worry." Packi fell into step alongside her. She liked Kimberly, or at least the normal woman beneath the self-conscious preening. She hoped her reassurances would reach that inner person. "Beth and the rest of the team say great things about you."

Kimberly stopped and grasped Packi's arm. "But Beth already put me in a match next week." Her eyes widened and her mouth gaped. "Court four. I'm scared to death!"

The woman's drama bugged Packi, but she understood. Two years ago, every match turned her insides upside down too. "Remember, it's only a silly game," she said, "and *nothing* compared to speaking to a television audience."

Kimberly bit at her lipstick and took on a worried look.

"You'll be fine." Packi abbreviated her sympathy. She had a question to get to before Kimberly hurried off. She paused only a moment.

"Did you play golf last week and have a problem with a foursome of men?"

Kimberly flinched. Her perfect complexion hardened and one well-defined eyebrow arched upward. "Yes." She peered sideways at Packi. "But how did you know?"

"I'm digging into an issue and asked questions at the pro shop."

Moisture formed on Kimberly's forehead. Her body tensed. Packi wondered how serious the altercation with the four men had been. She decided, for the moment, to let Kimberly off the hook. "A guy in a private golf cart may, or may not, have been stalking a young boy."

"You think it was one of those golfers? That's disgusting." Kimberly's polyester straps loosened as her shoulders relaxed, and well-disguised crow's feet deepened as she thought.

"Yeah. I can see any one of those guys being a stalker." She pursed her lips, heedless of the threat of permanent wrinkles. Anger creased her brow. "One of them recognized me from Toronto. From the show, I guess. Like he knew me." She punched the air with a tight fist. "Tried to pat my butt! The freak. No boundaries. I almost broke his arm."

The war between anger and professional control worked its way through Kimberly's body. "He wanted us—my three sisters came down to help me move in—to meet him and his drunken friends for drinks. Eight o'clock in the morning, and he already reeked of booze."

Packi was stunned by the depth of the woman's anger. She let a moment of silence pass while Kimberly got her emotions in line.

"Sorry." Kimberly still seethed but corralled her outrage. "I never got used to it. People pushing in, thinking they know me, that we're buddies."

Packi couldn't imagine the problems of celebrity but nodded and then nudged the conversation forward. "Did you ask the golf pro or course ranger to intervene?"

"Not really. I tried to blow it off. We asked for a different time slot and then . . ." Kimberly dismissed the rest of the story with clenched fist.

The vehemence surprised Packi. She wondered how far Kimberly's anger had driven her. She tucked away the thought, promising to mull it over after resolving the issue of Curtis's creeper.

"Can you describe the guys who harassed you? Did one have a cowboy look? Maybe younger than the others—tall, athletic?"

"That's the jerk I'm talking about." Kimberly ground her teeth. "He was in a cart with a fat slob who had drool running down his chin." She closed her eyes and waved her hand. "Well, not really, but you know what I mean. Disgusting."

"And the other two?"

"Old. Stupid. They sat in their cart leering at my younger sisters. I don't know how the club allows scumbags like that on the golf course."

Packi tamped down her excitement. Details were falling into place. She suspected that one of those scumbags would never bother Kimberly, or anyone else, ever again.

Kimberly was on a roll, and Packi wanted to keep her talking. "What else do you remember about the guy who patted your butt and almost lost his arm?"

The retired news anchor sniffed but then took on her journalistic persona. She lifted her chin and, without a TelePrompTer, recalled details.

"He, the douche bag, bragged about traveling the world. Singapore, Peking, Malaysia. Selling something, I think." Kimberly tapped her French manicure against her tennis bag. "He must have spent time in Toronto. He could mimic the intro to my newscast."

"So he was a fan?"

"More like he wanted to latch on to me to prove to his drinking buddies that he's a *somebody*." A soundless whistle blew from Kimberly's plump red lips. "Apparently, he didn't know I got the boot from TV land."

"You mentioned he's a salesman," Packi said. "What does he sell?"

Kimberly shrugged. "I wouldn't buy anything from that slime ball."

They reached the end of the walkway, but Packi wasn't ready to let Kimberly go. She was certain the aggressive fan was the creeper. "Did he give his name?"

"No." Kimberly shook her head, then stared at a passing cloud. "Wait—he did. Link or something. Lincoln."

That wasn't what Packi expected to hear. "Are you sure?"

Kimberly brought her focus back. "Yes. Lincoln Powers." She locked eyes with Packi but then startled suddenly. "I gotta run. Sam is waiting for me. Thanks for letting me vent, Patty."

Kimberly Stinson trotted across the court with her ruffled tennis skirt swaying with her hips.

22

Packi spent an hour flipping through cookbooks before deciding on a recipe for lavender cookies. Baking grounded her, cleared her mind, and allowed her to see the basics of things. For two hours she put aside thoughts of murder, gangs, and creepers and allowed luscious aromas to soothe her.

In spite of the break, she still worried about Curtis. Though she knew he was at school, she boxed up a dozen warm cookies and dropped them off at the Grant house. Mrs. Grant accepted the cookies and Packi's thanks for the donations to the homeless camp. She seemed surprised at Packi's concern for her grandson. Just in time, Packi realized Curtis hadn't mentioned his encounter with the thieves to his grandparents and was careful not to betray his trust. No doubt, he didn't want to worry them.

Packi packed another two dozen cookies to bring to the tennis league's Thanksgiving round robin that evening. She had agreed to help Beth and the others decorate for the event. She arrived early to tack up posters of turkeys and Pilgrims, string orange streamers, and pile hay bales, gourds, and pumpkins at the registration table. With the work done, the group rested in the shade on court-side bleachers to wait for the first of the players to arrive. Beth filled them in on her plan for the event, but the conversation then turned to the unsolved murder on the tennis court and the man in the golf cart who had spooked Curtis.

Beth sat with her elbows on her knees, listening to Packi's stories about golf cart identification and Kimberly's altercation with the drunken golfers.

"Well, of course, he'd pick an alias." The turkey on the ridiculous hat Beth wore bobbed up on down as she spoke. "If you're going to act like a jerk, you don't give your real name."

Packi wandered from one side of the bleachers to the other as she spoke. "But it doesn't match either the tee sheet or the tennis bag's ID card, though the initials are the same."

"That, right there, is suspicious enough." Kay slapped her hands on the tennis bag on her lap. "So you got it solved. They're all the same guy—the kid's creeper, Kimberly's jerk, and the dead guy."

Packi wasn't satisfied. She wanted to tie the details together and present a real resolution to the police in spite of, or maybe because of, Billy Teig's warning to stay out of the investigation. The next question was obvious. *Who killed the tennis player with the initials L.P.?*

"Who would have a gun?" Packi wondered aloud. "Who'd be angry enough to shoot him?" She paced in front of the group like a teacher on test day.

"You said Kimberly was mighty irate," offered Kay. "We don't know her very well. Could she . . ."

"Oh no." Marilyn put her hand on Kay's shoulder to stop her. "I played with her yesterday. She couldn't."

Beth rubbed her chin while her turkey hat bobbed. "Maybe this Lenny or Lincoln guy at the basketball court tried something creepy, something physical, and the kid got revenge."

The horror of the thought took Packi's breath away. "Curtis?"

"I'm just sayin'." Beth apologized with a shrug. "Is it possible the kid found a gun to defend himself? I know his grandfather owns one. I was practicing at the gun range last year—right after Rex gave me a nine-millimeter for my birthday. Well, anyway, I ran into Dr. Grant, shooting in the next lane."

Kay jumped on the idea. "If his grandfather owns a gun, maybe Dr. Grant . . ." She pantomimed aiming an imaginary gun and pulled the trigger. "If somebody messed with my kids, I'd have no problem shooting him dead."

Packi slumped onto the bleacher seat, thinking of Iris Grant. *This is too much. One of our neighbors is capable of murder. Too ugly.* She stewed in the terrible possibilities until the word *ugly* brought her mind around to the fat man who had nearly run her over in his golf cart. Confusion unscrambled.

"My money is on Oliver Graham," Packi announced. She was more than happy to deflect suspicions away from Curtis and his grandfather. The group pivoted toward her to listen as she explained her reasoning.

"Graham knew the dead man. Leonard Pritchard was his guest. Maybe he stayed at his house and they got into a fight. Maybe he insulted Oliver's wife with his lurid talk."

Marilyn gasped and put her hand over her heart. "Oliver couldn't possibly be a killer." Her soft-spoken words pleaded for that to be true. "The

Grahams are decent people. He works hard for this community, and Ursula played Mahjong with us."

As her assertions proved nothing, Marilyn's delicate skin crinkled at her temples and tears threatened. "Ursula does drink too much lately," she admitted with obvious pain. "She complains about neighbors butting in on arguments between her and Oliver." Marilyn sighed and removed herself from the conflict by concentrating on the hem of her tennis skirt.

"I heard that, too." Kay sniffed. "Their fights shake the tiles off their roof. They had a humdinger last week, and Jungle Jim came pounding on their door." Kay seemed to relish the gossip but shook her head. "Graham is *not* a decent person, Marilyn. He may be an active volunteer, but he's a vulgar clod who manipulates everyone. He blew a gasket with Jim Voss over that jungle around his . . ."

Beth jumped into the conversation. "Graham also got into a shouting match with the club manager at the board meeting. Accused him of wasting money on pickleball courts and financial mismanagement. Even claimed Vince diverted funds into his own pocket. Stuff like that."

The turkey hat wobbled side to side as Beth wound down. "In any case, nobody's going to insult Ursula to her face and get away with it. She's a bruiser. She can hit a golf ball two hundred yards."

Beth paused and raised her finger. "You know." She tapped the air in front of her as if weighing her next thought. "There's a rumor some of the golf couples on Periwinkle Lane got into that spouse swapping thing."

That was a shot out of left field. Packi flushed, remembering when Kay offered her husband to repair Packi's pool filter. Kay's territorial look had been unmistakable, but the awkward moment had been solved by an acceptable swap—a loaf of homemade zucchini bread.

"Pfft." Kay tossed her tennis bag under the bleachers. "Who'd want Oliver Graham in their house to do chores?"

"Maybe he trades tax accounting or computer repair," Marilyn suggested.

"No," said Beth. "That's not what I mean. I heard some of them swapped more than chores." She screwed up her face and waited for their reaction.

"You are joking." Kay gaped at Beth and looked to the others for confirmation. "Whoo, baby! I can't picture that."

Packi was speechless. Petty feuds and financial scandals were acceptable fodder for gossip, but real husband swapping shocked her.

"Just sayin'," said Beth. "Swap parties ran rampant in a community north of here couple years ago. Viagra and all that."

Packi's imagination filled in the blanks. *Had things gotten out of hand between neighbors on Periwinkle Lane? Maybe the murder victim got in on it, and his murder was a crime of passion.* Though she couldn't see Graham as a swapper, she could see him as an angry man and a killer. In her mind, Oliver Graham had the temperament, opportunity, and now motive.

* * *

The issue of wife-swapping was left hanging in the air when participants in the Thanksgiving round robin began to arrive. Packi sat at the registration table and handed out play schedules while Beth ticked off the players' names. Kay and Marilyn distributed raffle tickets and offered cold water and snacks. The gossip had left the team with extra color to their cheeks, and they laughed a little too loud.

While explaining how the schedules worked, Packi avoided looking male participants in the eye. She wondered if the idea of swapping chores had been perverted in their neighborhoods too.

Rumors are only rumors, she assured herself, but her mind continued to wander. Certainly, her Ron would never have taken part in such silliness. Neither would Mark. At least she didn't think so. A seed of doubt encroached upon her pleasure over seeing him the next evening, so she pushed aside the absurdity and focused on the Thanksgiving event.

Packi surveyed the tennis players milling about the courts waiting for instructions. They were a congenial, responsible, good-hearted bunch. None of them looked or acted like Oliver Graham. *He is the anomaly,* she thought. *Something was wrong in that house.*

Beth's publicity for the Thanksgiving event attracted enough players to fill the tennis courts. Packi wasn't needed and watched from the sidelines. The fun didn't hold her interest for long. She dwelled on her suspicions about Graham and itched to know more.

What the heck, Packi decided. She waved goodbye to Beth and slipped away, intent on visiting a certain veteran marine who might have information about his neighbors. Logic told her Jim Voss's anger during her last visit had been directed at his neighbors, not her. She blamed her panic in his backyard jungle on her fear of confined spaces. Still, a shudder ran down her spine. *I won't let my guard down this time,* she promised herself.

Packi parked the car across the street from the Graham house, short of the driveway, and cut the engine. The darkened residence had hunkered down with a secret, its doors shut like a prison on lockdown. Did a killer lurk inside?

In comparison, Jim Voss's jungle looked almost welcoming. Packi exited her vehicle and kept her eye on the suspect's house across the street. She inched her way along the side of her car.

"Evening, ma'am."

Packi's purse crashed to the pavement, spilling its contents. Her phone skittered under the bumper and coins rolled into the gutter. She dithered between a scramble after her stuff or the prospect of facing Jungle Jim.

"Hello," Packi said from her knees. She jammed her phone and keys back into her purse and began a search for loose change.

She reached for a quarter but pulled back when her fingers came too close to the toe of a large hiking boot. The leather was worn but well polished. The ends of the laces were secured in the cuff.

Muscles bulged from Jungle Jim's calves. She stared, mesmerized. Golden hairs curled on his shins. His seductive kneecaps flexed, snapping her back to reality. Packi recaptured control of her wandering eyes and reminded herself who she was. She snatched up the last of the coins and used the bumper to struggle to her feet.

Jungle Jim Voss stood over her carrying a large dog in his arms. The pit bull's tongue lolled from the side of its mouth as he rested his chin on the man's shoulder.

"You left mighty quick this morning." Jim grinned at her discomfort and hoisted the dog higher on his chest. "I didn't have a chance to say how much I enjoyed your visit."

Packi brushed dust from her knees and swiped her hands against her shorts. "Sorry.   I get a little claustrophobic." That part was true. Ever since she was a kid and got stuck in a culvert trying to reach a lost baseball, she panicked in small spaces. She didn't care that he was skeptical of her explanation.

Packi avoided looking at the man and focused on the animal in his arms. The dog looked like him, she thought: broad shouldered, virile, dangerous. Determined to appear calm and in control, she asked the natural question. "What's his name?"

"His tags say Winston." Jungle Jim scratched the dog under its chin and cooed to the animal. "I call him Ranger." He grinned, his teeth emerging from beneath his bristling white mustache.

"He's not your dog?"

"No. My wife's allergic." Voss nuzzled his face into the dog's neck. "When this one comes for a visit, I give him a real name."

A wife? The thought had never occurred to Packi. Had he thrown out that tidbit to catch her by surprise or to warn her away? She refused to show a reaction."So who's his owner?"

"The man's a maggot, but I love his dog." Jungle Jim inclined his head to the shuttered house across the street. "Point of fact, Ranger is Ursula's dog, but she ignores him. He escapes three or four times a week. Works for us both. I brush his coat and wrestle with him for a while before I bring him home."

The pit bull licked the man's whiskers to confirm the story.

Packi had never been a dog lover but admired the rapport between man and beast. Or was it between beast and animal? Her joke brought a tiny smile to her face. Jungle Jim took note.

"Stay here until I get him back home." The ex-marine motioned to the Graham house, but his heavy boots stood firm in the street. "Were you coming to visit me?"

"Oh." Interviewing him no longer seemed like a sensible idea. "I wanted to know . . . I wanted to ask you . . ." Packi wobbled a bit and steadied herself against the Audi before trying again. She cleared her throat. "There's been talk about . . . about your block. Parties where people . . ."

"You mean the swap parties? Haw!" Voss put the pit bull down at his feet and the dog raced back into the jungle. When the man straightened up to his full height, he looked down at Packi. His eyes were bright, his bronze face crafted into a smile. "Well, this may be my lucky day. Are you asking me to take part?"

Packi lurched backward. "What? No!"

Without the dog in his arms, Voss seemed bigger, more shirtless, more animal.

"That's not what I meant," she stammered. "I wondered if it was true. Do your neighbors . . . do that?" Her entire arm shook as she pointed at the Graham house. She noticed new crepey skin inside her elbow and tucked her arm back at her side. "It might be part of something else, a crime maybe."

Jungle Jim enjoyed a hearty laugh. "I am relieved, Mrs. Walsh. Didn't figure you for one of them." He chuckled, then crossed his arms over his chest and changed his demeanor. "Didn't I warn you not to get involved with them?"

Determination replaced her embarrassment. "Well, I'm following up on a suspicion and it's important."

He regarded her from beneath dark brows, but then snorted. “Come on then. Help me fetch that dog. I’ll pour you an iced tea and tell you what I know.”

She eyed his overgrown yard and fought back claustrophobia. “If you don’t mind, we can talk here. I don’t have much time. I have to go home to do something.”

“Have it your way.” He wasn’t buying her excuses but settled his cargo shorts against the fender of her car. “Okay. Shoot.”

“Well, like I said. I heard rumors about, uh, swapping and think it resulted in that man dead on the tennis court.”

“Could’ve happened that way,” he said but shook his head, rubbing his whiskered jaw. “Mrs. Walsh, I patrol this neighborhood every night. I see and hear things. A number of women started swapping husbands to do odd jobs. Did a few myself. Yard work.” He tossed a prideful glance toward his jungle. “Then a couple yahoos at the end of this street took it farther. Me and the wife got out of that group. Didn’t want to give the muckrakers on the block any more gossip to spread.”

“Were the Grahams part of that group?”

“Who’d have him?”

Good point. That dead end disheartened her. She sighed, fished in her purse for her keys, and clicked open the lock. Jim didn’t move.

He has more to tell me, she thought. *I just have to hit on the correct questions to lead him to it.* She had no idea why he’d make it difficult, but Packi figured he had his reasons.

What does he know? She watched the marine’s impassive expression and soldiered on. “There’s been a report of a guy leering at a teenage boy down at the basketball court. I think it might have been a guest of Mr. Graham.”

The frown carved into Jungle Jim’s forehead deepened. He raised his eyebrows and tapped the end of his nose. “Ask that deputy buddy of yours to check the passport of the deceased. Look into that. I bet you get your answer.”

Voss pushed himself off the car and whistled through his fingers. “Ranger!” He gave Packi a curt nod and marched away and into the thick vegetation of his yard.

Astonished, Packi watched the jungle swallow him.

23

Packi slept fitfully all night thinking about swap parties and passports. Suspects and sex offenders populated her half-dreams. Nothing made sense. She gave up on sleep and slapped the button on the alarm clock long before the set time.

Though dawn encroached, a slivered moon still hung high in the gray sky above the lanai. Below the crescent, Jupiter shone like a star. Packi used the bright planet as a focal point to maintain balance during her yoga poses. Moisture saturated the cool morning air as she rushed through her meditation. Her mind wandered. She had left the sliding door open to hear the phone. Deputy Teig no doubt got her message last night but would wait for dawn to return the call.

Packi showered, threw in a load of laundry, dusted the furniture, and paid bills on line. No phone call. She breezed through the crossword puzzle and the daily jumble and then listed suspect names in the margins of the newspaper. The clock clicked toward seven thirty, but Billy still hadn't called. She left a strident message for the deputy and rushed out the door.

* * *

"What got you riled up?" Kay asked as Packi ran onto Court Three where Beth and the others warmed up before practice.

Packi huffed and hung her bag on a hook, shaking her head. Tennis drills seemed too exhausting. She slumped onto the bench. "The murder, wife-swapping, and sex offenders had me up all night. I couldn't . . ."

"Whoa. Whoa." Beth let a ball drop at her feet and stopped with her racquet in midair. "Did you hear more about wife-swapping? Wait." She whistled to the other players and waved them over. "Don't say anything until everybody gets here."

"No, Beth. Don't tell them." The last thing Packi wanted was to hold a public hearing on her speculations, but it was too late. Seven players gathered at the canopy as if lottery tickets were being handed out for free. Even Helen stood close enough to listen, though she feigned disinterest.

"Squeeze in here, girls," Kay said. "Packi's got some juicy stuff."

"Ok. Dish," Beth demanded when they all got settled.

"Nothing juicy," Packi protested. She stood and backed away. "Sorry I said anything. I was thinking out loud." She retreated to the water fountain and took a long sip. Her teammates waited as she pulled a towel from her bag and dabbed her lips. "Seriously, I don't know anything."

"Tell us the part about wife-swapping," Beth urged. "Was I right?

Before Packi could reply, Grace interrupted. She hadn't been part of the previous discussion and pointed her racquet at the team captain to get clarification. "You mean husband-swapping."

"What's the difference?" asked Diane who was equally confused. She looked to Kimberly for support, but the ex-news anchor blushed and turned away.

Kay explained. "Some of us trade husbands to do chores. Like my Mike cleaning Packi's pool filter." She paused for effect. "Wife-swappers trade for the entire night—if you know what I mean." Her leer left no doubt as to her salacious meaning. She swaggered over her inside information. "They swap wives up in Crescent Cove, north of here. Heard about that at the nail salon."

"And I heard it might be happening here in Paradise," added Beth.

The entire team gaped in a moment of silence.

"Jesus, Mary, and Joseph. I thought that was a joke." Grace's pale Irish skin lost all hint of color. "The nuns from Saint Christopher's would faint if they could hear us now."

Packi imagined Franciscans falling to the floor but suppressed a snicker. "Now wait a minute. We don't know anything like that. I was tracking down clues on the guy who was bothering Curtis and followed up on a rumor. That's all." She made eye contact with Beth. "It's still just a rumor."

Helen sniffed in disgust. "You're messing where you don't belong." She kicked a ball across the court and turned away from the group. She didn't leave.

Beth rolled her eyes at the cranky woman's back and dismissed her with a toss of her hand. "So, nothing new with that," Beth said. "What did you find out about the creep who was lurking at the basketball court?"

On safer ground, Packi relaxed and updated the team on her conversation with Jungle Jim. "He seems to think Oliver Graham is guilty of something."

"Ew." Kay grimaced as if smelling rotten fish. "Like wife-swapping?"

Grace put her hand over her heart. "Oh, please. We're not back to that, are we?"

"No." Packi was happy to leave that subject behind and smiled at the motherly woman. "We talked about Leonard Pritchard, the murder victim. He was Graham's guest. Jungle Jim suggested I find a way to check out their passports, though I don't know how it's relevant. Maybe Pritchard was a criminal in a foreign country, smuggling drugs or some such." Packi let her hands fall in her lap. "I don't know. I'll call Deputy Teig again to see if the Sheriff's department has access to passports."

Grace perked up. "Didn't the Grahams need passports for that big trip to Asia last year? I remember pictures on Facebook. If you want, I'll search their page for that trip."

Grace's computer savvy impressed Packi, and she accepted the offer. "Anything you can find will help. Thanks, Grace."

"The fastest growing rate of STDs are among senior citizens." Marilyn's soft voice caught everyone's attention, and the odd segue produced a long silence. The women pivoted toward Marilyn for an explanation.

"STP?" Beth stopped working the strings of her racquet and gave Marilyn a quizzical stare. "Motor oil?"

Packi chuckled, remembering the old race car commercials but muffled her laughter by dabbing her face with her towel. Kay wasn't as generous and laughed out loud. The outbursts unsettled Marilyn, and she shrank back against the bench.

Beth defended herself. "Well, I didn't hear her. What she's talking about?".

Marilyn recovered her nurse-in-charge demeanor. "Sexually transmitted diseases," she explained with a bit of impatient annoyance. "Central Florida is the hotspot for new cases."

Wary about being the butt of a joke, Beth narrowed her eyes at her tennis partner. "What?"

"I read that, too," said Packi. "Sounds comical but think about it. For the first time since college, newly widowed or divorced and retired people with time on their hands are dating. Free love, like in their youth in the sixties."

Marilyn's cheeks bloomed a lovely pink, but she lifted her chin with a trace of a smile. "And the men have Viagra."

"Ha! So, the old hippies are having fun!" Beth's bullhorn laugh brought attention from irritated players on the next court.

"Oh, good Lord." Grace edged away from the cluster of women and put her hands over her ears. "La, la, la, la."

"Yep." Kay continued the joke by singing 'Love the one you're with,' the old Steven Stills song. She sounded like a rusted door hinge, and the group joined in on the refrain with a laugh. Kay ended her musical silliness and dropped her smirk. "You think that's what this wife-swapping is all about?"

"I don't know." Packi shrugged. "I'm only interested if it's connected to the murder victim."

Kay stuck her finger up as if to say something but lowered it slowly. She put her chin on her fist, deep in thought.

"Years back, there was also gossip about parties on Pelican Lane." Beth offered the information without relish. Sexy stuff in other communities was fodder for jokes. Close to home, it got personal. Lives changed. People got hurt.

Marilyn nodded and sighed. "Two divorces out of that one."

"One couple moved back north," said Kay.

"This is too much." Grace's ample chest heaved, straining her formfitting tennis shirt. "First murder and sex offenders, now this. Aren't we here to play tennis?" Grace motioned for others to follow and bustled onto the court. She beat the air with her racquet as if fighting back mortal sins.

* * *

Questions and suspicions were driven from Packi's mind as she sprinted and volleyed. Sweat dripped from her hair, soaked her clothes, and washed away sunscreen. Opponents vied for points with earnest aggression but then switched partners for a new set. Between games, Packi kept watch on the clock in the eaves of the canopy.

After the last set, Beth gave Packi a little nudge. "Got a hot date or something?"

Packi toweled her face to hide the rising blush. "Not really."

Kay had been bent to drink from the fountain and quickly straightened. "Not really? That means yes." She wiped her mouth on the back of her hand, eager to bite into juicy news. "Mark? Or somebody new?"

"We need details, girlfriend," said Beth, giving Packi a come-on gesture.

As well-meaning as her teammates were, their attention seemed an intrusion into her personal space. Intimate revelations were outside Packi's comfort zone, but she cautioned herself to trust these friends.

"Not a date." Packi couldn't stop the tiny smile that formed at the corner of her mouth. "Mark says he has something to show me." She turned away to zip her racquet into her bag. "He asked me to wear a dress."

"Ha!" Beth laughed in triumph. "That's a date."

Kay and Beth bobbed their heads and grinned, apparently satisfied they'd ferreted out her secret. Perhaps they imagined romantic moments for her or recalled snippets of their own dating years.

Marilyn sat alone and frowned up at Packi. "Is it downtown? He's picking you up, right?"

Kay seized the idea and grabbed Packi's arm. "You're not driving alone? Your last date downtown almost killed you."

Adrenaline stung Packi between her shoulder blades. She needed no reminder of the evening that ended with her trapped in an abandoned penthouse. "I don't know where we're going but don't worry, he's picking me up."

Kay nodded and then brightened. "If you're getting dressed up, do you want to borrow my heels again?"

Packi flinched. On that last date, she had lost those shoes in the lobby of the high rise. They then saved her life by leading rescuers to her the next day. She pushed the memory away and took a deep breath.

"Thanks, Kay, but Mark suggested casual shoes. It's a trick to climb in and out of his truck." Packi glanced at the clock and slung her bag over her shoulder. "Gotta run."

24

Two hours later, coconut oil soap and a hint of floral cologne replaced Packi's layer of sweat. She felt fresh and feminine. With Beach Boys music filling the house, she twirled in front of her bedroom mirror to watch the jersey sundress swing around her knees. Her hair shined as it curled around diamond earrings.

I'm trying too hard, Packi thought. She lost enthusiasm for the dance and studied herself in the mirror. "Do I look desperate?" she asked the woman in the glass.

You look needy, said the reflection. *Calm down, girl.*

Packi blotted away most of her lipstick and replaced diamonds with simple silver loops. For five minutes, she dithered between blue or beige flats. When the doorbell rang, she rushed to tone down the music, smoothed her skirt, and steadied her breathing. She slipped her feet into the beige shoes and opened the door.

The sinking sun backlit Mark. His cornflower blue eyes were bright against his deep tan and matched the softness of his neatly pressed polo shirt. She wondered how long he'd labored over the ironing board.

Time floated as she surveyed him; he on one side of the threshold, she on the other. He cocked his head to the side and returned her stare, keeping his eyes on her face.

"You're beautiful," he said.

His compliment broke the spell. Startled into etiquette, Packi stepped back. Her hands fussed, inviting him inside. "Come in. Come in."

Mark captured her fluttering hands and held them to his chest. "It's so good to see you." He pressed the door closed, held her at arm's length, and ran his eyes over her bare arms, her dress, her legs. She enjoyed his approval.

While the Beach Boys sang *Good Vibrations*, he lifted her hand and guided her into a slow, graceful circle. Her skirt swung around her knees, and she danced to whatever music playing in his head.

The pirouette ended with his arm around her waist, their bodies close and face to face. Heat radiated from his chest. Her nostrils flared and picked up the scent of fabric softener and a hint of aftershave. He leaned down, and she raised her chin, waiting.

He whispered close to her ear. "We should go. The sun sets at five forty."

"Oh." That wasn't what she expected. Packi lowered her chin and pulled away, unnerved by her misinterpretation. "Let me grab my purse." She rushed to turn off the CD, threw a sweater over her arm, and locked the door. Flustered by her foolish expectation, Packi looked away as Mark took her hand and led her down the walkway. She noted her hibiscus were a fluorescent red and in full bloom.

Mark squeezed her fingers and tugged her to a stop at the edge of the driveway. With a grand sweep of his arm, he said, "Your chariot awaits." His flourish indicated a Buick SUV with sunlight bouncing off the blue metallic surface.

Still uncertain of how to react, Packi shaded her eyes against the blinding glare. "What happened to your truck?"

"This is a loaner." Mark grinned, enjoying his surprise and heedless of her discomfort. "My friend on Metro needed his kitchen painted, and I needed decent transportation for a special lady." He then bowed like a loyal chauffeur.

Pleased and willing to be a little foolish, Packi took on the role of grand duchess. "Thank you, kind sir." She waited for him to open her door, then breezed past him with an imperious air to settle into her seat. The interior smelled of Windex and leather polish. The dashboard sparkled. She watched him hustle around to the driver's side and wondered if other royalty fell in love with their chauffeurs.

* * *

The season had begun. Snowbirds crowded the grocery stores, roads, and restaurants. Daniels Parkway's congestion ran fast, glutted with service trucks, RVs, and employees leaving work. In spite of the chaos, Packi relaxed because Mark drove with steady confidence. He wasn't a crazy, red-light-running local nor a slow, hesitant retiree. He kept his eyes on traffic while asking about her tennis matches and friends.

Packi bided her time, waiting for the first long light to have his full attention. "Mark?"

He turned his boyish grin on her and raised his eyebrows.

"I haven't yet thanked you in person for rescuing me at the homeless camp," she said. "Those gang bangers meant to hurt us, especially Curtis. Scared me to death. So, thank you."

"My pleasure." Mark covered her hand with his and pressed gently. "But in fact, I should thank you. It made me feel young again, running through the woods to rescue my lady." He winked at her.

Packi blushed and turned her hand over in his. Palm-to-palm, she laced their fingers together. "I'm sorry I went to the camp without you, Mark. I didn't understand that their world is so different."

"It is." Mark scowled at traffic for a moment, then shook his head and glanced back at her. "I was scared to death for you too. Fear made me shout at you. Stupidly. I apologize. You were trying to do the right thing."

Packi nodded her acceptance and studied his hand in her lap. She loved his hands and what they had accomplished. She ran her finger tip over the calloused thumb, a scraped knuckle, and his scrubbed-clean nails.

"What I don't get," she said, "is why the campers didn't protect us from the gang. Why don't they even protect themselves?"

Mark sighed and gave her a wan smile. "I had to be out on the street myself before I understood, Packi. Maybe I still don't get it." The light turned green, and Mark withdrew his hand. "Most of those men are beaten down. Their self-worth is gone. They can't imagine why you'd want to help them, and they accept that gang bangers are a part of nature, like a hurricane. Can't do anything to stop it."

As they drove along, each in their own thoughts, Packi sent a thank you skyward for the blessings life had given her. She also looked more closely at people at bus stops and those riding battered bicycles or trudging along the sidewalks.

As cars whizzed through the intersection of Winkler and Evans, she realized they were headed downtown. She suspected he had splurged on reservations at the expensive restaurant where he used to maître d'. *Such a waste.* Packi worried about Mark's finances and meant to ask about their destination and to protest, but he had begun a story about one of the campers.

While concentrating on a left-hand turn, he paused the story, and Packi took advantage of the break. "You know, Mark, we don't have to go to a fancy place. I'll be happy anywhere."

He took his attention off the road for a split second to wink at her and reached over to pat her knee. "It's all taken care of."

As he turned back to his driving, a momentary concern seemed to cast a shadow over his face. Packi sensed a slip in his confidence and worried anew that he might have financial problems. As they arrived in downtown Fort Myers, she vowed to refuse to enter the elegant Victoria House, if that's where Mark had made reservations. She hated to make a scene but wouldn't enjoy an extravagant dinner. She tensed as they neared the street.

But Mark drove on. He meandered through the historic streets as if showing off his shiny blue Buick to any friends they might pass along the way. He pointed out landmarks as if he were a tour guide. She enjoyed his historical accounts even though she'd heard most of them before. They cruised along the river road, past the boats bobbing at the docks, and onto MacGregor Boulevard between rows of stately royal palms.

"Here we are." He slowed as the road paralleled a white picket fence and turned the Buick into a short driveway.

"This is the Thomas Edison museum," Packi said bewildered but pleased. "Aren't we supposed to park across the street?" She leaned forward to survey the beautiful estate beyond the entrance marked Gate 14. "It's too late. Everything is closed." She slid a look at Mark, hoping he wasn't too disappointed with his spoiled surprise.

Mark's fingers danced on the steering wheel to a tune on the radio. "No problem. I've got friends in high places. This is the service entrance to the caretaker's house where they allow private parties." He grinned and pointed through scattered flowering shrubs toward the small white house.

Party? Are we going to a party? Excitement crept in as Packi sat forward to scan the house and lawn for friends or other cars.

Only a stout woman with an apron tied around her belly trundled down the driveway. With each step, her feet threatened to split through her ragged sneakers. Mark waved through the windshield and waited as she removed a heavy padlock from the gate. She walked both sides of the white picket gate open and stepped aside as Mark pulled forward.

"Good evening, Dolly. Thank you for waiting for me."

The woman's heavy pink jowls appeared in the window, and a whiff of pine cleaner and sweat blew in. "Well, ain't you a sight? You clean up pretty good." With red, chapped hands, Dolly grasped Mark's wrist as if she wanted to take him home. She glanced past him to take a look at her rival.

"Hello," said Packi, leaning over Mark to smile at the woman.

Dolly's puffy eyelids closed to slits. She straightened up, still holding Mark's hand. "I'm 'bout done with my work." Her fingers played along his forearm. "Park back there at the end. Clyde and Andy's on security. One of 'em be round to lock the gate after ya leave."

Mark withdrew his arm and must have winked at the woman. She chortled, shook her head, and stood aside as the car inched forward, crushing coquina shells beneath its tires. Packi twisted in her seat to watch the cleaning woman hang the open lock in its hook. "What was that all about? Why are we here?"

Mark stopped the car in front of a three-stall garage attached to a cracker-style house with wide overhanging eaves. Signs said, 'Gift Shop' and 'Open to the Public.' He squeezed Packi's fingers. "I want to share something with you." He rubbed his palms together, then jumped from the car to run around to open her door. "Let's go, or we'll miss the big show."

Mark's surprise was a front row seat to one of nature's best displays. He led her down a walkway bordered by bamboo, palms, and flowering plants, each marked with a white plaque announcing its name and origin. A small fountain made of rough natural rock marked an intersection where they turned away from the historic buildings. The pavement ended at a wide expanse of lush grass with the glittering Caloosahatchee River beyond. They stopped on a beaten, dirt path at the water's edge, and Mark drew Packi to his side.

"We'll watch the sunset from here."

"It's a wonderful view," Packi said, well-satisfied with the surprise. She relaxed and gave herself to the experience.

Though buildings jutted above thick stands of vegetation to her right, she imagined the scene as Edison would have seen it. Across the river, maybe a half-mile away, a low, irregular line of trees marked the far shore. To the left, beyond the river's mouth in the open gulf, a heavy sun hovered on the horizon. Two boats, under full sail, glided through the scene. *Perfect.*

A light wind riffled the hem of her skirt. Packi pulled her sweater around her shoulders and inched closer to Mark. There was no need to talk.

A fine floral scent drifted by. Packi filled her lungs, capturing the fragrance as if it were a message meant for her. Jasmine, she thought. She memorized its exotic richness which sketched pictures in her mind of a luau fire and brown girls in grass skirts and orchid leis. The images became clear and vivid as if they'd been her own experiences. She squelched the urge to track down the source of the scent and to analyze and identify the flower as was her habit. Today, the fragrance was enough.

After a long minute, Mark echoed her sigh of satisfaction. He then pointed to the right to a forest of bamboo which formed a border near a large pavilion. "That's where we worked yesterday."

With her face still warm from the luau fire, she smiled at the man who'd brought her into the moment. "You have a job here? What do you mean?"

"Not a job exactly." He plucked a dry leaf from a shrub and twirled it between his fingers. "I volunteer four hours a week. I wanted to learn landscaping, so what better place than the Wizard of Menlo Park's experimental gardens? Yesterday I helped slash out bamboo."

"You're amazing."

Mark's lips parted as if caught between words. He cocked his head to listen harder, then shook off the compliment. "Nothing like digging in the dirt to get a sense of history. Henry Ford and Thomas Edison both walked through these gardens. Firestone too. Edison planted trees from around the world, experimenting with them to make rubber. He tried bamboo for his light bulb filaments."

Packi had heard the stories before, had even been on a tour of the estates. This was more intimate, more real. She let Mark talk. *What a place this must have been before Edison built his winter estate,* she thought, *when MacGregor Boulevard was a cattle trail and wilderness lay on the opposite shore.*

Mark led her to a bench at the water's edge where Edison's dock had jutted into the river. Rhythmic ripples sideslipped the remaining stubs of wooden pilings and lapped at the rocky shore. They sat in silence, as if in a church pew, while the warmth of his shoulder protected her from the chill blowing in from the gulf. Thin strands of clouds, low on the horizon, split the sun's color and sent an orange glow into the dusky sky. Mark rested his arm across her shoulders until the last arc of orange extinguish itself in the water.

Nature's show lasted only a few minutes but left Packi at peace. "This is absolutely lovely."

She leaned against his chest, more at home than she'd felt in years. His fingers explored her sweater's shoulder seam. Her thigh heated up against his. She must have purred.

"Hmmm. Me too," he said.

She felt the warmth of his whisper in her hair, above her ear. If she looked up and tilted her head, he'd kiss her. Knowing was enough. She gave her smile to the darkening river as the last hint of day brushed the horizon.

25

Mark had a few more surprises. They strolled in the dusk along the soft dirt path at the river's edge. At the far end of the estates, behind Henry Ford's garage, Mark trained a flashlight on the oddest tree Packi had ever seen. At its huge base, roots bulged from the ground like a tangled swarm of serpents.

"It's a Mysore Fig," Mark said." A hundred feet tall. From China, if I remember right."

He interrupted his litany of facts when headlights appeared and glided along the walkway behind the Ford house. Mark waved at the golf cart. A dark silhouette returned the greeting.

"That's Clyde seeing if we're okay."

"Should we leave?"

"No. We're fine." Mark said, taking her hand. "I got approval for an hour. Come on, there's one more thing to see."

They retraced their steps to the stone fountain. The water was now inky black, lit only by a rising moon and security lights on the museum property. Dolly must have gone home.

Mark guided Packi behind a small building and through an arbor, holding aside a dangling angel trumpet vine with gorgeous seven-inch blossoms. "And this is Myna's moonlight garden."

Mark switched on his flashlight and played its beam over tall red azaleas and white-flowered shrubs along the borders of the small area. He spotlighted a shallow rectangular pond, dotted with floating lily pads and edged by worn flagstone. Royal blue stone pots, planted with greenery, marked the four corners.

Packi found a stone bench almost hidden in the azaleas, while Mark clicked off the light and continued to wander. She sat and contemplated the little pond as Mrs. Edison might have done on a summer's evening.

Her last tour had been in daylight. Now twilight's intimacy enveloped her, and white flowers and soft leaves glowed in the moonlight. She couldn't identify the flowers and didn't care. The quiet was a pillow on which to rest her mind.

A wonderful place for a tryst. The idea startled Packi, and she shot a quick glance at Mark. Had he read her mind? Could he tell from her face? No, he seemed intent on examining a row of pale, nodding flowers.

Packi sighed in contentment and closed her eyes. She'd always wanted a tryst. The word conjured up romance, passion, and clandestine entanglements. Her thoughts took her to those places but never left the little garden's fragrance and warmth.

Packi awoke from her moment of daydream to find Mark standing before her, his grin plain as day in the moonlight. *He knows!* The private smile fell from her face. Shamed by discovery, she dropped her gaze to her hands. *What now? What do I do?* She kneaded her fingers as if in fervent prayer.

Suddenly at peace and emboldened by shadows and the garden's long-held secrets, she allowed her smile's slow return. Packi raised her eyes to his. Behind his silhouette, stars pricked through the black night, and she wondered at their brightness. As a woman met for a tryst, she rose toward those stars and slid her arms around his chest. Mark drew in a long breath and took her face into his large, workman's hands. His kiss was certain and sure but did not demand. She welcomed him.

Mark was first to pull away, yet his fingers continued to roam through her hair. She rested her head in his hands and allowed him to explore her eyes, to see her. In wonder at her good fortune, she traced her finger along the crease of his dimple, the ridge of his nose, and the softness of his ear lobe. She meant to memorize him and every moment of their tryst.

"Your carriage awaits, m'lady," Mark whispered. He stepped back and gave a gentleman's bow.

Packi acknowledged his gallantry with a ladylike nod and lifted the flare of her skirt to respond with a proper curtsy. Her hand slid into his palm as if it had always belonged there, and they strolled away from Myna's oasis in comfortable silence. Their steps synchronized, and their rhythms matched as they moved through the darkness.

Away from the security lights, where their feet crunched over the coquina driveway, Mark opened the Buick's door and helped Packi into the passenger seat. Though she felt like a pampered princess, reality began to return.

"I'll get the gate," she offered, remembering how Dolly had walked it open.

"Not tonight, Mrs. Walsh. Not tonight." Mark insisted on his gentleman's role, jumped in and out of the car to open and close the gates, and then secured the lock.

As traffic streamed by on MacGregor Boulevard, Packi held on to the memories they'd just made. Vowing to return, she turned in her seat for a last look at Edison's homestead behind the white picket fence. Amid the tourists, she'd have a secret—their tryst in Myna's moonlight garden. She squeezed Mark's hand to thank him for the gift.

"Tonight we celebrate," Mark announced, turning onto a quiet residential street two blocks from the old mansions along the river.

"My goodness. What else do you have in store for me?" Bones in the middle of her chest tingled, but she dared not hope or expect too much. It wasn't in her nature to want more than she already had.

"This part of the plan is a little more personal." He flashed a brilliant smile, then flinched as if his happiness suddenly wavered. "I hope you like it."

"How could I not?" She reached to meet his hand on the steering wheel and traced the muscle running through his wrist. "You continue to amaze me."

Mark huffed his satisfaction and drove another block before stopping at the curb of a small house. A proud lamppost at the sidewalk shined brighter than the overhead street lights. Manicured bushes led to the front door. More light flooded from the entry where a coral-colored door sent out a welcome.

"This is it."

"Your house? The one you're rehabbing?" The house reminded her of a dollhouse she'd loved as a girl.

"It's finished." Mark hopped from the car and ran around to her side. "I think I even have a buyer," he said as he helped her from her seat.

Pride swelled in Packi's chest as she studied the little house with groupings of thin palms waving at the corners of the low roof. The exterior walls appeared to be a soft beige with a darker trim. Fresh white plantation shutters completed the Floridian look. The cozy home put the rest of the block to shame.

Mark caught her eying cars under repair parked in the driveway of the tired house next door. "The neighborhood is on the rebound," he assured her. "The younger generation wants to be near downtown and the water. I'm betting on a resurgence here, and my clients are willing to buy in early. If all goes well, we close next Tuesday."

"That's so exciting." She clasped her hands in front of her chin. "I love it, Mark, and they will too. You did a wonderful job."

He gained a bit more confidence and took her elbow. "Let me show you the inside."

The aroma of fresh baked bread met her at the door. Gauzy white curtains brightened every window and ruffled in the breeze from the river. The clean, inviting rooms were chic in their simplicity. Solid wood craftsmanship impressed her, but she wasn't a bit surprised, except to wonder how he had pulled it off.

"These are expensive materials, Mark. Did you get your credit back?" She knew it was none of her business, but she worried for him.

"Relax, my friend. I'm a wily old guy, and I'm making new business connections." He caressed the cabinet's wooden surface, then motioned to a stool. "Go ahead and sit. I'll pour you a glass of vino."

Packi propped herself on the opposite side of the kitchen island. Its surface gleamed with smooth black granite, streaked with whorls of gray and white. He lifted the top of a crock pot and aromatic steam swirled upward.

"Mmmm. Beef stew?"

"More high-class than that, dear lady. I give you boeuf bourguignon." He kissed his fingertips like a French gourmet and gave a sly tic of his eyebrow. "This is a recipe from Victoria House."

"Does Chef know he shared his recipe with you?" Packi teased, accepting a glass of white wine.

"Ah, Madame!" Mark lay his hand over his heart and feigned a mortal wound. "Perhaps it was I who gave Chef this wonderful recipe." He winked, clinked his glass against hers, and gave the stew an elegant stir.

Mark refused her offer of help, so Packi sat at the cool stone countertop in complete contentment and watched him work. He adjusted the flavoring in the pot, tossed a salad, and sliced bread. His movements in the tiny kitchen were so efficient, she imagined him the chef at Victoria House, not the maître d' he had been.

While his hands were busy with meal preparations, Mark told stories about his previous life. He had been a successful residential builder and later gambled on building a high-rise condo complex.

"I have to confess. I've always been a bit of a pack rat, saving leftover material from every job I ever did," he said with a little boy's grin. "Scraps of wood, granite, pipe, rejected fixtures."

Packi nodded and laughed. "My husband was like that too. You never know when you might need three feet of copper tubing."

Mark stopped with his spoon poised above the spoon. "You never talk much about your husband. What did he do?"

"Oh." Perhaps the wine had loosened her tongue. She hadn't meant to say anything. "Sorry, I guess I don't." Packi dawdled over a sip of wine, then took a deep breath. "Ron was a plumber. Had his own business for the last twenty-three years. I ran his office, did payroll, handled union issues, and all the boring stuff."

Mark must have picked up on her reluctance to bring her past into the present. "Sorry. I didn't mean to pry," he said.

"It's okay." Packi smiled over the rim of her wine glass. "The business was good to us. We sold at the right time and had several comfortable years of retirement before Ron got sick." She paused with a sigh and then tipped her half-empty glass toward Mark. "So what did you do with all the scrap you hoarded?"

Mark seemed to catch onto her wish to back away from her history. "Stored it all in a warehouse in Cape Coral." He shrugged as if none of it mattered, but a shadow passed through his eyes. "Of course, I lost the warehouse in the bankruptcy too."

He gave the stew a few vigorous stirs and then wagged the wooden spoon at her. "Last year I contacted the new owner of the warehouse." He raised his eyebrows in real surprise and his glass as if for a toast. "Now he needs the space cleared, and he's paying me to remove the *junk*!"

Packi laughed at Mark's incredulity. "Like I said, you're amazing." She enjoyed his carefree manner but also understood his moments of anger. Most of all, she admired that he had clawed his way back after his finances and family had been destroyed in the housing collapse—from homeless and unemployed to this. Her gaze wandered the spotless little kitchen.

Mark noticed her studying the carved molding on the creamy white cabinets. "These came from a remodel I did a month ago in Gulf Harbor. They're only six years old, but the woman wanted dark maple." With his oven mitt, he buffed away a smudge from a cabinet door. "I get such a kick out of repurposing other people's rejects. Come on, I'll show you the best part of this house."

He put a basket of sliced bread in her hands and carried the steaming crock pot through a set of French doors. On the darkened patio, he flipped a switch with his elbow. Hundreds of tiny lights came to life, twinkling along the upper edge of the screened-in lanai. Colorful flowers cascaded from large stone pots arranged in the corners. In the center was a bistro table covered with white linen and set with two place settings, glassware, and a bottle of wine.

Enchanted, Packi entered the fairyland, holding tight to the basket of bread. She could almost forget the rest of the world existed—no tennis matches, no murder to solve, no homeless camp—just serenity and peace.

"Oh, Mark. This is wonderful."

"My maître d' experience comes in handy." He set the crock pot on a side table and took the bread from her hands. With a white napkin draped over his arm, he bowed. "Please be seated, madam. Tonight we dine alfresco."

As he lit the candle, his face shined brighter than the flickering flame. He knew he'd done well.

He had indeed. His boeuf bourguignon filled her with its rich flavor. The salad had been an interesting variety of fresh veggies. The bread had the perfect crunch. She had eaten like a truck driver, then daintily dabbed her lips with a linen napkin.

While Mark carried empty plates to the kitchen, Packi wandered around the small lanai admiring the collection of plants. His neat arrangement of stone pots spilled over with greenery and impressed her more than Jungle Jim's lush and wild yard.

"What do you think?" Mark put two colorful desserts on the table and joined her at the floral display.

"They're lovely, Mark." She gestured to the flowers and to a stately, and expensive, Bismark palm outside the screen. "But how do these plants fit in the budget for this house?"

"Ah, Packi. You worry too much." He took her hand and led her to the table. "I trade muscle for plants. When we thinned the gardens at the Edison estate, I rescued these from the waste pile." He tapped her dish with a spoon like guests do at a wedding. "Now eat."

After a simple dessert of yogurt topped with roasted strawberries, Packi held her wine glass in front of the candle's dancing flame. She marveled at the rich ruby color of the merlot and could almost smell California's sun warming the grapes to ripeness.

"Mmmm. This is wonderful." Her words sounded dreamy and far away. *You're drunk,* Packi warned herself. She set the glass down but kept her fingers on the fragile stem.

Mark watched her with a warmth of his own. He had eaten less than she and then leaned back in his chair with his arms crossed over his chest. His hands grasped his biceps, belying his casual posture. Tiny lights behind his head beatified him.

Packi's eyes rested in his gaze and wouldn't leave. A wine-induced smile gave away her thoughts and seemed to help him make a decision.

He leaned forward and slipped a small packet into her hand. Surprised, she examined the thin blue tissue for a moment before tearing a bit of tape from the edge. She glanced up at Mark and he urged her to continue. After she unfolded several paper layers, a silver chain slid out onto the table cloth. It sparkled against the linen, reflecting light from every source.

Mark picked up the dainty bracelet and suspended it between his work-worn fingers. A row of tiny tennis racquets dangled from the chain, each one adorned by a glittering stone.

Diamonds! The extravagance shocked her. "Mark," she whispered. "This is too much. I remember what it's like to have nothing, to be poor. I can't accept it."

Shadows flinched across his face in sync with the candle's flickering flame. Confusion changed to hurt. "No." He closed the chain into his fist and pointed a stubby finger at her. "I've *never* been *poor*, Packi, though I've been plenty broke and homeless. *Poor* is a state of mind. A lack of belief in your future—a lack of hope."

Taken aback by his intensity, she covered her gaffe by catching his fist between her hands. She wondered how much to say, how much his pride would allow. A few words stumbled out. "Mark, I'm so sorry. Bad choice of words. I should have said, I know how hard you work." She chose her words with more care and watched for their effect. "An expensive gift like this makes me uncomfortable."

Mark's brows arched and he put his head back to look at the stars. A long, low groan rolled from his chest. He rubbed at his clean-shaven jaw and covered his mouth. He suddenly leaned forward and put his elbows on the table. Tears glistened in his eyes.

Packi shrunk in her chair and berated herself for hurting his feelings. *Why do I do that!*

"Packi," His lips tightened and a dimple creased his cheek. He was trying not to laugh. "Packi, when I stage my rehabbed houses, I shop at garage sales for furniture. The little tennis racquets reminded me of you. That's all. I didn't mean for it to be a problem."

"Garage sale?" She studied the chain in his hand and watched it sparkle. "You bought this at a garage sale?"

Mark pleaded guilty with a slow nod.

"That is so . . . I love it." Packi laughed at herself and picked the bracelet from his palm. She held out her wrist for him to fasten the chain.

"So you're okay?"

"I'm delighted."

While he bent his head and struggled with the delicate clasp in his swollen fingers, she studied him. She wanted to touch the soft network of lines above his collar and across his cheek. He was her age. She loved the way his white hair bristled and how his blue eyes flashed and then softened. His smooth nose and firm chin. Charming. Patient. Fun.

"Thank you, Mark."

26

The next morning, the scent of Mark's shoulder lingered. The weight of the dainty bracelet on her wrist proved it hadn't been a dream, and joy swelled within her ribs. The sensation followed her from her bed and outside to the gray-blue dawn. As was her habit, she moved through silent exercises on the lanai, next to the pool. She closed her eyes to revisit Mark's scent, the sunset, the moonlight garden, and the dinner he had prepared for her.

A nearby noise interrupted her memories. Wary, she froze in mid-pose to listen to the sharp, insistent scratching. *Was it another warning? Curtis? An alligator?*

Exposed and ready to run, Packi's eyes roved to the bushes beyond the screen where dawn's weak light had yet to penetrate. There, shadows moved. Her breath caught in her throat until a large raccoon dropped to the ground from a palm tree. Two babies followed. Packi chuckled and released her wound up nerves.

She watched the little gifts from nature. The mother chittered at the two kits and chased them back up the tree trunk. Each time she turned her back, the youngsters dropped to the grass again. The universal maternal problem amused Packi throughout the remainder of her routine.

The ding-dong of the doorbell jarred the morning and sent the trio into hiding. Packi abandoned serenity and trotted through the house, muttering to herself about the earliness of the hour. She peeked through the window to see a young woman dressed in blue coveralls and a baseball cap.

"Who is it?"

The girl's long blond ponytail swung over her shoulder when she turned toward Packi's voice. "FM Towing. I have a delivery for Patricia Walsh." She held up a letter-sized envelope.

Towing? What's this about? Leery of again opening her home to strangers, Packi spoke through the door. "Leave it on the bench please."

The woman shrugged, tossed the envelope on the bench, and jogged across the lawn to a black truck at the curb. Packi waited until the vehicle lurched into gear and disappeared down the street before unlocking her door to retrieve the envelope.

She examined the envelope, half expecting another bloodstained warning, but all seemed normal. Her name and address were scrawled across the front. *FM Towing* was printed in the upper left-hand corner.

Packi tore off the end of the envelope and slid out two sheets of paper. As she unfolded them, something fell and clinked on the cement at her feet. She bent to pick up two small keys, dulled by age, on a thin metal ring. *What's this about?* The keys seemed familiar in her hand.

The stiff, legal looking paper answered the questions but raised others. *Bill of Sale* was printed in bold letters at the top. Packi scanned the typed information: "2010, Yamaha, $25, Seller—Harold Baskin," she read. "Buyer, Patricia Walsh!"

She looked again at the keys in her hand and then at the service ticket from FM Towing. "Paid in full" was stamped on the thin yellow paper.

Thinking to chase down the tow truck, Packi hurried down her walkway. She stopped in her tracks when she spotted a green golf cart with a striped canopy and shiny new tires parked in her driveway.

"Oh no. He didn't." Packi sighed to herself but like a kid on Christmas morning, climbed into her new toy. The thick dust that had covered the vehicle while in the Baskin garage had been washed away. The beige leather seat was supple and clean. She checked out the storage compartments and other accessories.

"You getting serious about golf?"

Packi jumped but quickly recognized Kay's voice. She raised her hand in greeting and shook her head. "No, it's a gift."

Kay walked her bicycle up the driveway and stood astride it next to the golf cart. "Some gift." She arched both eyebrows to put a suggestive slant on the remark. "You got a secret admirer?"

"No." Packi gasped. "At least I hope not. Harold Baskin wanted to thank us for coming to their aid when they were mugged downtown."

"Us? Where's *my* golf cart?" Kay asked with a false pout.

"I . . . I . . ." Packi jumped out of the cart. "I guess I was in the right place. You can have it. We can share."

"Relax," said Kay. "I'm kidding." She waved away the entire issue. "We need a fourth for tennis at two o'clock. Me, Grace, and Helen. Can you play?"

"Sure." Packi ran her hand over the cart's smooth green fender. "He offered it to me for twenty-five dollars but didn't even take that. Do you think I should return it?"

"Heck, no." Kay turned her bike toward the street and hopped on the pedals. "If the old coot has a thing for you, take advantage. Enjoy!" She was gone before Packi could protest or even blush.

* * *

The phone was in mid-ring when Packi dashed into the house. She snatched it up before it rang again. "Hello?"

"You okay?" Deputy Teig asked without greeting.

"I'm fine, Billy. Why?" She listened to his lungs working to get air through his large body and wondered what it was he wasn't saying.

"Tryin' to be sociable, Mizz Walsh."

"Kind of early for that. Did something happen?" She gripped the phone tighter and worried about her friends, about her neighbors. Maybe Teig had found the murderer. She waited, sensing urgency or maybe relief in his silence. "You're not going to tell me, are you?"

"There's nothing you need to know."

His tone told her otherwise. Something *had* happened. Police policy or his cantankerous nature kept him from talking. She gave up, promising herself to try again later. "Can you at least do me a favor? I need you to check the passport of Len Pritchard."

"Not gonna happen. That case got closed up tight."

"What does that mean?"

"Means we can't butt up against the FBI, so whatever you got to tell me, I don't need to hear."

"FBI? There's been a federal crime?" Her mind flew through possible scenarios. "Was Pritchard a spy or something?"

"That would be CIA," he said, "and I doubt it. Just be careful, Mizz Walsh. Have a nice day."

"Please tell me, Billy." She took on a sweet tone. "What's going on with the investigation? Did you find the killer?"

She waited for him to realize she had a right to know.

"Billy?"

A dial tone irritated her eardrum.

"Ack!" Packi slammed the phone into its cradle and stomped through the house, grousing and fuming at the man's refusal to see her as anything but a helpless old lady. Between surprise gifts and infuriating deputies, her morning serenity had been destroyed. The clock clicked and she shot it a dirty look.

"Oh, shoot." *Tennis practice in thirty minutes.*

She rushed into the shower and gave her hair and skin a vicious scrubbing. Hot water cooled her frustration and allowed her to think.

So the case was closed. She didn't know if she should be relieved or disappointed. *Is that why he called?* She scrubbed at her teeth and spit into the sink, then pointed at the mirror with her brush. *If they found the murderer, why is he worried about my safety?*

The question followed her as she dressed and rushed from the house with the golf cart keys in hand. *The cart will be faster*, she reasoned.

She turned the key. Nothing happened. She twisted the forward and backward knob. Nothing happened. "Arrgh!"

With no time to figure out the new toy, Packi jumped from the cart and grabbed her bicycle. "Worry about that later." She glowered at the useless vehicle in her driveway and sped toward the tennis courts, still wondering what it was Deputy Teig refused to tell her.

* * *

"Wait up!" Beth shouted from a half block away.

Packi stopped and watched her team captain's powerful legs pumping and covering the distance between them in five seconds.

Beth slid to a showy stop. "Hey, what's up? I hear you got a new ride."

The speed of flying rumors impressed Packi. "The golf cart?" She feigned disinterest, afraid Beth, like Kay, thought she should share the gift. "I can't keep it. It wouldn't even start."

"Are you crazy? Of course, you'll keep it. Probably a dead battery or something simple." Beth pulled her phone from her tennis bag. "I'll text Rex to take a look at it."

Packi accepted Beth's need to control every situation and didn't argue. As they pedaled side by side, Beth launched into an account of the singles match she played at Riverside Racquet Club. During a pause, Packi slid a glance at her team captain. "Beth, did I miss any news? Some Paradise Palms gossip?"

"The only news we need to talk about is your date last night." Beth waggled her eyebrows and smirked.

Packi imitated Beth's signature eye-roll and ignored the suggestive tease. "Deputy Teig called this morning. He didn't really say anything but wanted to know if I was okay. He's keeping information from me. I can feel it."

"Hmmm," said Beth. "Yeah. Kind of odd." She steered her bike closer to Packi's, their handlebars inches apart. "Maybe I do have something for you. A neighbor might have called the cops last night about noise pollution on Periwinkle Lane."

"What do you mean, noise pollution?" Packi couldn't quite tell if Beth was joking or not. "And how would you know someone complained?"

"Denny Gladding," Beth announced with slight bravado. When Packi failed to recognize the name, disappointment fluttered across Beth's face. "You know, the baseball player."

"Oh, yes." Packi pretended to remember him, though she hadn't attended a Red Sox or Twins spring training game in years.

"Anyway." Beth waved away the baseball player's importance. "He was on the elliptical machine next to mine at the gym this morning. He rents two doors down from the Grahams. Says his neighbors had a shouting match so bad he had to close his windows and turn up the AC last night."

"Did he say which neighbors?"

"Nope, but it sounded like a regular problem." Beth swerved away from Packi's handlebars to avoid a crash. "Gotta think it was Oliver and Ursula Graham. Or your Jungle Jim. The three of them are famous for their hot tempers and loud mouths."

Beth's own loud mouth conveyed their conversation to everyone on the street, but none looked up from their dog-walking or jogging. Rather than spew gossip like confetti in the wind, Packi braked and hopped off the pedals.

Beth rode on, engrossed in her monolog, until she realized she was alone and glanced over her shoulder. "Something wrong?" she called.

"No. I'm okay." Packi leaned against her handlebars and weighed her priorities while Beth circled back.

"You mind if I skip practice today, Beth? I'm not scheduled for the match Wednesday and want to check out your baseball player's complaint." Packi jerked her thumb toward the Eagle's Nest neighborhood a mile away. "I'll ride down Periwinkle and maybe call Teig again."

"Sure. Sure." Beth looked torn between joining Packi and being a responsible team captain.

Packi didn't wait for her to figure it out and pedaled off.

27

Periwinkle Lane still slumbered. Only a family of wood storks trooped across a lawn on the left side of the street, high stepping through Bermuda grass. Mist hung in the shrubbery, waiting to be burned off by the sun. Shutters were closed. Drapes were drawn.

Jungle Jim's place stood out in the row of nearly identical houses with its wild vegetation crowding properties on either side. Packi cycled down the center of the street, keeping an eye out for Jim Voss. After her abrupt exit from his yard two days earlier, she was almost reluctant to find him.

Have a little courage, she reminded herself. *You can handle him, and he may know something.*

As she approached his mailbox, she stared into his jungle, searching for a hint to his whereabouts. Too focused on her left, she missed movement on her right. Her peripheral vision caught only a streak of white. She refocused in time to identify a large dog, running hell-bent into the street and straight at her. Startled and unable to stop, she gripped the handlebars and careened into the path of the animal.

At the last second, the dog skidded, his nails scratching at the asphalt as he tried to veer away. Her front tire hit him broadside with a solid thud. He gave one high-pitched yipe and fell backward onto his rump.

Packi pitched forward. Her ribs slammed against the handlebars, and the crossbar came up hard between her legs. Her vision blurred.

A dense moment passed before she came to terms with the pain and sucked breath back into her lungs. She exhaled slowly and opened her eyes. At her feet, the injured animal reeled on uncertain legs.

As an apology, she reached out a hand of comfort. She murmured to calm him, but the pit bull eyed her with feral suspicion. He planted his feet, reared on coiled muscles, and sprang at her.

"Down, Ranger! Stop!"

Her commands failed to control the frantic animal. His claws raked her bare thigh as he barked into her face. Saliva flew from his mouth as she stared down his red throat.

Packi shielded herself behind her bicycle and shoved it into the dog's chest. He yelped again and jumped away. He sped in a circle around her in a panicked run, trailing a stream of slobber. Packi circled too, keeping the bike between herself and his claws until he broke off and darted into Jim Voss's jungle.

Packi's heart thumped in her ears. Her knees wobbled. She propped herself up against her bicycle and ran her fingers over her tender ribs. Abrasions burned her palms. She realized then that she'd grabbed the rubber handle grips, not the brake levers. "Idiot." Her carelessness had injured the poor dog and nearly gotten herself eaten.

Ranger continued to bark from within Jungle Jim's yard, but the pitch changed. An aluminum door slammed.

"Easy, Ranger," Jim Voss said. "There you are. Good, boy. Can't play today." His voice was smooth and deep, loving. "What the hell! What happened to you?" Marine-style curses preceded Voss as he emerged from his yard, carrying the dog. His determined march halted when he spotted Packi inspecting her broken spokes. He hugged the dog tighter. "Mrs. Walsh! What the hell happened?"

"It wasn't my fault. He lunged at me and knocked me off my bike." She pointed to the evidence of her innocence —angry welts on her thigh.

"Did he bite you?" Voss glowered, not a bit interested in the claw marks. "There's blood in his mouth."

"No," she was relieved to say. "No. He didn't bite me." *No doubt, that would have been my fault, too.* She didn't dare mention her bruised ribs and damaged bike.

Jungle Jim ended his concern for her with a sharp nod and then lowered Ranger to the ground. "Now what's got you riled up, buddy? That's a good boy." He examined the dog's mouth, frowning in spite of his soothing words. "Where did all these cuts come from?" He shot a glance at her as if she had answers.

Packi gave a helpless shrug, and the man returned his attention to his buddy. He cooed and scratched behind the dog's ears as it rested its head on his knee. Nothing else mattered to either of them. It would have been a wonderful scene, if her ribs and everything else didn't hurt. Eager to get away from them, Packi examined her bike and picked up an L-shaped spoke from the ground. Another spoke hung from the aluminum rim. She tried to straighten the metal and wondered if she should walk the bike home.

The man, still kneeling next to the dog, offered no help and seemed lost in thought. A storm gathered in his eyes as he ruffled the fur at Ranger's throat and ran his hands along his sides. When Ranger yipped, Voss lifted his hand. Blood streaked his fingers.

"Damn it, Graham! You've gone too far!" The retired marine jumped to his feet and stomped up the neighbor's driveway. Ranger trotted at his heels.

Oh geez. He's going to kill him. Packi laid her bike in the grass and ran after Ranger's vengeful champion. Maybe she could stop Voss from beating the older man, and keep one out of the hospital and the other out of jail. She'd be the peacemaker and bring calm to the testosterone-fueled confrontation.

Every step jarred Packi's ribs and forced her to slow to a walk. She kept the man in sight and rounded the back of Oliver Graham's house in time see Jungle Jim jerk open the lanai's screen door. The door slammed in Ranger's face. The faithful dog crouched on his haunches in the grass and waited.

Packi held back too. She cradled her ribs and watched Voss storm across the lanai into the house through the open sliding doors. She dreaded the argument and waited outside for the shouting to begin.

When none came, she followed the silence inside.

The house was quiet. A news reporter's face flickered on a flat-screen television on the wall, his mouth moving without sound. With his back to Packi, Jim Voss stood over an easy chair, blocking her view of its occupant. She saw only two slippered feet, propped up on an ottoman, pointed toward the TV. Beneath the chair, dark red grout lines crisscrossed the white tile. Animal footprints smeared the red and trailed out to the lanai. She looked for a weapon in Jungle Jim's hand.

"Call the cops," Voss said.

Packi shook herself out of inertia and found a phone in the kitchen. She dialed 911 and stretched the phone cord around the wall to keep an eye on Jim Voss. His hands were empty. He backed away from the body, taking care to step over the streams of dried blood. She could now see a mug and spilled coffee on the far side of the chair. She assumed the slumped body, large belly, and blue plaid pajamas belonged to Oliver Graham. "Is he dead?"

"Very." Jungle Jim lost some of his stature, seeming to shrink inside his bloodstained shirt. Grief or some other dark emotion ruined his face. He returned to the lanai where she heard him consoling the dog.

When the dispatcher came on the line, Packi answered questions the best she could: location, victim's name, her name. *What happened? No clue.* She returned the phone to its cradle and tucked her hands under her arms to avoid leaving her fingerprints at the crime scene, if that's what it was.

Packi smelled fear. Was it her own or did it belong to Oliver—or his wife? The metallic odor of blood tainted the woman's home. "Ursula?"

Familiar with the floor plan of the house, common to Paradise Palms, Packi tiptoed down a short hallway to the master bedroom. "Mrs. Graham?"

A rumpled quilt had been thrown back from one side of the king-size bed. A pillow was crushed up against the headboard. In the bathroom, a heap of clothes lay on the floor. A towel filled the sink. A blue toothbrush leaned in its holder. "Ursula?"

Packi listened for breathing, for any hint to the woman's presence, but the house gave no answers. She moved from room to room, nudging open closets with her elbow.

Ursula was not home. Satisfied there was no second body, no more blood, Packi tiptoed back to the living room and past the body slumped in front of the TV. The dark bloom on Oliver's light blue pajama top was a larger version of the stain on the murdered tennis player's shirt. Packi averted her eyes and escaped into fresh air.

"What'd you do in there?" Jim Voss sat on the end of a chaise lounge with the pit bull between his knees. His fingers looped into the dog's collar as he urged Ranger to sit still. Anger, or maybe worry, carved deeper lines in Voss's face.

"Nothing." Packi shot the man an irritated glance but softened when she saw he had wrapped his shirt around the dog's bloody belly.

"I had to see if Ursula needed help, but she's not home."

Voss stroked the dog's wide head, slowly, gently, as if removing himself from the reality of the body in the house. "Course, she's gone. Shot him and got outta Dodge."

"You can't know that," said Packi.

"Heard 'em goin' at it last night. Don't blame her for killing him, the old fart." Voss stooped to take Ranger into his arms. "Easy, boy. I gotcha." He nodded to the open house. "You can take care of this. I gotta get him to a vet."

Packi sputtered. She had expected an ally while reporting to the police. "But . . . but I . . ." *Is it even legal to leave? Why is he in such a hurry?*

The man's stone expression permitted no argument. She ran ahead to open the screen door for Voss and the injured dog. "Was Ranger shot, too?"

"He'll be okay."

The dog, too exhausted to raise his big head from the man's shoulder, licked Voss's neck. Jungle Jim hugged him closer. "See that hole there?"

She followed his glance to a metal panel around the lower perimeter of the lanai, obviously designed to corral a pit bull with a habit of running loose. Near ground level, where sections of the barrier met, was a gash in the metal with the edges bent outward. Canine teeth had pockmarked the vicious shards of aluminum.

"He chewed his way out," said Voss, scratching under Ranger's chin. "Scraped his belly up somethin' fierce squeezing through. Ran from the murder, I guess."

"Or wanted to tell you about it." Packi gave Jungle Jim a slight smile and walked beside them to the front of the house. "You go on. I'll give the report to the police, but they'll probably want to talk to you, too, you know."

"Later." Voss cocked his ear to the sound of sirens in the distance and hurried his steps across the street.

28

A minute later, Voss's car pulled away and a squad car, followed by an ambulance, turned onto Periwinkle Lane. Packi recognized Deputy Teig's white Ford sedan with its low-slung rear end. *He's not going to be happy.* She stood in Graham's driveway to wave them in.

"Mizz Walsh! Are you hurt?" Deputy Teig called over the door of his car as he stepped out. He moved faster than Packi had ever seen and hustled up the driveway.

"I'm fine, Billy. Just shaken."

Teig put his hands on both her shoulders and stroked her biceps as if testing her solidity. Satisfied with her health, he glanced at the nearest house. "Did you make the emergency call? You found a body?"

Packi put her hand on his solid chest and felt the reassurance of his bulletproof vest. "Not me exactly."

"Then who?"

"Jim Voss. He lives across the street there." She pointed to the jungle and wished again Voss hadn't left her to be the only witness to finding the body.

Teig nodded, already forgetting his concern for her and becoming impatient with her answers. "And where is he?"

"At the vet."

"What?" Billy puffed his cheeks out in frustration. "After finding a body?"

"The dog was badly injured. Bleeding."

"What dog? What happened here?"

"Now, Billy, calm down. You're getting red in the face. Remember your blood pressure." She used the same soothing voice she had when her Ron had vented about all manner of injustices. "It'll be okay. Ranger was cut escaping from the lanai."

The deputy's eyes bulged, trying to see through her explanation. "Why are you here? You'd better start from the beginning."

"I am, Billy." She meant to calm him with a benign smile, but that seemed to have the opposite affect. She smoothed the air with her hands. "Now, listen. I rode my bike here to talk to Jim Voss about . . ." She stopped short before admitting her investigation of the wife-swapping parties. "Well, never mind. Ranger, the pit bull, knocked me off my bike. He was very agitated after finding Oliver's body. He, Oliver Graham, is the owner. Well, Ursula is, but she's gone."

"Stop." Deputy Teig took her hands. "Stop. Where is the body?"

Packi motioned to the Graham house. "Billy, I think . . ."

Teig put up a traffic cop hand to silence her and waved for the EMTs to follow him. "I'll talk to you later," he said, pointing to the ground at her feet.

She nodded, waited, and then walked a respectful distance behind the gurney as the EMTs headed for the front door. "It'll be easier getting in the back," she called. "The patio doors are unlocked and open."

Deputy Teig turned away from the locked front door, scowled, and then pointed again to her feet. He motioned to the EMTs and marched around the garage to the backyard.

Packi did her part by guiding several additional squad cars to the correct house. Even a firetruck pulled up and parked as if waiting for something to explode.

A skinny young man, whose uniform bagged across his chest, exited the passenger side of a Lee County SUV with a roll of yellow crime-scene tape in his fist. He couldn't have been more than twenty. She darted to the side of the Graham house and circled around back before the earnest young cadet could rope off the area.

Packi watched the officials at work from behind thick hibiscus bushes outside the lanai. They hadn't moved the body. She ducked down when Teig stepped outside the sliding doors to speak into his radio. "Need Baker's team here. Leland too. One fatality. Gunshot." He gave the address but turned away as he spoke. He paced between the pool and the patio furniture, then seemed to make a decision and stopped.

"Mizz Walsh, please come here."

"Yes, Billy." Packi rose from her crouched position and walked to the side of the lanai, rehearsing her defense. She figured a meek and conciliatory response might diffuse his anger.

Deputy Teig exited the lanai and motioned to a banana palm. His leather holster creaked as he hiked up his belt and waited for her to join him in the tree's shade. He removed his mirrored sunglasses and stared down at her. "How you holdin' up?"

Packi sighed in relief and nodded.

"Did you go inside?"

She looked toward the open doors and the half-dozen uniforms milling about. "Yes." She startled a bit. "But I only touched the phone. That's it."

"Relax. I trust you." One chubby cheek threatened to dimple, but Teig controlled it. "What about the man who found the body? Did he touch anything?"

"No." Packi raised a finger to correct herself. "I don't think so. I didn't go in immediately. Maybe one minute behind."

"Why were the two of you here?"

"The dog," Packi said. "He always escapes and Jungle . . . I mean, Jim Voss, from across the street brings him home. This time the dog was bloody and Jim got upset. They didn't get along, Mr. Voss and Oliver Graham."

"Did you know the victim?"

"Not really. He was an unpleasant man." Packi took a long sigh. "So, he was shot? The wound looks a lot like the one on the body at the tennis courts. Do you think his wife did this?"

"Do you know Mrs. Graham?"

"I never met her, but Beth says they fight often, and Mr. Voss . . ." She hesitated, not wanting to put words in Jungle Jim's mouth. "He said he heard them arguing last night."

"We'll interview him." Teig pulled a notebook from his pocket and put a pen between his fingers. "You said Voss and Graham didn't get along. Did he say why?"

Packi shrugged. "People say Mr. Voss and Oliver argue at homeowner's meetings about Voss's overgrown yard. We call him *Jungle* Jim, you know. Oliver's on the board and fined Jim, threatened to sue him, put a lien against his house. Stuff like that.

Teig bit at his upper lip as he listened and tapped the pen against the notebook's cover.

"And the dog," said Packi. "Ranger. That's not his real name. Oliver and Ursula didn't seem to take care of the dog. He'd escape whenever they'd open the door and run to Jim to be fed and played with. So today he got out, but he was bloodied and Jim was livid."

She pointed to the gash in the metal mesh around the lanai. "See that, Billy? Ranger chewed his way out. Must have taken more than an hour. He busted out of his cage in the laundry room, too. The blood on the floor has dried. I figure Oliver's been dead at least two hours."

Teig humored her. "So sometime during the night?"

"Oh, no. It was dark but closer to dawn."

"Go on." He pressed his lips together, masking his amusement.

What? He thinks I'm cute? She chose to ignore his patronization in favor of getting her conclusions on record. "Put this in your report." She tapped his notebook with a confident finger. "He's still in pajamas, but he was drinking his morning coffee. The sliding doors were wide open, like people do first thing in the morning. He got up before dawn, because he was upset over their argument."

Packi gasped and looked with narrowed eyes from the sliding doors to the bushes where she had been crouched. "Now I get it." She tugged at the deputy's sleeve. "Have your guys check behind the hibiscus."

"The what?"

"Hibiscus, Billy. The bushes with pink flowers where I was hiding. I mean, where I was watching. I bet you'll find footprints or something."

"Yours?"

Packi clamped her mouth shut. "Sorry. I didn't figure it out until this minute. That spot has a perfect view of Oliver's easy chair. There's a small hole in the screen about a foot above the metal dog barrier. I bet that's where the bullet tore through." She shook her head at her failure to interpret the hole sooner. "So. Write this down, Billy. While it was still dark, someone hid in those bushes and shot him. Out of nowhere. Straight shot."

Billy raised one quizzical eyebrow. "Did the wife do it?"

"No, she's gone." Packi pointed at Billy to make sure he listened. "I bet she left him permanently. Only one person slept in that bed last night. Her toothbrush is gone and there's an empty dresser drawer."

"Maybe she came back."

Packi faltered only a moment as she reconsidered her own conclusions. "No. Ursula is a big woman. Strong. This was personal. If she was angry, she'd use her strength up close, not hide in the dark at a distance."

"Then who?" He was ribbing her again, but she didn't care.

"The same person who shot the guy on the tennis court." Her theory solidified as she sounded it out. "Len Pritchard was Oliver's house guest, you know. They were shot the same way—from a distance. Somebody who knew them both, but I don't believe it was Ursula."

Teig dropped his chin to his chest. "Not Ursula?"

"Nope. Find out where Ursula stayed last night. I bet she has a solid alibi." Packi caught a glint of true interest in the deputy's eyes and stated her case more firmly. "Someone wanted them dead but didn't want to face them. You might want to question the other two guys in their foursome when they played golf a few days ago."

Proud of herself, Packi stuffed her fists into her pockets and rocked back on her heels.

"We'll check it out." Teig awarded her with a real smile. "You're a headache, Mizz Walsh, but you have a good eye for detail." The smile disappeared, replaced with a hard stare. "Except that you're standing on an anthill. Hold still," he warned. "Don't excite them."

Packi glanced down, horrified to see a dozen fire ants crawling over her socks. She swatted at them and danced around to shake them loose. Teig grabbed her elbow to pull her further from the sandy mound and bent to brush several ants from her bare legs.

Too late. Her skin reddened where three painful bites dotted her right ankle. She sucked air between her teeth to absorb the sting.

"Sorry, should've seen that hill." Teig gave her a sheepish look. He stomped his big boots, shook out his own pant legs, and then stuck a stick in the ant hill to warn others. "My mother always had us put ice and antibiotic cream on the bites."

Billy's condescendence was gone but so was his friendly smile. She'd become a bother again. Her ankle itched like mad and her ribs still ached. "I'm going home."

Packi trudged to the front of the house where crime scene tape held back curious neighbors. Detective Leland had arrived in an unmarked car. Squads blocked the street. Packi decided the professionals had it under control, and she could put down her responsibility to the dead man. She suddenly felt every one of her sixty years and more.

Deputy Teig exchanged some unspoken communication with the detective and then took Packi's elbow to turn her away from the buzz of activity.

"That your busted bike in the grass?"

Packi nodded in misery.

"Come on," he said. "We'll throw it in the trunk of my cruiser."

29

Packi was still ensconced in her cushioned chair where Billy Teig had left her. She must have dozed. Sunlight streamed through the plantation shutters at a different angle. Shadows had changed their pattern on the white tiles. Her foot was still propped on a pillow, but the comforter he had tucked around her had fallen to the floor.

Tea in her favorite cup had cooled on the side table. She closed her eyes to recall how Billy's big hands protected the steaming cup as he took slow steps from the kitchen. The porcelain had clinked in its saucer. His leather had creaked as he bent to place the delicate cup on the table, careful not to spill.

Is this how he had cared for his mother before she died? Is this what it's like to have a son?

She began to stretch and breathe deeply but stopped, mid-stretch, fearing pain would stab at her ribs. No pain came. She exhaled by inches and then adjusted her position and breathed again. The ibuprofen had done its job. The fire ant venom must have dissipated too, leaving only a manageable itch to ignore. She flexed her foot and slid out of the chair as a nagging need to track a bit of information pulled her from her comfort.

Something wasn't right. The bullet hole in Oliver Graham's lanai screen bothered her. She bent over the sink to splash water on her face, hoping the shock of cold water would clear her thinking. *Was the hole even made by a bullet? Could a rock been thrown by a mower, or a stick poked through by landscapers?* She wished she had studied the screen before throwing out that theory to Billy Teig. No wonder he thought of her as a doddering old lady.

Packi buried her face in a thick terry cloth towel and breathed in the dryer-fresh scent. She paused to enjoy the simplicity. *How did life get so complicated?* A muffled sound caused her to lift her face from the towel. The doorbell rang again, followed by several sharp knocks. Reluctant to face a handyman or landscaper, she grabbed her phone and swiped through several screens to the security camera app. A picture flickered on.

"Oh. I'm coming!" Packi trotted through the house, hugging her ribs in fear of pain. She swung open the front door to be greeted by her team captain's big grin.

Beth stepped back and pointed at the bicycle parked next to the golf cart in the driveway. "What'd you do? Crash into a tree?"

The grin fell apart when Beth spotted the claw marks on Packi's thigh. "Holy crap. You really did!"

Packi raised her hands to the heavens. "It's been quite a day. Come on in. I'll tell you everything."

Beth insisted Packi sit in a comfortable chair on the lanai while she found her way around the kitchen and poured ice tea for both of them. Packi watched her friend open and close cabinets and itched to jump up to get the lemon, the cutting board, the cookies she baked two days earlier. She fought back the urge to protect her domain. While Ron was alive, he seldom entered the kitchen, except when grazing for snacks. The granite countertops always shined. Fingerprints never marred the stainless steel appliances. She had served him and he'd expected it, but in truth, she wanted to have control of that one room of the house.

Now, Packi forced herself to sit. Beth's movements in the bright white kitchen lacked grace, but her thoughtful intentions gave Packi an odd, but pleasant feeling. She allowed Beth to wait on her which seemed to suit them both.

Beth plunked down a plate of cookies next to the glasses of tea and then settled herself at the table. She raised her eyebrows. "Tell me everything."

Words spilled from Packi's lips as if they'd been waiting for release. She stirred the ice in her glass, watching the cubes eddy and swirl, as she described her run-in with Ranger, the body in the chair, and her discussion with Deputy Teig. The telling didn't make the day any less troublesome.

Beth refilled both glasses and slid the sugar bowl toward Packi. "So you don't think it was Ursula?"

"That's my hunch." Packi shook her head and squeezed another lemon wedge into her tea. "But maybe I just can't imagine a wife shooting her husband."

"Happens all the time." Beth tapped crumbs from a cookie and popped it into her mouth. "Mmm. These are good. What's in 'em?"

"Lavender. I brought them to the Thanksgiving event."

"Mmm. They were gone by the time I got to eat." Beth sucked up crumbs from her hand. "Could've been Jungle Jim, you know. If you weren't there to find the body with him, they'd think he did it." She reached for another cookie. "Lucky man."

Excellent point, Packi thought. *Maybe too lucky.* She nibbled at her cookie and pictured again Ranger knocking her over and Jim Voss appearing. It had happened so fast. *Is it possible he set the stage for me to be a witness?* She frowned at flecks of lavender on her napkin. *No, he's too . . . too . . . sexy.* She slammed the door on that thought and her image of the shirtless man. *Anyway, he wouldn't do that to the dog.*

"Ranger was really bleeding," she said aloud, but she tucked the coincidence away to examine later and maybe mention to Billy Teig.

"Poor dog," Beth mumbled with yet another cookie in her mouth.

When the women had had enough tea and talk of murder, they leaned back and watched clouds scud across the perfect blue sky. Condensation ran down the side of the tall glasses and left hexagonal rings on the cloth place mats. Egrets pecked for food at the edge of the pond. An osprey dropped out of the air, splashed into the water, and made a show of flying off with a fish hanging precariously from its talons.

After the bird disappeared into the trees, Beth filled the silence. "You missed a great tennis lesson. Sam had us working on power volleys."

Packi slid a glance at the team captain, looking for some sign of reproach for her having skipped the drills. She decided Beth only meant to make conversation. "Yeah. I need to work on stronger volleys." Packi groaned. "I should have gone to practice rather than sticking my nose into another police investigation."

"But you're so good at it." Beth smirked and knocked her fingers against Packi's arm. "Hey, I forgot to tell you. Rex stopped by to fix your new golf cart." She sat up and put her hands on her knees as if it was time to go. "He said you should drive it around and let him know if anything else goes wrong. Should we do that now?"

"Sure." Packi caught up to the sudden change of pace and began to clear the table. "What was wrong with it?"

"Disconnected battery cable. All fixed now."

Beth balanced the remainder of the dishes in her arms and tromped into the house. She dumped the things on the granite counter with a clatter, snatched the last cookie, and headed for the door. "Get your shoes," she called over her shoulder.

Though it pained Packi to ignore the kitchen's disarray, she grabbed sandals and rushed to follow.

* * *

Beth slid over smooth leather into the golf cart's passenger side and examined the various cubby holes and compartments. "Pretty cool. You got a steal."

Packi tried to read her friend's demeanor. Did she begrudge Packi's good fortune or think Harold had been unfair to her?

"Do you want to drive?" Packi asked, reluctant to take command and willing to share or give the thing away to keep the peace. "Mr. Baskin should have given this to you. You did much more to save them from the muggers than I did."

"But *you* went to visit him." Beth patted the seat beside her. "Come on, get in."

Packi sensed no animosity and hopped into her new ride.

Other than the reverse switch in an odd place, Harold Baskin's cart operated the same as those used on the golf course. After a jerky start, the cart glided out of the driveway. Packi tested the accelerator, the brake, and a top speed of about twenty miles per hour. With the windshield down and open sides, wind streamed through, giving the sensation of extra speed. Like a ten-year-old behind the wheel of a go-cart, Packi forgot the troubles of the day.

Beth nearly lost her phone as the cart wheeled around the cul de sac on its test run. "Yikes! Slow down, girl." She had been texting the team to meet at the pool to tell them about the second murder. "They'll meet us at the snack shop in fifteen—if you can get us there in one piece."

"Sorry. I'm taking my aggression out on this new toy." Packi grinned and settled the miniature vehicle into its standard mode. Satisfied the old cart had plenty of life left, she drove back down the street, waved to Curtis shooting baskets in his driveway, and headed for the center of Paradise Palms.

People are more friendly when you wave from a golf cart, Packi decided. Even though she had no bag of clubs strapped to the back, the golf community seemed to embrace her and the dutiful little vehicle. Packi hugged the curb, allowed cars to pass, gave plenty of room to cyclists, and greeted everyone equally.

At the intersection of Eagle's Nest and Spoonbill Drive, a big car inched beyond the stop sign, seeming impatient for her to clear the street. Packi floored the accelerator and the golf cart did its best. She waved an apology as they puttered past, but sunlight glinted off the car's windshield preventing her from seeing the driver's response. She hoped he returned the wave.

"My mother had a Grand Marquis," Packi told Beth. "Gold, same as that one. It was so big, Mom felt protected. She was very proud of it."

Beth glanced back at the car at the stop sign. "Yeah. I hear it's like driving a floating sofa."

Packi mused over memories of her mother and then, with a start, recalled she'd seen that car before. The memory mingled with the smell of paint and dust.

"Hey! Watch out!" Beth screamed.

Panicked, Packi gripped the steering wheel and whipped her head around to find the source of the danger. Right behind them, the Grand Marquis gunned its engines and aimed at them. An old woman drove with her fingers white laced around the steering wheel, her mouth open, in shock. From the passenger seat, a white-haired man grabbed at the steering wheel. They seemed to be screaming and fighting for control of the vehicle.

The screech of crushing metal terrified Packi as the impact ejected her from the cart. A split second of freedom released her body from gravity. Wind whipped through her hair. Spears of light streaked past. A shuddering thump took her breath away as her hip, then her shoulder came back to earth. Her spine settled into a cushion of grass, and she stared up at blue sky framed by palm fronds with clusters of green coconuts.

Am I in pain? Packi took inventory. *Breathing works. No headache.* She blinked, tested her shoulder, and bent her knees. Nothing new hurt, but her ribs reminded her of the collision with Ranger. She gingerly rolled to her side and tried to make sense of the scene. Ten or twelve feet away, the golf cart now lay on its side. Beth sat beside it.

Across the street, the Grand Marquis rested with its front bumper hiked up against the base of a thick palm tree at the edge of the golf course. The door gaped open. Inside the car, Dora Baskin seemed to blame her husband for the deflated air bag hanging in her lap. She hit and screamed at him. Harold raised his arms to fend off her tiny fists until, finally, she screeched like a wet cat and half tumbled, half jumped from the car. Dora straightened her sweater on her boney shoulders, reached into the car for her purse, and stalked away. Ten feet further, she realized she had but one shoe. She glared back at her husband for the insult and kicked her other shoe into the pond.

People stared from the golf course, from a parked car, from down the sidewalk. A golfer stopped Dora at the edge of the seventh green and put his arm around her shoulders. Mr. Baskin struggled with the passenger side door. Beth sat in the grass, cursing and kicking at the toppled golf cart, trying to extract her leg from beneath its roof.

Packi realized then that they needed help and began to crawl back toward Beth. She forced herself upright, staggered a bit, but then found her balance.

"Are you hurt?" Packi asked, surveying the cart's metal frame and wondering how to lift it.

"I'm stuck," Beth said between grunts and curses.

Packi put her shoulder against the cart and pushed, but it wouldn't budge. The edge of the fiberglass roof had embedded itself in the sod. Each time she lifted, more color drained from Beth's face.

"Stop. Go take care of him," Beth panted. "I'll wait for some muscle."

Harold Baskin had struggled out of the Grand Marquis and made it to the rear of the vehicle. He stood there, as if on spindly stilts ready to splinter, then teetered and fell against the car. Packi ran across the street as the old man slid down the fender. She caught him and lowered him to the grass, protecting his head. Mr. Baskin acknowledged her with a grimace and then crushed the fabric of his shirt in his right fist.

"Someone call an ambulance!" Packi yelled at a group of people gawking from beyond the car. No one moved. She singled out one woman and glared. "Dial nine-one-one."

The woman blanched but nodded.

Packi brought her attention back to the helpless man and softened her voice. "You're all right, Mr. Baskin. Now stay still."

Terror sharpened his eyes as his fingers raked at her sleeve, wanting something from her. She leaned closer to his dry, crackling breath. "I did it," he rasped.

"No, no. It was an accident, Mr. Baskin." Packi reassured him, but she couldn't understand why he'd claim crashing into them. Dora had lost control. Packi had seen her crazed eyes. "Don't you worry. Help is on the way."

Harold Baskin shook his head and gasped for air. "B . . . Bang . . . Bangkok." Before he could say more, his jaw went slack.

Afraid she'd lost him, Packi searched the crowd for help. They murmured and shuffled backward. She huffed her disgust, but had no time to berate them. *What to do?* She racked her brain for first aid instructions, CPR, General Hospital, anything.

Packi put her ear to the old man's chest and struggled to shut out life around them. There it was. A faint thump, thump. She thanked him for living and brushed a wisp of white hair from his forehead. With his limp hand in hers, she waited for the sound of sirens.

Cold metal in her palm surprised her, and she opened her hands. His wedding ring, worn and dull, slipped around his knuckle. She straightened the ring and puzzled over his devotion to his disagreeable wife. When she looked into his face to wonder, his eyes were upon her, green and intense, but half hidden beneath lids too weak to fully open. His mouth moved with silent words.

Harold Baskin exhaled one faint word. "Confess."

Packi leaned in and waited for more, but the effort had used his last reserve of air and energy. His body was spent, and he again slipped beneath the surface of consciousness. She could only hold his hand, watch the rise and fall of his chest, and wonder. *Did he say* confess*? Confess what?* He had seemed too upset, too worried for the confession to be about the car accident. *Why is he telling me? Why now?*

No answers came from his placid face. *How could this kindly gentleman, in his shiny dress shoes and buttoned-down shirt, be guilty of anything?*

Seconds later, a familiar voice, muffled by the murmuring of the crowd, washed Packi with relief.

"I'm a nurse. Excuse me. I'm a nurse." The wall of people parted and Marilyn Scott pushed through. "Packi! What happened?" She knelt beside the old man without waiting for an answer and began to assess his condition. "Did someone call nine-one-one?"

"I did." A woman at the side of the car raised her hand.

Packi nodded her thanks. "He collapsed after his car hit the tree," she told Marilyn. "I think he has chest pain."

Marilyn threw her purse at Packi. "There's baby aspirin in the side pocket." She put her fingers beneath Harold's jaw and then listened for his breathing.

Packi juggled the purse in her lap and found a packet of aspirin as ordered. She tried several times, in different ways, to tear at the packet, but her fingers seemed too big for her hands. She resorted to ripping at the paper with her teeth until the tablets fell into her palm.

Marilyn grasped her patient's chin and pushed the aspirin beneath his tongue. Her calm efficiency impressed Packi while her own uselessness weighed on her. "Is there anything else I can do? Do you need me?"

"Don't think so." Marilyn kept her eyes on Harold and positioned herself at his head. "All I can do is monitor him and stabilize his spine until the

EMT's get here." On her knees, she crouched to put her hands on either side of his neck. "His breathing and pulse are low, but I don't see any injuries."

"Okay," Packi whispered. "I'll go check on Beth."

"What?" Marilyn's eyes darted around, but her elbows remained planted on the ground, protecting her patient's neck. The crowd blocked her view. "Beth?"

"Not bad. She's okay." Packi squeezed Marilyn's shoulder. "Mr. Baskin needs you more."

Marilyn nodded, regained her nurse's demeanor, and turned her attention back to the old gentleman while Packi slipped away.

Beth stood on one foot at the side of the upright golf cart, shaking hands with several women. "Thanks," she said. "Thanks for your help."

"How's your leg?" Packi asked when the women moved away.

"They lifted the cart, but my foot . . ." Beth caught her lip between her teeth, and her cheeks paled. Her shoulders seemed to bear the weight of a boulder.

The only time Packi had seen the stoic woman so dejected was after losing a brutal three-hour tennis match. "You'd better sit."

"Crap." Beth hopped into position and let herself fall onto the seat of the golf cart. "I hope it's not broken." She propped her leg on the seat and rested her head against the back. A sharp line of purple bloomed above her ankle.

Packi wanted to help but was afraid to touch the injury. "Keep it elevated," she said. "The ambulance will be here soon." She sympathized with her friend who wasn't the type to be mothered.

Beth glared at her ankle and groaned as if disgusted with herself. "Those old people okay?"

"The husband is breathing," Packi said. "Marilyn came running and is with him now. It looks bad."

"Marilyn's here? That's lucky." Beth perked up a bit. "And the crazy old bat?"

Packi suppressed a grin. "Somebody's taking care of her."

"Huh." Beth prodded her inflamed ankle, poking her finger into swelling flesh. "I don't know. Maybe it's only a sprain."

Packi watched her friend explore the injury and picked at a clod of grass clinging to the roof of the golf cart. "I think he confessed to something."

"Who?"

"Harold Baskin," Packi said. "It was like a deathbed confession. I thought he meant the accident."

"What? That's who it was? His loony-tunes wife aimed right at us!" Beth snorted in disgust. "I guess she wanted her golf cart back."

"Possible." Packi shook her head at the absurdity. She stood on tiptoe but could no longer see Harold on the ground, nor Marilyn amid the growing knot of people around the Grand Marquis. "I think," she whispered, "he also said *Bangkok*. I wonder what happened there."

"Didn't Grace say Oliver and Ursula traveled to Thailand?"

"Yeah, and now Oliver's dead."

Beth glowered and pulled herself to the side of the seat. "You think the old man killed him?"

"I can't imagine, but we have to consider it. He wanted to confess to something that really disturbed him." Packi plucked off the last of the mud from the roof and threw it aside. She also picked at the idea of Harold Baskin as a murderer. *Was he the violent sort, maybe in his youth?* She'd seen his willingness to battle the muggers. "Could he have known the first victim, too?"

"His wife would know, don't ya think? Let's question her." Energized and eager for action, Beth slid off the seat to stand. The moment she put weight on her foot, she sucked air through her teeth and sat back down. "Whew, baby."

Packi reached out to steady her friend. "Do you want me to get you to the ER? We can drive this cart to my house to get my car." She bent to peer at the underside of the golf cart and pulled the crushed fender away from the back wheel. A large chunk of fiberglass came off in her hand, and she threw it into the cart's basket.

"Don't bother. This thing is trashed," said Beth, lifting her foot to rest on the dashboard. "We'll wait for the ambulance. Besides, I want to see if the cops arrest your Mr. Baskin."

30

A cadre of ER staff hustled in and out of the next cubicle. From amid hospital sounds, announcements, and alerts, Packi honed in on a stream of mournful beeps. They echoed Harold Baskin's beating heart. She was unfamiliar with the proper cadence, but the timing seemed off, too slow. Guilty of something or not, she wanted him to live.

Several times, the staff had chased her from Harold's room. *Someone should be with him,* she thought. *Someone should hold his hand.* An orderly finally closed the door to her, so she waited in Beth's empty cubicle while Marilyn tracked down the ER supervisor.

"MRI is backed up." Marilyn slid into the molded plastic chair next to Packi's, both facing the space where Beth's gurney had been. "But they should bring her back soon."

Marilyn seemed more confident here, in the ER, than on the tennis court. Packi pictured her tending to patients in a spotless white uniform. So much mystique had been lost, Packi thought, when nurses renounced the old uniforms and their origami-shaped hats. Now nurses appeared ordinary. Everyone in ER wore scrubs or printed smocks: paisley, animal print, floral. They were wired into efficient electronic devices which beeped and pinged and took their attention. Packi wondered what else had been lost along with the white uniforms.

"Did you ask about Dora?"

"They haven't seen her," said Marilyn. "An EMT said she refused treatment and someone in the crowd persuaded her to at least see her own doctor. I suppose they drove her there."

"She should be here." Packi wanted to dislike Harold's wife but realized the woman might have been in shock after the accident. "He could die."

Hospital minutes dragged on into an hour. With time to think, Packi wondered what kept the Baskin's marriage together. "Dora doesn't even seem to like Harold," she said aloud, though she didn't expect Marilyn to hear. "Why have they stayed married for fifty years? Loyalty?"

"Habit?" Marilyn glanced up from the magazine she'd been flipping through. "Marriage vows? I can think of several couples we know in Paradise Palms who have simply called a truce."

"Really, a truce? Who?" Packi said, but then held up both hands. "No. Don't tell me. None of my business." She stood up to pace the cramped cubicle. "You never know what other people deal with."

The flatness of her relationship with her own husband bothered her. Of course, for many years she had covered up and put on a happy face. Friends and family never guessed—or maybe they did. Now she wondered—had Ron lived, would they have developed a joyful relationship like Beth and Rex, or would they have called a truce?

Familiar hospital routines, smells, and sounds brought back the heavy weight of memories of interminable days at Ron's bedside. His release from the hospital had given her hope, even joy, but he had had his own plans. Ron intended to die on *his* terms. Still, it disturbed her that she hadn't been at his side.

"Dora should be here."

"Are you all right?" Marilyn appeared from behind in her own quiet way and put her hand on Packi's arm.

"Yes, of course." Packi shook off her melancholia and cleared traces of emotion from her face. She felt naked to Marilyn's probing concern and turned away. "I was thinking. What makes Dora so angry? What are the Baskins covering up?"

Marilyn squeezed Packi's arm in silent agreement to sidestep the real issue. "Beth should be down soon. If she feels up to it, we can call on Dora and persuade her to visit her husband. Maybe she needs a ride."

Minutes later, Beth's voice sounded from down the hall a full thirty seconds before her wheelchair came through the double doors. She and the volunteer pushing the chair joked about swamp buggy racing. Beth had found a local who shared her love of Everglade mudding and apparently forgot her casted foot.

The party atmosphere irked Packi. Her time would have been better spent fetching Dora or even tracking down clues to Oliver's murder.

Packi soon regretted her lack of sympathy and understanding.

Beth's convivial mood disappeared the minute she flopped into the back seat of Marilyn's car. "Take me home," she begged. She winced as she lifted the Velcro boot onto the seat. "Good god. This is only a sprain. I'd hate to have a broken leg." She tried to find a comfortable spot for her painful ankle, then lay her head back and closed her eyes while Marilyn pulled the car into traffic.

"I saw the old guy being wheeled upstairs," Beth said without opening her eyes. "He looked bad."

"I agree," Packi said, "but they wouldn't tell me anything." She worried about the Baskins but was also disconcerted to see Beth in her weakened condition: pale, exhausted, relying on others. It wasn't right.

"Do me a favor," said Beth, peeking from one eye. "Find out why that crazy old bat rammed into us."

31

Nothing happened when Packi rang the doorbell at the Baskin house. She rang again and then dropped any pretense of etiquette and stared through the lace at the window. The light within the house shifted, and she heard stirring behind the faded front door—faint and inconsequential sounds, like a squirrel rustling leaves somewhere in the forest. Packi waited for a face to appear at the window, but none came. The lace curtain riffled, so she offered a small friendly wave to the unseen occupant. Locks clicked and the door cracked open.

"Yes?"

"Hello, Mrs. Baskin."

"Who are you?" Dora seemed smaller now, as if another vertebrae collapsed in the last few hours. She scrutinized Packi through the screen.

"I'm Patricia Walsh, Dora." Surprised by the lack of recognition, Packi worried the elderly woman had suffered a head injury in the accident, a concussion maybe. She inched open the screen door without Dora's notice. "I've come to offer you a ride to the hospital."

"I don't want to go to the hospital."

Neither the accident nor the mugging incident had softened Dora's sharp edges.

"To see Harold."

"He's not home." Dora stepped outside in slippered feet and glanced down the street, as if expecting her husband's return. She blinked in disappointment.

Packi noticed poorly applied Band-Aids dotting Dora's legs. "Mrs. Baskin, I see you were cut in the accident. May I take you to the doctor to have them tended?"

"Harold's coming home." Dora wrapped her sweater around her bones. "He's getting the car repaired." She shuffled past Packi into the house and disappeared behind the door.

Packi had been dismissed, but her conscience wouldn't allow her to leave the confused woman alone. Before the door slammed, she put her foot in its way and spoke through the crack. "Mrs. Baskin, may I come in? I want to talk to you about your husband."

Dora leaned her ninety-five pound body against the door, squeezing Packi's shoe. The attempt to bar the entrance was too much for her, and she abandoned the effort with a sour look thrown at her visitor. The door swung open.

"Thank you," Packi said as she stepped into the dim interior.

The smell of neglect rushed at her from the cluttered room. Heavy drapery trapped years of dust and blocked out the healing Florida sunshine. The furniture, popular up north thirty years ago, was littered with newspapers, books, and half-completed crochet projects. The kitchen counter was heaped with a week's worth of dishes. Obviously, cleaning had fallen to the wayside long ago.

Packi wondered how the couple, so formal and neatly dressed, could live in such disarray.

"Mrs. Baskin, have the police been here to check on you?"

Dora went rigid. Pink rouge stood out in contrast with her white powdered cheeks. Her unsteady slippers threatened to topple her.

"Dora." Packi reached out to the delicate woman, but Mrs. Baskin shrank away, sidling toward the bedroom door. "Dora, Harold is in the hospital. After the accident, his heart bothered him. Do you want me to drive you to the hospital to visit him?"

"No, no." Dora rubbed and kneaded her knuckles. "He'll be home soon and you shouldn't be here. I don't want you poking around in our business."

"Of course not," said Packi as if to a toddler. "Do you remember the car accident? You were driving and collided with the golf cart."

Dora jumped and bristled like a cat thrown into a bathtub. Her shoulders rounded, ready to pounce. "You stole my golf cart," she hissed through gritted teeth. "How dare you?"

Taken aback at the woman's vehemence, Packi had no defense. She circled away from the woman's exposed claws. "Please, Dora . . ."

"Stay away from my husband, you hussy. We have a reputation in this community." Dora grabbed a chair to support her anger. "He rejected you, so you want to ruin him. Ruin him!"

"That's not it. I want to help." Packi stuttered, desperate to ease Dora's anxiety.

"How dare you pretend to be my friend?"

"I am your friend, Mrs. Baskin, and I barely know your husband. I was investigating . . ." She stopped. *How can I tell this poor woman about Curtis' stalker now? Can she handle news of the murders?*

Dora's rage collected in her eyes. "Liar!" She grabbed a framed picture from a side table and sidearmed it, Frisbee style. Packi ducked as the frame flew past her head and crashed against the television, sending splinters of glass skittering across the tile floor.

Dora had her eye on another family photo, so Packi maneuvered to intercept and distract. "Please listen, Mrs Baskin." She dare not touch the woman but reached out across the space between them. "Anyone can see Mr. Baskin loves you. He's a good man and no one can ruin him. I'm your friend. Let me help you."

Doubt wormed through Dora's anger. Hesitation undid her determination. Backed up to the sofa and with the next picture frame out of reach, the old woman ran out of steam. She seemed to reconsider her tirade and dabbed at the spittle at the corner of her mouth. As fight drained away, Dora slumped onto a footstool and put her fists between her knees. Robbed of an enemy, she began to cry.

"Those filthy men," Dora whispered.

Packi listened harder. "What men are you talking about?"

"They deserved to die." Dora absentmindedly reached down to scratch at her ankle.

Nodding as if she agreed, Packi's mind flew through scenarios and searched for a connection. "Mrs. Baskin." She lowered herself onto the sofa, ignoring the newspapers beneath her. "Did Harold travel to Bangkok with those men?"

Dora pursed her lips as if fighting back sour truth. She gave a curt nod. "With that club."

"A travel club? What sort of club?" Packi leaned forward to study the woman's face. *What is she trying to tell me?*

"They tricked him."

“The men in the club?” Packi asked, fishing for whatever Dora was on the verge of telling.

The older woman’s expression hardened, but she didn’t answer. Instead, she growled from deep within her throat and jumped to her feet as if powered by an inner demon. Packi stiffened and raised her arms, ready for an attack.

Dora shoved past Packi to get to a bookshelf next to the cracked television. Glass shards skated out from beneath her slippers. She pushed aside skeins of yarn piled in front of a set of encyclopedia and pulled a heavy volume from the middle of the alphabet. The book fell open to a section marked with photographs.

“He thought I didn’t know about these.” She flung a handful of pictures at Packi.

Instinct caused Packi to duck, but the photos fluttered harmlessly around her. She picked one from her lap but immediately dropped it. Too late. The sickening image scorched her memory. A child with a naked man, very similar to the photos in the gym bag belonging to Leonard Pritchard. The same sort of picture assaulted her from the coffee table. She turned the repulsive pictures face down on the table with the finality of throwing dirt into a grave. “Your husband got these in Bangkok?”

“He quit thirty years ago, but they tricked him.” Dora hurtled the encyclopedia to the floor at her feet.

This is what Harold was hiding, thought Packi. *Is this why he shot Pritchard? Oliver Graham, too?*

“He left, flew home.” Dora paced in circles, muttering and wringing her hands. “He didn’t . . . he couldn’t . . . not children. We have grandchildren, for God’s sake!”

What is she saying? Packi thoughts thickened and churned in slow confusion. She couldn’t bring herself to imagine kindly gentlemanly Harold would participate in . . . in . . . in what the pictures suggested. She felt sick and glowered at the backsides of the photos as if they should burst into hellfire.

Think, Patricia. While Mrs. Baskin paced, Packi sank back into the sofa and stared at the broken TV to mull over what she knew.

Is it possible Harold was being blackmailed? It became too much, she reasoned, *so he shot Leonard Pritchard at the tennis court. That explains the clay grit she’d seen in the Baskin garage.*

Packi could almost hear the crunch beneath his dress shoes as they removed the tarp from the golf cart. She remembered the cluttered garage:

tools, decorations, old trophies. The smell of tempera paint was there, too. *Had Harold thrown painted tennis balls into her home to warn her away?*

No. Packi stared at the broken TV, deep in thought. *A woman had been seen at her house.*

Dora?

Packi sat straighter and pulled herself out of the deep cushions. Ideas clicked. Her mind's eye saw the trophies in the garage more clearly. Shooting awards. The golden figure on top of each wore a skirt.

Dora? Dora shot Pritchard. Why? To protect her husband's reputation?

Another click, audible this time, brought Packi back to the present. She suddenly realized the house was too still. Dora had gone quiet. Another sound came from behind. Metal on metal, mechanical. Packi twisted in her seat.

Mrs. Baskin stood in the bedroom doorway, posed like the figure on top of her trophies, with a rifle aimed at Packi's back.

32

Packi rose from the sofa in slow motion. Her limbs and her mind moved through a sludge of fear. As she stood, her phone slid deeper into her pocket, out of reach. That lifeline was gone; a call for help, impossible. Beg, she told herself. The words wouldn't form. She pivoted and reached out her hands as if her palms could stop a rifle bullet.

"Now you know." Dora's chest heaved, but her gun remained steady. "I tried to warn you, but you kept poking around in our business. You'll tell everyone. His reputation is too important to let you live."

"No, Mrs. Baskin," Packi stammered. "I wouldn't tell anyone. I like your husband."

Too late, she remembered the woman's jealousy. "I mean, *everyone* likes your husband. He's respected in this community." She squeezed images of the pornographic pictures out of her mind and babbled on. "Everyone knows he's a good person. You don't have to do this."

In a panic, Packi realized she could not reason with a deranged person. She transfixed on the gleaming steel and an errant thought popped into her head. *Why a rifle?* Len Pritchard had been killed with a handgun. *Where is the other gun?* Packi would have preferred the smaller weapon but did it really matter? No doubt, the trophies meant Dora Baskin was proficient with both, and Packi was her paper target at the end of a practice range.

Dora's eyes sighted down the long barrel and held no empathy, only determination and certainty. She motioned with the barrel of the gun. "Get away from the sofa. I had it cleaned yesterday."

"Okay, Mrs. Baskin, please. Please relax. We can fix this." Packi inched along the dirty sofa, grabbing hold of its thick seams to steady herself. Her stomach lurched at the thought of her blood staining the cream-colored fabric. She sidled behind matching recliners and hoped Dora valued them as much as the sofa.

In spite of her joints stiffening with terror, Packi looked for an opening, a moment to disarm the old lady. She envisioned herself crouching low, under the rifle, and hurtling herself at the woman's knees.

"Please listen, Mrs. Baskin," she begged, trying to mask her desperation. "You don't want to shoot me. I can be your witness and tell the police that it was Pritchard's fault." Packi looked for her chance to spring. "He was a filthy man, wasn't he?"

Every grandmotherly wrinkle around Dora's mouth distorted with hate. She glared at the scattered photos. "He tempted my husband with those," she hissed, "but I ended that. No more traveling. No more . . ."

Packi saw her opening. *Almost there.* She flexed her reluctant muscles, ready to pounce, but then stopped. The old woman's words sunk in. Mrs. Baskin was about to confess to murder. The opportunity to attack slipped by.

Keep her talking.

"Of course, your husband is a gentleman and nothing like Pritchard," Packi said, soothing the woman, reeling her in. "Oliver Graham was dirty and vulgar too, wasn't he? Did you take care of that situation?"

"Yes, I did. The filthy pig." Dora lifted her chin with smug satisfaction. That man sat at the pool every day watching the little ones, wanting . . ." The rifle shook. "Harold never. They traveled to Thailand to . . . to get . . ."

The point of the gun lowered a few inches, perhaps weighted down by Harold's guilt. Dora's skinny arms could no longer keep the heavy weapon steady, or maybe her determination to kill faltered. The chance to disarm the woman wouldn't get any better.

"You got those bites on your legs from fire ants behind Graham's house, right? The night you shot him?"

Dora glared down at her Band-Aids and seemed plagued by the urge to scratch.

With that split-second distraction, Packi sprang from behind the chair and jumped over the footstool. She dove around the sofa and landed in a crouch, ready to grapple with the woman. Too late. The lethal gun barrel swung around with Olympic confidence. Inches from Packi's forehead, the bullet couldn't miss. She froze with the smell of gun oil and sulphur threatening her nose.

"You shouldn't have taken my golf cart." Dora's bird-song voice contradicted her murderous eyes.

"Now, Dora." Packi itched to rub the burnt gunpowder smell from her nose, but she dare not move. She played the supplicant from her crouched position. "Let's think about this. The judge will listen when you tell him you killed Pritchard and Graham because they abused children. People might even say you're a hero. You can tell them Harold tried to trap them, tried to make them stop."

"That's true." Dora concentrated on the new idea and the gun wavered to the side. "He certainly did. Yes, Harold trapped them. He's a hero."

"Yes." Packi tamped the thought into place. "Harold's a hero. His reputation is safe. It's better . . ."

The doorbell shattered the fragile connection.

33

Dora snapped the gun back to its target. Her eyes blamed Packi for the doorbell's interruption, and the rifle warned her to be silent.

In the standoff, Dora's gun hand tightened, but her gaze sneaked to the front door. Packi eyed the wavering gun and seized upon Dora's hesitation. She batted the rifle away with her most powerful backhand tennis stroke and launched herself at Dora's stomach. The frail woman fell back like a stick figure with her arms thrown over her head. Her trigger finger let loose an explosion. Glass shattered nearby. Stunned by the avalanche of noise, Packi fell back as the gun's retort reverberated from wall to wall.

Still reeling with ear pain, Packi scrambled to her knees and threw herself spread-eagle on top of Dora. She grappled for control of the rifle. Beneath her, she heard a sharp gasp and the crack of bone. Dora wheezed.

The sound of splintering wood and glass broke into their fight, but Packi's only thought was to grab the weapon on the floor above Dora's head, still in her hand, still lethal. Packi crawled toward the gun with Dora pinned beneath her. The ninety-year-old groaned each time Packi crushed her with her body, but Dora would not release the rifle. Packi lay chest-to-chest with the woman, struggling to control the gun hand, while Dora bucked beneath her and scratched at her face.

"Hey!"

The powerful scream forced a split-second pause in the fight. Packi squinted from between their entangled elbows to see a large tennis shoe swing out and give a mighty kick. Dora's rifle skittered across the floor, spinning and ricocheting off chair legs until it came to rest under the dining room table.

Dora cried out at her loss. Spent and defeated, she shrank into her body and went still. Exhausted, Packi rolled off Dora and lay flat on her back.

"Beth?" Packi struggled to focus on her friend, towering over her.

"What the crap! What's going on?"

Dora groaned in pain and curled up like a dead caterpillar.

"Beth! Oh, thank God you're here." Packi heaved a heavy sigh. She cradled her ringing ear and huffed for breath. "But why are you here?" She dragged herself to a sitting position and leaned against the sofa, feeling every ache and aging a hundred years. "How . . .? Your ankle?"

Beth glanced down at the black Velcro cast as if seeing it for the first time. "Oh. I forgot." She paled and felt behind her for a chair. She sat, lifted her sprained ankle onto the footstool, then slumped into the cushions. "Adrenaline, I guess. I heard the gunshot and thought . . . well, I panicked and slammed through the door." She gave Packi a weak smile. "Actually, it was half open."

The little bit of humor revived Packi some. "Why are you here? I thought Marilyn took you home."

"She did, but I got to thinking you shouldn't come here alone. If that crazy old bat rammed us with her car, she could do anything." Beth threw a glance at Dora, winced and settled back. "Anyway, Kay's getting her hair cut, and Marilyn got called in for a shift at the food pantry. So here I am. I can drive with only one foot."

"Well, thanks. It might have turned out different." Packi shook her head at Dora, still on the floor, snuffling and groaning as if her heart was broken. Perhaps it was.

"What was that about?" asked Beth.

"Mrs. Baskin confessed to shooting both Pritchard and Graham. She was protecting her husband's reputation."

"And you were about to expose them."

"Right." Solving the crimes didn't bring Packi any joy. "We should call for help. I think I cracked one of her ribs."

"My phone's in the car." Beth struggled to get out of the chair but gave in quickly when Packi pointed at her.

"Sit still. I've got mine." Packi felt for the phone, but her pocket was empty. "Well, I know I had it. Must have gone flying." She used the sofa arm to haul herself up. She searched the cushions, beneath the coffee table, amid the stacks of newspapers, and under a half-crocheted afghan.

"That it under the book shelf?" Beth asked from her chair.

Packi crawled across the area rug to retrieve the phone from amid broken glass. The effort to stand seemed too great, so she propped herself against the bookcase. "I've got Deputy Teig on speed dial."

Beth nodded and laid her head back in Harold Baskin's chair. "If you don't mind, I need a rest. The drugs are taking a toll."

"Billy?" Packi didn't bother with hello. "I'm at the Baskin . . ."

Her words stalled in her mouth when she saw movement under the end table. Dora had dragged herself behind Beth's chair. She upset a basket of yarn, pulled out a handgun, and aimed the weapon at Packi.

There it is. Packi thought stupidly. She had only a second to lurch to the floor and roll before an explosion shook the walls. A solid thwack hit the coffee table. Packi upended the table and scuttled behind it, pushing like a bulldozer toward Dora.

Another shot rang out, killing the overhead fan. Screams battled.

When the shrieking turned to grunts and whines, Packi peeked over her shield.

Dora hung suspended from Beth's fist like a prize fish on the end of a line. Dora writhed and fought, the gun still clutched in her blue-veined-hand. Beth finally wrested the weapon away and tossed it down the hallway. Dora screeched her frustration, and Beth lowered the defeated woman to the floor.

"You want me to sit on her?"

"We may have to."

Packi retrieved her phone from amid scattered glass and put Deputy Teig's fears to rest.

34

Deputy Billy Teig slowed the cruiser enough to avoid pedestrian injuries and jerked to a stop behind Packi's car in the driveway of the Baskin house. Mizz Walsh scared him. Scared him like it was his little Mikey in danger. Scared him like his mother being smacked around by his father on a drunken tear. Scared him . . . He ground his teeth and focused on business. *She said the shooter was subdued, but ya never know. Trouble follows that woman.*

He unsnapped his holster and jumped from the car. Gapers stepped into his path to offer their opinions and observations.

A blonde woman tugged at his arm. "I'm Mrs. Homolka, neighborhood watch . . . "

"Stand aside, please." He rushed past her. "Make room for the ambulance."

He couldn't breathe.

Before he could crash through the door, Mizz Walsh flung it open. Her tiny figure stood out against the shadows behind. He studied her pale face for fear or pain. She almost smiled and put her hands on his chest, as she always did. Her calm reached him through his bulletproof vest, and he exhaled.

"Come in, Billy. The crisis has past but thank you for coming."

"Is everyone okay? Any injuries?" Teig's eyes adjusted to the murky light and surveyed the room. Beth Hogan stood over an ancient woman in a chair who sat as prim as a Sunday school teacher with her hands folded in her lap.

"Oh." The old lady turned in her chair and began to rise. "I'll make tea for our visitor."

Mizz Hogan pushed the woman back into the cushions with a firm hold on her shoulder. "Packi and I are no worse for wear, but this one may have a broken rib."

"Billy, this is Dora Baskin," Packi said as if introducing him to her great aunt.

"Pfft." Beth rolled her eyes and gave him a stern look. "Mrs. Baskin is your shooter. She tried to kill us both. I think that's a nine-millimeter on the floor in the hallway."

"Anyone else here?" He scanned the hallway and spotted the gun at the far end. *Big weapon for a little lady.* "You got her under control?" He pulled his Glock from his holster and moved toward the hallway.

"No one else is here," Mizz Walsh said, cupping her ear as if it hurt. "Her husband is in the hospital."

"Gotta check. Stay put."

The house was a mess. Each room strewn with clothes, boxes, and hobby supplies. A rifle lay beneath the dining room table, and he wondered if there was an arsenal hidden somewhere. *What the heck went on here?*

The overstuffed garage and lanai didn't harbor anyone either, so he holstered his gun. "All clear," he said to his backup who appeared at the front door, their guns drawn.

"I don't think we have enough tea," said Dora Baskin.

Deputy Teig gave a brief report to the new arrivals and then pulled handcuffs from his utility belt.

"You don't have to do that, Billy." Packi moved between him and the old lady. "She's confused and can't hurt anyone now."

"Are ya kiddin' me?" Beth said. "She's a fake. She could have guns stashed in any of these yarn baskets or hidden in the furniture."

A sudden fear widened Beth's eyes. With a rough hold on Dora Baskin's shoulder, she shoved her other hand into the cushions behind the woman and searched the sides of the chair. Satisfied the old lady hadn't hidden another weapon, Beth let out a dramatic huff and flopped onto the sofa.

"It's procedure, Mizz Walsh." Billy helped Dora to her feet, running his hands over her body so quickly, she seemed oblivious to being frisked. Miranda rights rolled off his tongue as he drew her arms behind her back and locked her hands in cuffs.

Dora winced and scowled at Mizz Walsh. "Arrest that woman," she demanded. "She stole my golf cart."

* * *

While waiting for medical help, Mrs. Baskin sat stiff and erect on the footstool, her eyes fixed on the cracked television screen. She seemed unaware of her injuries and predicament and would not, or could not, answer Deputy Teig's questions.

What's going on in her head? Packi wondered. *Apparently, her mind is absent.*

Packi found it hard to believe the ninety-year-old had shot at her and had planned and executed the murder of two men. She began to question her own conclusions and memory of events.

Packi paced out of earshot a few feet away, while Deputy Teig took Beth's report and the backup team searched the Baskin home. A female deputy arrived to take charge of Dora Baskin. When the young woman realized the elderly lady with her hands cuffed behind her back was her assignment, an eyebrow twitch revealed a crack in her professional mask.

"Her mind's not right," Packi explained, "and she needs a doctor. I think I broke her ribs."

Suspicion passed through the deputy's eyes as she searched for Packi's guilt in the matter. She put her hand on the cuffs hanging from her belt, ready to take Packi into custody, and looked to Teig for direction.

Deputy Teig took his young associate aside and spoke to her in low tones. He then gently guided Dora to her feet. "Keep the handcuffs on her," he said.

The female officer cast a last dubious glance at Packi and escorted Dora out the front door to an ambulance. In spite of the growing number of police officials in the small house, tensions eased with Dora gone. Packi's pacing slowed.

After Beth gave her version of events, she wandered outside to the lanai. Deputy Teig motioned Packi into the kitchen and sat across from her at the table. "So, Mizz Walsh, tell me what happened."

Sensations and emotions rushed at Packi. Though she had reviewed the scenario six times, thoughts jumbled and refused to make sense. She would have felt better to busy her hands by serving something. Dora had mentioned tea, but Packi shook away the idea and forced herself to sit still. "Where do I start?"

Billy surprised her with his patience. His blue eyes seemed to smile and encourage her to calm down. He took her hands. "Why were you here?"

"I wasn't investigating," Packi assured him. "Mr. Baskin insisted I needed a golf cart and delivered one to my house."

The deputy's eyebrow arched, but he let her talk.

"Dora was jealous and upset about the gift. Called me a hussy."

Billy's professional demeanor almost slipped and a dimple formed, but not as deep as it would have been a few months ago. *His cheeks are thinner,* Packi thought. She glanced around the table to see his belly. Extra shirt fabric bunched beneath his belt.

"You've lost weight."

"Few pounds." He tugged on his loose Kevlar vest and then got back to business. "Go on with your story."

Packi sighed and focused on a pile of newspapers on the table, one of them folded back to a half-completed crossword puzzle. *Is that Dora's neat printing? Or Harold's?* She wondered only for a moment, then forced her thoughts into alignment. She described the car crash, the woman's crazed eyes, and Harold's wish to confess.

Her hip and shoulder ached with the telling. "Mr. Baskin is in ICU, and I came here to offer Dora a ride so she could be by his side. I hope he's still alive. Will they allow her to see him?"

"Doubt it."

"Could you try?" She leaned forward and took Billy's hand. "Seeing him might calm her, and she could answer more questions."

Teig didn't respond. He glanced around at the mess in the living room and the hallway beyond, where a deputy was bagging the handgun. "Tell me about the guns."

Packi blew air from her cheeks as she had seen Billy Teig do when he was exasperated. "After Dora calmed down, I sat in the living room piecing it together. I suddenly realized the grit on the garage floor the day I looked at Harold's golf cart was from the tennis courts. Then, I recalled seeing the shooting competition trophies at the same time and knew they were hers. It also dawned me that she was scratching at fire ant bites on her legs like those I got behind the Graham house. She was the shooter. Before I could react, Dora had a rifle pointed at my back. We fought over the gun, and it went off. Beth heard the shot and crashed through the door."

Only Billy's big paws around her hands kept them from shaking and allowed her to get her thoughts organized. "Dora's tricky and stronger than she looks." Packi sat back and kneaded the soreness in her neck and left shoulder. Her muscles remembered the fight better than she did.

"I thought she fainted. Both Beth and I thought she was done. That's when I dialed your number. But Dora snuck that big handgun out of her yarn basket and shot at me." Sweat broke out on Packi's forehead as if she needed to dive for cover again, but she held her seat.

"Before the fight and the shooting, I had Dora talking. She seemed to say that Harold used to collect pictures like those. Years ago." Packi pointed toward the upended coffee table in the living room and the explicit pictures scattered about. "Oliver Graham angered her by tempting Harold and giving him pictures."

Packi worked her fingers into a knot that had formed between her eyebrows. "After Mr. Baskin was injured in the car accident, he mentioned Bangkok and seemed to confess to something. Dora was livid about him joining a club to travel there. You need to follow up on that."

Teig ran his big hand over his jaw as if mulling over how much to say. "Leonard Pritchard was the pornographer. His personal perversion was teenaged boys."

Stomach acid burned in Packi's throat. Confirmation of her suspicions about the body on the tennis court gave her no satisfaction. "So Pritchard was the creep watching Curtis play basketball?"

"Curtis pointed him out in a photo lineup."

Packi groaned. She mourned the loss of the boy's innocence, but realized Curtis was more street-smart than she. He had been unfazed by the men at the homeless camp, stood up to the gang members, and knew when to ask for help. He'd be okay. It was *her* innocence tipping off kilter.

"Sorry, Billy. I've had enough." Packi jumped to her feet, rushed past Teig, ducked around deputies in the hall, and ran to the bathroom. No amount of soap could scrub away the filth that clung to her hands.

35

The next day, Packi, Beth, and a few other non-playing team members sat on the bleachers in the shade while their team battled women from Estero out in the hot sun.

Kay and Helen struggled against strong opponents on Court One, but the game in Court Two was going well for Paradise Palms. Grace's playful humor and motherly calm worked on Kimberly who was holding up under the pressure of competing on a higher court. Packi regretted ever including the attractive Canadian on her list of murder suspects, no matter how briefly. Packi and Beth cheered quietly, as tennis etiquette required, each time Grace or Kimberly aced their serves or fended off Estero's power shots.

There was less to cheer about on Court One. They had begun the second set and were still behind. Helen tossed the ball up to serve, but then caught it and glared through the fence. Packi glanced around to see what caused the delay.

"Uh-oh." Beth poked Packi's ribs. "Here comes your buddy."

A Lee County uniform moved along the sidewalk on the other side of the windscreen. Packi slipped off the bleachers and hurried to meet Deputy Teig.

"Come this way." She motioned Billy to a pavilion far enough away from the courts so their voices wouldn't disturb the matches. The shaded sitting area provided benches and a soft breeze, but she was too wired up to sit, especially with him pacing the small space.

"Did something happen, Billy?"

"There will be a story in the paper tomorrow and maybe on the news tonight." He took off his hat and turned the brim in his hands. "I wanted to tell you myself."

"Oh, no." Her heart withered. "Is it Harold? Did he die? The hospital wouldn't tell me anything when I called this morning."

"The old man's hanging in there," the deputy said. "He regained consciousness for a few minutes. Detective Leland asked a few questions, but Mr. Baskin only worried about his wife. Claimed *he* shot Pritchard and Graham."

"He can barely stand," Packi protested.

"I know." Deputy Teig shushed her with a hand gesture. "We also questioned Dora in the ER. She ranted on about the pictures, revenge on those filthy men, and you trying to run off with her husband."

"I never . . ."

Teig gave the hand gesture again to interrupt her objections. "It's clear Dora goes in and out of reality. She thought I was her son. She also said the painted tennis balls were to scare you away from poking into their business." Teig made little quotation marks in the air and gave her an I-told-you-so look.

Packi imitated one of Beth's eye rolls. "Go on."

"Dora confessed to killing Pritchard and Graham and was coherent enough to say which gun she used, time of day, and where she hid. She could cite the details. Her husband could not." Billy took a huge breath. "And the footprints you found outside the tennis court matched shoes we found in the Baskin garage. Women's size five."

Teig glanced down at Packi's shoes, and she held up a foot for inspection.

"Size six," she said.

"Thought you might have trampled the evidence."

Packi tensed, ready to argue, but spotted his almost invisible smile and backed down. She caught a hint of pride in the way he frowned down at her.

"Forensics found the bullet hole in the screen at Graham's house," he said. "I'm betting the gunpowder residue matches Dora's handgun. If I'm right, we have a tight case against her."

Packi appreciated Billy's acknowledgement of her contributions to the investigation, but there seemed no cause for celebration. "That's good. I guess." She was relieved Dora had been stopped. Now she worried for the couple's conditions, one mental, one physical. *How will Harold survive without his wife*?

"Does Mr. Baskin know Dora was arrested?"

Teig shook his head. "Detective Leland assured him Mizz Baskin is safe in the hospital with minor injuries from the accident. That eased him some."

"Poor Harold."

He had brought the blackmailers upon himself, but the gallant, old gentleman had protected his wife from the muggers, from whatever dementia was taking her mind, and now from the consequences of murders she had committed. Packi envied the devotion they had for each other.

"Will he have to go to jail for having the pictures or for covering for Dora?"

"Mizz Walsh." Billy put a gentle hand on her shoulder. "Packi, the doctor says he won't last two days."

"Oh." Sadness weighed her down onto a bench. She could see the old man's face, his kind eyes. "Harold knew he was dying," she said, certain that she'd seen an aura of finality about him. She sighed, but admired his clear objective planning. "He gave away his possessions and paid off debts. Now I realize he gave me the golf cart because he wanted me to feel obliged to befriend Dora."

"I s'pect so." Billy sat on the bench beside her and leaned close as if to take her into his confidence. "You should feel proud though."

"Why's that?"

"The gym bag you recovered contained Leonard Pritchard's list of business contacts." Deputy Teig paused and seemed pleased his statement perked Packi up. "The list gave the FBI what they needed to close in on a child pornography ring they've been working for months. This morning they did a sweep across the state and arrested a hundred sixty men. That's what will be in the newspapers."

The extent of the pornography plague astonished Packi. The arrests should have been good news, but the knowledge burdened her. *What is the world coming to?* Unable to find joy in the circumstances, she rested her head against a post and worried for the unknown children. "And Harold?"

"Mr. Baskin was not on their radar."

A small comfort, Packi thought. She stared at the women playing tennis fifty yards away without seeing them. She tried to wrap her mind around the news and its irony. "Dora was so obsessed with Harold's reputation, she killed two men and ruined his reputation." Packi closed her eyes for relief from the bright sun and the enormity of the situation. *This all started with a scrap of paper and chasing after a garbage truck.*

Deputy Teig reminded her he was there by shifting his weight on the bench. "Might've done the world a favor," he muttered. "The FBI's been on Oliver Graham for eleven months, monitoring his computer. He spent hundreds of hours logged on to child porn sites and paid thousands of dollars for it with his charge cards."

Packi's stomach churned. She hated that she ever spoke to the disgusting man. "Marilyn used to visit Ursula to play Mahjong. She mentioned Oliver locked himself in his office the entire time, and everyone thought he was working on his computer."

"He wasn't working." The deputy set his jaw as if ready for a fight. "Detectives tracked Ursula down at her sister's and is cooperating in exchange for immunity."

"Immunity for pornography? You mean, she knew what he did?" Packi was shocked. "How could a woman, a mother even, put up with such filth under her own roof?"

"Maybe that's why she left." Billy gave a perplexed shrug. "Graham hid stuff all over their house. Our department brought in a dog specially trained to sniff out a chemical used in SD cards, thumb drives, and any electronic devices that store digital content."

"That's amazing." Packi didn't understand the technical terms, but was reassured to hear technology could be used to fight back.

Billy nodded but slumped as if his bulletproof vest was too hot and too heavy. "The FBI's also been after Pritchard for years. He travelled the country under different names selling godawful pictures, CDs, and even playing cards with porno pictures on them. He'd find one customer and pressure that one to bring in friends to form a club for overseas travel."

"Thailand?"

"That's one. How did you know?"

"Ursula posted pictures on Facebook last year."

Teig's big face gaped at her. "You kiddin'?"

A moment passed before Packi realized the kind of pictures the deputy assumed. The horror in his eyes ignited hers, and she covered her mouth with both hands. "Not that kind!" She jumped up and backed away from him. "Oh, no, Billy. No. Tourist stuff Oliver sent back to her. Mountains, temples, huge golden Buddhas."

Teig donned his sunglasses and covered his embarrassment with bluster. "Pritchard's trips weren't for tourists. They catered to perverts."

Packi couldn't look at Billy, but tamped down revulsion to think. "Like the photos in the gym bag and the pictures Harold hid in the encyclopedia." Her knees wobbled. She felt for the bench and fell onto it, clutching her stomach to keep its contents contained. "Harold Baskin could be one of them."

"Still questionable." Teig patted her knee. "There's no history on Baskin. He might have been new, lured in by those pictures on a trial basis."

"Dora claimed he came back early from Bangkok," Packi said. She wanted to believe in the old man's innocence. Her mind reeled, searching for some safe haven for her memory of Harold Baskin. "I suggested to Dora that Harold planned to turn Pritchard and Graham in. Maybe he saved the pictures as evidence against them. Maybe the Baskins imagined themselves as avengers, protecting the children."

"Could've, but they were in dangerous territory. Pritchard made big money giving men access to . . ." Deputy Teig shook himself and reddened as if loath to even think disgusting thoughts in front of a lady. Maybe he thought of his eight-year-old son.

"Well, anyway." The deputy cleared his throat. "Pritchard had bosses who demanded more money, so he blackmailed club members to bring in new members. Oliver Graham was the local recruiter. Baskin was probably his next blackmail victim."

"Like a pyramid scheme." Packi's depression grew as she wondered if the sordidness had wormed its way through the entire country. Heck. If it's here in Paradise Palms . . . "I suppose Oliver lied to Harold about the trip, told him it was a tourist thing."

"Could be he reeled him in slow. We found nothing else in the Baskin house, besides those few pictures." Teig lifted himself to his full height and flexed his shoulders to adjust his holster strap. "It's over now, at least in Florida. Pritchard and Graham would've been rounded up in the sweep, if Dora hadn't gotten to them first."

The successful raid should have buoyed Packi's spirits, but the pervasiveness of the crimes sickened and baffled her. "Dora didn't seem to know about blackmail threats."

"Don't believe she did," Teig said. "Days ago, the FBI got an anonymous call from a woman using the Paradise Palms clubhouse phone. I suspected it was you."

"Not me."

"I know. I called you to find out how much you knew." Leather creaked as he hiked his utility belt back up to his waist. "And I worried about you getting in over your head again."

Packi shot him a warning look, but calmed herself when she saw only genuine concern. "It was Ursula Graham who tipped them off, wasn't it? She left the night before Dora shot Oliver."

Teig nodded and tapped his hat onto his head. "She called the FBI a second time wanting immunity and protection. Months ago, she figured out the charges on their credit card bills and went snooping on his computer. She even made an audio recording of Pritchard threatening Oliver and a discussion of their next, um, travel plans."

The deputy stepped out of the pavilion and Packi followed, thinking Ursula was the hero of the story.

"Thank you for telling me, Billy." Packi knew he'd gone out of his way to find her and offered her hand to show appreciation for the update. He accepted the handshake as an equal would do, and she ignored the pain of his grip. "Please let me know what you hear about Harold, and if I can help."

"Will do." Teig motioned to the gaggle of women at the tennis courts. "But for now you have plenty for the mother hens to peck over." He gave Packi a sad half-smile, and headed to his squad car.

36

Packi walked back toward the tennis court drained of energy, in need of her friends. Court Two was still in play, so she paused at the corner until the point ended. The small group of spectators and her teammates sat on the bleachers, craning their necks in her direction. They wanted news, but Packi vowed not to feed the rumor mill any more than necessary.

Beth met her halfway down the sidewalk. "I think the man is losing weight," she said, aiming her index finger at Deputy Teig. "His pants are getting baggy."

Packi glanced back at Billy, unlocking his car in the parking lot. He looked good, she realized, and moved more like an athlete than a cop with a diet of bagels and cream cheese.

"He's trying. The other day he turned down my fresh baked cookies."

"You're kidding." Beth licked her lips. "What kind?"

"Oatmeal raisin with pecans."

"Mmmm. He's serious about dropping the pounds." Beth laughed aloud, but then leaned down to Packi's ear level. "You gonna tell us what's going on?"

"Can we wait until we're alone?"

But the group on the bleachers wouldn't wait. In spite of the game in play on the court, Marilyn tapped Packi's shoulder to ask about Harold's condition. Diane and Mary had been discussing the shooting of Oliver Graham and wanted to know if that murder tied into the one on the tennis court. Many ears listened for Packi's short, factual answers as she tried to fend off gossip.

"But why did the police come here?" asked Chris, who had won an easy match on Court Three. "Did something new happen?"

"Yeah." Helen sniffed. "How am I supposed to play my best with distractions from the cops?" She glared at Packi and jammed her racquet into her bag, still feeling the sting of her loss. Her irritation silenced the group only for a moment before they pressed for more information.

"Helen's right," Packi said. "It's not fair to our players to hold this conversation here." She glanced at the spectators there to support the Estero team. Half of them were intent on the tennis match, but others listened for news about the Paradise Palms murders.

"It's all solved," Packi whispered. "Read the newspaper tomorrow."

Rebuffed by the abrupt ending, Kay pulled back. She stewed for a moment and then poked Packi with an elbow. "Good job."

Satisfied with Packi's answers or not, everyone turned their attention back to the action on Court Two. Grace and Kimberly had come from behind to win the second set, sending the match into a ten-point third-set tiebreaker. The Estero women were strong at the net, but had trouble running for Grace's well-placed lobs. The teams were neck and neck at nine to eight.

Beth perked up suddenly to watch a fast volley. "Yea! Paradise!"

Kimberly had put away a sharp angle shot to end the match. She and Grace hugged as if they'd won the lottery, and then went to the net to shake hands with their opponents. Applause acknowledged all four players.

"Great game, everyone!" Beth shouted.

Forgetting her TV-anchor cool, Kimberly squealed and bopped off the court to be greeted by her team with hugs and congratulations.

For the moment, spectators and players put aside the sordid crimes that had invaded Paradise Palms. Joy won the day. The joy of competing well; the joy of well-used muscles; the joy of being among friends and teammates.

* * *

Beneath oversized umbrellas on the terrace outside the clubhouse, the tennis team ordered their celebration lunch, replayed the high points of the tennis match, and cross-examined Packi and Beth on the details of Dora's arrest.

When curiosity died down and conversation turned to grandchildren and doctor appointments, Packi sat back for a quiet moment. From her vantage point, she could see golfers in the distance teeing off on the tenth hole. To the left, children splashed beneath waterfalls at the pool. To the right, she heard a boisterous game of bocci ball. Between them, a profusion of colorful impatiens lined the walkways.

Packi loved it all and gazed above the towering royal palms to send thanks to her husband for bringing her to Paradise and forcing her into a new life. *Thank you.*

She sat up with a start. *Thursday is Thanksgiving. Thanks is certainly in order. Maybe Mark will help cook a big meal.* The idea grew. *I'll invite Billy and his son, and Curtis and his grandparents. I'll roast the turkey. Mark can . . .*

"Listen up, people." Beth stood at the head of the table, waving her cell phone. "We need a team picture for the newsletter. Everybody get over here by the bushes."

Nobody ever argued with Beth, so they scraped back their chairs to get into position. The ten women jostled to squeeze into lines, with those with healthy knees crouched in front and tall or shy women hidden in the back.

Their server watched the chaos with a full tray of drinks at her shoulder. "I'll take the picture," Brittany said, as if eager to get in on the celebration. She set her tray on the table and took Beth's phone.

"Ready?" Beth asked. "Grab the neck of the person in front of you."

Packi hadn't heard right and glanced back at the captain from her crouched position. "What?"

"Like this," Kay explained. She put her hand on the nape of Packi's neck and pulled loose skin back. "See? Takes ten years off."

Embarrassed, but willing to be drawn into the foolery, Packi did as instructed. "Next time, I'll bring duct tape and make it permanent."

Beth hooted. "Everybody got it? Smile."

Somehow the picture got taken, Brittany served their meals, and the team chatted and laughed over their lunches.

After dishes had been cleared, Kay clinked her knife against her wine glass. "I think." She stood up to make her announcement. "That we should meet every week to form a crime-solving club. Packi will be the president. We'll call ourselves the TTL Investigators."

She waited for the inevitable question with an impish grin.

"I give," said Beth with her signature eye roll. "What's TTL?"

"Tennis Team Ladies!" Kay's excitement caught the team's imagination. "It doesn't have to be big crimes. We've had enough murder around here. We could figure out why the coffee budget is so big and why we spend more on golf cart leases than other clubs."

Marilyn raised her hand like an obedient student. "I want to find out where the homeless men went after their camp was shut down."

"And who's shooting at the eagles in North Fort Myers?" Beth pointed around the group as if they might have had something to do with it. Kimberly put her hands up to proclaim her innocence.

Grace cleared the table in front of her and pulled her laptop from her tote bag. “I’ll search the newspapers and Lee County public records for unsolved cases.” Her fingers flew over the keyboard. “This is so exciting.”

Packi watched her team come together into one mighty force of combined energy, experience, and enthusiasm. She knew they had untapped power. They could do so much more than tennis and golf. With the TTL on the job, the crime rate around Paradise Palms would plummet.

I love these women, Packi thought, *for being exactly what they are.* Her Thanksgiving invitation list just got longer. *Deputy Teig won’t know what hit him.*

37

Thanksgiving dinner was a success. Fifteen people stuffed into her dining room and spilled out onto the lanai. It had been decades since Packi hosted a big meal, but no one minded the crowded seating or mismatched plates. Bumping elbows, juggling dishes, and a potluck menu only added to the festivity. Her house had never felt so small. Never so homey.

Mark got to Packi's house hours early. He had insisted on bringing a twenty-two pound turkey which he had soaked in brine overnight. "Saw the chef at Victoria House brine turkey and wanted to try it, but never had a crowd to use as guinea pigs."

"Oh great, now my guests are guinea pigs," Packi had moaned. "I don't know what I was thinking when I invited everyone. I just don't know how to do this."

Mark laughed at her desperation and lay his hand against her cheek. "Relax. They'll love every minute of it." And they did.

Beth, Kay, and their spouses had arrived right on time, loaded down with their family-favorite vegetable dishes. Kimberly came alone, dressed impeccably, and offered a dainty endive appetizer. Grace brought a bottle of Irish cream, stayed only for appetizers, and then shuttled off to dinner with her sister's family.

Packi was pleased to finally meet Deputy Teig's son. Mikey stood back a step in his father's shadow, but bravely put out his hand for a formal handshake. He seemed as nervous as she, and she'd resisted the urge to hug the little guy. Mikey sat stiffly at Billy's side, but perked up when he spotted Curtis at the front door.

The teenager had ditched his hoodie and had his grandparents in tow. Iris Grant put a warm sweet potato pie into Packi's hands. The elegant woman apologized for the humble dessert, but beamed with pride as Packi breathed in the luscious aroma.

Curtis nodded to Deputy Teig and his son and enticed the eight-year old away from the adults by suggesting they play a game on his phone. Billy Teig raised an eyebrow and shot a warning look at Curtis. The teenager grinned and held up the phone for the anxious father to see. "It's rated G," Curtis assured him, and Mikey had a new hero. After they ate, the boys bounced a basketball between them in the driveway and then changed into swim trunks and dove into Packi's pool.

The doorbell had rung again as the food was being served. Marilyn had warned she and her husband would be an hour late. As was their tradition, they had served a Thanksgiving dinner to the homeless at the church downtown. She glowed with enthusiasm for the turnout of diners and volunteers. "Thanks for setting up tables last night," she told Mark. "Your buddy, Murphy, came later and says hello."

"Sorry I missed him," Mark had replied. "Did he say where the new camp is? The guys would appreciate any leftovers we have." Marilyn told him what she knew and the two of them made plans to deliver extra turkey, sides, and treats the next day. Packi wrapped the dishes immediately, relieved she'd have the temptations out of her kitchen.

Diane, Chris, and other team members had stopped by after dinner, bringing still more desserts, but staying only a short time before going back to their own Thanksgiving celebrations.

Now the guests were gone. Except Mark.

Packi scooped the tablecloth from the dining room table and heard him rattling around in the kitchen. He insisted on fussing with the turkey carcass and making soup stock. She threw the linens in the laundry basket and then lingered in the kitchen doorway to watch him.

As if the white cabinets and gleaming granite countertops were his own domain, Mark whistled a soft tune. He piled pots upside down to drip dry and found drawers to store spatulas and carving knives. His back was to her as he washed his hands and then dried them on a ruffled apron. He wore it well. The silly apron, tied with a bow around his waist, accentuated the width of his shoulders and the muscles of his back.

It seemed only right to slip up behind him and slide her arms around his chest. She rested her cheek against his shoulder blades and closed her eyes.

Mark tensed for a split second, but then let out a long breath. He covered her hands with his and traced her wrist bone with a fingertip. "Well, Mrs. Walsh. Your dinner was a big success."

"Thanks to you." She nudged his back with her chin. "Your experimental turkey was delicious. Crispy on the outside and juicy inside. I'm afraid you won't have much to share at the camp tomorrow."

"They'll appreciate anything we bring." Mark twisted around within Packi's embrace and wrapped his arms around her. "You'll come with us, won't you?"

Packi leaned her forehead against his chest and shook her head. "Of course, I will. I can make up for the mess I made of the last visit."

"Good." Mark kissed the top of her hair and released his hold on her. "This time I'll pick you up. I'll bring a cooler for the food. Is nine o'clock okay?"

"That's fine. Yes. Nine." Packi's body lost heat as he moved away from her, heading for the door. The homey feeling that had filled the house all evening, began to seep away and loneliness surged into the widening gap.

She grabbed for his hand just in time. "Mark, it's late."

He halted in mid-stride, turned to her, and seemed to stop breathing. That puppy-dog look came into his eyes as he took a step forward. His direct stare stole what little confidence Packi had, and she didn't know how to ask.

"I mean, you've been on your feet all day." She bumbled over the words. *What will he think of me?* "You should put your feet up. There must be a football game on and you could . . . you should stay."

"Packi." Mark took her face in his gentle hands. "Are you asking me to stay? To leave my truck in your driveway overnight?"

Yes. He understands! She trembled with relief. "Yes, your truck will be safe in the driveway until morning. It's a good . . . ."

Whatever else she might have said was silenced by his lips. She rose to her tiptoes to reach for more and floated off her feet within his arms. His heart's rhythms matched her own and a thought drifted through her trance. *This is home.*

END

Serve It Up

The Tennis Team's Favorite Recipes

Life in Paradise Palms revolves around tennis and food. The TTL support each other and solve problems by whipping up a batch of cookies, a casserole, or a special drink. They seem to think better while eating. Here are a few of their favorites.

Enjoy!

These yummy cookies are Packi's go-to sweet. She got the recipe from the back of the Quaker Oats box, but made several very important changes. She bribed Deputy Teig with these cookies in *Gator Bait* and later served them with tea to Billy in *Killer Serve.* He was able to resist and stuck to his diet. What willpower!

Gator Bites - Oatmeal Cookies

1 stick Butter, softened
½ cup Sugar
½ cup Brown sugar
2 Eggs
1 tsp. Vanilla

1 cup Flour
1 ½ tsp Cinnamon
½ tsp. Salt
1 tsp Baking soda

3 cups Dry oatmeal
¾ cup Raisins
¾ cup Pecans, chopped

Preheat oven to 350. Beat butter, sugars, and eggs. Stir in flour and spices by hand. Fold in other dry ingredients. Batter will be very thick, so bring your muscles. Drop dollops onto cookie sheet and, to make them a bit crispier, press down with fork. Bake for 10-12 minutes. Cool. Makes about thirty cookies.

There's nothing Packi likes better while reading a good book than a cup of hot tea and a small slice of homemade dessert. This easy coffee cake is colorful, sweet, and tart.

Raspberry Coffee Cake

8 oz	Cream cheese	½ tsp.	Vanilla
1 cup	Sugar	¼ tsp	Salt
½ cup	Butter, softened	½ tsp.	Baking soda
1¾ cup	Flour	1 tsp.	Baking powder
¼ cup	Milk	2	Eggs

1 cup	Raspberries, fresh or frozen	¼ cup	Sugar

8 oz Whipped topping

Preheat oven to 350 degrees.
Mash raspberries with ¼ cup sugar or less and set aside.
Beat cream cheese, one cup sugar, and softened butter until fluffy. Add eggs, milk, and vanilla. Sift the flour with baking powder, baking soda, and salt. Combine dry ingredients with wet and beat until well mixed. Spread batter in a greased and floured 13x9 inch pan. Spoon raspberry mixture over batter and swirl into the batter. Bake for 35 minutes. Serve warm with a dollop of whipped topping (optional). Or once the cake is cooled, spread the whipped topping like frosting.

While trying to wheedle information out of Deputy Teig, Packi misinterpreted Billy's refusal of her baked goodies. She thought he blamed his heaviness on her and responded, "Oh, come on! My cupcakes and cookies didn't do all that." Oops. Here's one of the culprit recipes.

Banana Nut Muffins

1 cup	Butter, softened	2 ⅔ cups	Flour
1 cup	Sugar	3 tsp	Baking powder
3	Eggs	1 tsp	Salt
2-3	Bananas, ripe	¼ tsp.	Baking soda
¾ cup	Raisins	Dash	Cinnamon
¾ cup	Pecans, chopped		

Preheat oven to 325 degrees. Cream butter with sugar and beat in eggs. In another bowl, mash bananas. In a third bowl combine flour, soda, powder, salt, and cinnamon. Mix all ingredients together by alternating dry ingredients, bananas, and wet ingredients. The batter will be thick.

Fold in nuts and raisins. Spoon into a greased muffin pan or line cups with paper.

Bake muffins for 35 minutes.

The day after Thanksgiving, Packi threw the turkey carcass into a pot of water to make soup stock. After simmering for hours, she and Mark skimmed out the bones and skin, left in bits of meat and filled two-cup containers. They froze the stock plus extra turkey meat and saved them to make this yummy soup.

Turkey Kale Soup

This is a very forgiving recipe. Feel free to delete items you don't have and throw in any other vegetables. In a crock pot combine:

2-4 cups Turkey soup stock, plus 3 times that much water.
1-2 cups Turkey meat, diced.
½ cup Groats (hull-less oats) Or try barley. Rice can be used, but it doesn't hold up as well, so add it later in the cooking process.

In a large frying pan, saute in a small amount of oil in this order:

2 stalks	Celery, diced	¼ Cup	Onion, diced
2	Carrots, diced	2 cloves	Garlic, minced
¼ cup	Red bell pepper, diced		
2	Kale leaves. Tear leaves into one-inch pieces. (Slice stems and saute with celery.)		
½ or ¼	Jalapeno pepper (optional), minced		

Packi had herbs growing in pots on her lanai, but dry can be used. Add herbs and spices to the liquid last:

½ tsp	Sage	6 leaves	Marjoram or 1/8 tsp. dry
¼tsp	Turmeric	3 leaves	Basil or ½ tsp dry
2 tsp	Salt	4 leaves	Cilantro (optional)
2 dashes	Pepper	2 pinches	Nutmeg
¼tsp	Thyme	¼ Cup	Parsley, fresh or 1 tbl. dry

Cook for several hours or until groats are soft.

Packi's last minute Thanksgiving dinner brought the neighbors and tennis players together. Iris Grant, a gentle Southern lady and Curtis's grandmother, offered a fragrant sweet potato pie made from a recipe she had memorized in *her* grandmother's kitchen.

Sweet Potato Pie

1 lb.	Sweet potatoes	1 cup	Brown sugar, packed
½ tsp.	Salt	3/4 tsp.	Cinnamon
1/8 tsp.	Nutmeg	1/8 tsp.	Ginger
12 oz.	Evaporated milk	1 dash	Allspice

Bake the sweet potatoes for 45-60 minutes, depending upon size, until they're soft. Let cool and scoop out meat. Beat until smooth.

Preheat oven to 425 degrees. Beat eggs in a large bowl. Add sugar, spices, salt, and mashed sweet potatoes. Pour milk slowly into mixture. Use less milk if you like a thicker (less custardy) pie. Pour into a chilled nine-inch pastry shell.

Bake at 425 for five minutes. Then reduce heat to 325 and bake 40 minutes until a knife cut comes out clean. Do not over bake. Pie will set as it cools.

There's no shame in using a refrigerated pie crust, but if you have time . . . Combine 1½ cups flour and ½ tsp. salt in a large bowl; cut in ¼ cup shortening and a half stick of butter until crumbly. Sprinkle in 4 tablespoons of ice cold water, one spoonful at a time. Mix with a fork until pastry holds together and leaves sides of bowl clean. Keep ingredients and bowl chilled. Roll out dough on waxed paper or floured board. Fit into a nine-inch pan and crimp and trim edges.

When the tennis team throws a party, everyone brings a dish to add to the table. Beth brought this cheesy rich asparagus mushroom casserole to the Thanksgiving feast, and everyone went back for seconds.

Baked Asparagus and Mushroom

1 bunch	Asparagus. Remove the thick stubs, chop the spears in to 2-inch sections and parboil a few minutes.
1 lb	Baby portobello mushrooms, sliced
6 strips	Bacon. Baked, microwaved, or fried until crispy. Crumbled.
½ cup	Sour cream
½ cup	Mayonnaise
½ cup	Cheddar Cheese, shredded

Layer the parboiled asparagus in the bottom of a 9" x 9" pan. Mix all other ingredients and pour over the asparagus. Bake at 350 degrees for 35 minutes. This dish can be assembled the day ahead and then baked just before party time.

Sinfully rich but, oh, so good.
Serves six as a side dish.

Packi makes iced tea every other day and cools off with a tall glass after a hot and sweaty game of tennis. She served the refreshing tea to Billy when they sat in her kitchen to figure out why fake-blood stained balls had been thrown into her house. She also had a pitcher in the fridge, ready to go, when Beth came for a visit.

Iced tea a necessity in Florida's tropical heat.

Florida Sun Tea

2 quarts cold water
5 individual sized black tea or orange pekoe tea bags
Lemon slices (optional)

Fill a glass jug or clear lidded pitcher with water. Trap the tea bag strings in the lid and suspend all five bags in the water. Set the pitcher outside in full sun light for several hours. The sun will slowly heat the water and give the tea a mellow flavor. When the tea is dark, it's ready. The tea can be saved in the refrigerator, but it's best when still hot.

Pour the heated tea over a full glass of ice and listen to it crackle. Add lemon slices or bit of sugar, if you wish.

ABOUT THE AUTHOR

Jeanne Meeks belongs to Mystery Writers of America, Gulf Coast Writers' Association, and the Women of Mystery critique group. She loves to attend mystery writer conventions to learn the finer points of forensics and hang out with mystery authors who like nothing better than studying blood splatter and learning new ways to kill off their characters.

When not writing, she backpacks, kayaks, volunteers with the local historical society, and plays tennis, pickleball, or golf. She is on two competitive 3.5 tennis teams .

Jeanne's 2016 adventure was a five-day, unsupported bicycle ride across Illinois. With three women, she rode from the Indiana border, 217 miles across Illinois, to dip their bike tires into the Mississippi River.

Jeanne writing career began with poetry in 1990. She belonged to Poets and Other Writers and gave poetry performances as part of that group. She also published a book of poetry, *My Sister's Quilt*. Later, she wrote human-interest articles for *Schoolhouse Life* news magazine. Her novel, *Gator Bait,* was nominated by the New Lenox Library and became a finalist for the 2015 Illinois Soon To Be Famous Author project.

Married in 1969, she lives with her husband on Florida's gulf coast and in a suburb of Chicago. After twenty-eight years in business, Ms. Meeks and her husband sold their security surveillance company in 2005. While in business, Jeanne was recognized by the Illinois governor as the Small-Business Person of the Year. She was also the Tax Collector for New Lenox Township, the President of the Chamber of Commerce, on the board of a local bank, and on Silver Cross Hospital's Community Trustee Board.
Now "retired" she has time for adventures and for writing.
Life is good.

GATOR BAIT - A Tennis Team Mystery

Book 1 in series

Can the Paradise Palms tennis team save their favorite alligator after he drags the body of a flashy real estate developer to the bottom of his pond?

A volunteer at the nature preserve spots a body bobbing in the pond at the same time as Big Joe sees his next meal. Convinced of the gator's innocence, Packi Walsh rallies her new tennis team, the fourth-grade science class, and the local motorcycle gang to campaign to save Big Joe's hide.

Packi's snooping uncovers real estate fraud and irate investors, an affair between a trophy wife and her tennis pro, and a connection between the friendly neighborhood pharmacist and the New Jersey mob.

Now someone is trying to make Packi gator bait.

* * *

"A delightful read . . . doesn't rely on foul language and over-the-top sex to tell a good story." Mary Baker, Illinois

"Wow. Another can't-stop-reading-it novel." - Beverly Ferris, Montana

"I loved it, especially getting to know Packi and Deputy Teig."
- Nancy Sorci, Illinois

RIM To RIM - Death in the Grand Canyon

Backcountry Mystery series. Book 1

A novice backpacker becomes prey for a murderer on the rim to rim trail. Can a backpacking trip across the Grand Canyon rebuild Amy Warren's self confidence or will the trek break her and leave her clinging by her fingernails to the edge of the abyss?

The awesome Grand Canyon scenery is marred when Amy and Sarah find a mangled body in a ravine. The women, who each hike for their own reasons, must face the physical hardships of the five-day trek *plus* stay alive as an eerie danger stalks them.

* * *

"Empowering Women, Dispensing Adventure. Ladies take note: Jeanne Meeks has created a first novel that puts her up in the company of fine adventure/mystery writers..." -- Grady Harp, Los Angeles reviewer

"Couldn't put it down. You owe me a night's sleep."
--Kathy Eversman, Rhinelander, WI

Rim To Rim was nominated for a Lovey Award - Best First Novel at the 2014 Love Is Murder writers convention in Chicago. It is available in e-book and print from Amazon, Barnes and Noble, from the author, and from other retail outlets. The audio version is available from www.Audible.com.

To sing along with the very cool *The Ballad of Rim to Rim* (lyrics by Jeanne Meeks, vocals by Mary Beth Hafner, and keyboard, bass, and guitar by Mike Evon) visit my website at_www.JeanneMeeks.com.

Wolf Pack- Mystery on Isle Royale

Backcountry Mystery series, Book 2

Can a backpacking trip to an island famous for its wolves mend the relationship between Amy and her grown daughter? Will blackmail and betrayal bring them together—or bury them on Isle Royale?

Emboldened by her adventures in the Grand Canyon, Amy Warren again laces up her hiking boots. She ferries with her daughter, Meagan, to Isle Royal National Park. When volunteer ranger Sarah Rochon is accused by a co-worker of assault and theft, Amy is torn between spending precious time with Meagan and clearing her best friend's name. When Amy rescues Remington, a pampered Havanese show dog, from the frigid waters of Lake Superior, he becomes her champion. Together they sniff out clues to the evil that threatens the natural tranquility of the magical island.

* * *

Her fresh voice and captivating story will have you reading well into the night.

- Lydia T. Ponczak, Author of *Reenee on the Run*

I loved the book! Can't wait for your next one!

- Mary Baker, Illinois

Wolf Pack was nominated for a Lovey Award - Best Amateur Sleuth Novel at the 2015 Love Is Murder writers' convention in Chicago. It is available in e-book and print from Amazon, from the author, and from other retail outlets.

Dear Reader,

I hope you've enjoyed the TTL's adventures as much as I enjoyed writing about them. Do me a favor? Will you help spread the word about these stories? Your opinions will help another reader decide to open the cover and visit Paradise Palms.

I'd appreciate your feedback in any of these ways:
* Leave a comment on Amazon or Barnes & Noble,
* Write a review for Goodreads.com,
* Pin a picture of yourself with the book on Pinterest,
* Post your opinion on Facebook and Twitter
* Request that your library carry my books
* Or simply mention my novels to your friends.

Do you belong to a book discussion club, civic group, or women's club? I'd be more than happy to visit your group to discuss my novels or speak about my publishing experiences or outdoor adventures. Contact me and let's talk.

Amazon Author's Page - www.amazon.com/author/jeannemeeks

Review at: http://bit.ly/KillerServe-Goodreads

Website - www.jeannemeeks.com

Pinterest - http://pinterest.com/jeannemeeks

e-mail me - ChartHousePress@aol.com or Jeanne2Meeks@aol.com

If you wish to receive notice of new writing adventures, appearances, and updates, send me an e-mail, and I'll put you on my Favorite Reader list. I'd love to hear from you. Thanks so much for reading.

Jeanne

Made in the USA
Lexington, KY
09 September 2017